More praise for Vincent Czyz's *Adri*

D1003793

"Written in hauntingly lyrical prose, C
vivid tapestry that is held together by ⌊the⌋ thread of human experience." –*Newark Star Ledger*

"Czyz is more than a bit mystical; indeed, he searches for rapture ... What
he's really after, however, is to find mystery within mystery, to have
experiences he cannot live without yet cannot pin down. [...] It is as if
shredded maps occupy Czyz most, transparencies and fringes, people
whose identities do not have clear outlines, for themselves or others."
–**Paul West**

"Certain books require a patient reader, one with the ability to concentrate closely and intently. Sentences are not straightforward or transparent, but long and labyrinthine, like intriguing yet shadowy dreams.
The writing, more like poetry than prose, calls attention to language,
to the fullness of a word, a sentence, with the purpose of expressing
inexpressible emotions and experiences. Think of Proust's Remembrance of things Past or Faulkner's The Sound and the Fury or, more
recently, William Vollmann's Fathers and Crows. [...] Vincent Czyz's
Adrift in a Vanishing City is just this sort of work: lyrical and pensive, an
odd and often beautiful portrait of longing." –**Capper Nichols,
Minnesota Daily**

"I could speak at length about how much I admire Czyz's considerable
talent, his fictive range, his willingness to plunge naked into the gutter,
leap after stellar contrails, his grasp of how ravenously one body grasps
another, or of how his impossible apostrophes out of the night are the
necessary utterances that make life possible, confronted with the silence
of the day, with the deafness of those who never hear."
–**Samuel R. Delany**, preface to *Adrift in a Vanishing City*

"Reading Vincent Czyz's book is like visiting someone else's dream. He
has a gift for vivid and surreal imagery, lush muscular prose and
strangely mesmerizing landscapes. In this, his first book, he's created a
dark-side-of-the-moon original." –**Peter Blauner, author of *The
Intruder* and *The Last Good Day***

"In poetic prose that flouts conventional fictive forms, Czyz draws on
classical myth, fable, folklore, Shakespearean tragedy, and other genres
to create a metaphor of modern alienation." –**Joe Castronovo,
New Jersey Herald & News**

Full citation from Allan Gurganus:

"There is something of Virginia Woolf's toxic perfume, the tincture of bemused sadness, the glorying in the jewel-tones of the half-healed bruise, the thing that – in being left one-quarter undone – is therefore promising forever.

"The writer is in love with difficulty. The writer is forced to buy many magazine subscriptions that will never produce even the first month's issue. And yet this fiction is always listening, constantly forgiving, in love with the material world and its home-made, self-defensive talk-dat-talk genius.

"Behind the flash, there waits a patience.

"Beyond technique, we feel a wise heart, expecting little while hoping for everything. We find someone making, as all true artists do, a great deal from a little of everything.

"The seasick rodeo of 'Zee Gee and the Blue Jean Queen' recalls a country and western ballad when you're newly drunk enough to hear it plain–without snobbism, without irony, without the upstaging tooth of self-pity. This tale recalls the very second when the Pain and the Bourbon go on a first-name basis, when the Pain and the Bourbon, buddies suddenly, start not just talking, but telling and telling unto that accidental byproduct and salvation we call Singing.

Here is a song to the weird sweetness behind loving the wrong person perfectly."

Adrift in a Vanishing City

Vincent Czyz

Rain Mountain Press
New York City

First Printing March 2015

Adrift in a Vanishing City
Copyright 2015 © by Vincent Czyz

ISBN: 978-1-4951-0605-7

Rain Mountain Press
www.rainmountainpress.com
New York City

Printed in the USA
Design: Sarah McElwain
Cover art: Ric Best

"Overhead, Like Orion" first appeared in *Archaeopteryx, The Newman Journal of Ideas*, Vol. 2, 2014

For Stevie Pallucca and Millo Farneti,
who taught me that stories start in the middle of things,
that instead of middles they have some ballast
that slides around and about kilter, and that no,
they never really do end.

ACKNOWLEDGEMENTS

I would like to acknowledge a creative debt to Paul West and an even deeper one to Millo Farneti; without Millo these stories simply would not exist, and I can only hope they constitute some sort of repayment. I would also like to thank Rocco Gratale, Michael Trotman, and Peter Blauner for their encouragement and wisdom; my brothers, Robert and Anthony, who have been Theos to this Vincent; and Frontenac natives, Kenny Krumsick and Tom Moody, who took me in as though we all grew up under the same roof. Special thanks to the New Jersey Council on the Arts, whose support helped make this collection possible, and to Joseph J. De Salvo, Jr., Rosemary James, Allan Gurganus, and the Pirate's Alley Faulkner Society. Special thanks also to Michael P. Dyer of the Kendall Whaling Museum, the only scholar able to help me track down documentation of the semi- or wholly fictional *Octavius.* My deep gratitude also to Gil Roth, the original believer, and Samuel R. Delany for offering his time, his literary expertise, and his inimitable touch both to me and this collection. Finally, I'd like to acknowledge Stephen R. Pallucca, who led me to many a place not on any map.

TABLE OF CONTENTS

Like every one of the last three dozen MFA theses I've read, the following text is neither a novel nor, really, a collection of stand-alone stories. Familiar characters – Zirque (rhymes with Jerk), Blue Jean, the Duke of Pallucca – disappear or are abandoned, reappear or are revisited tale to tale. But equally clearly these are not novel chapters. Our young writers seem unhappy with the strictures of both genres and are struggling to slough them.

If you are a reader convinced of the irrevocable sociality of fiction, I warn you: By and large, the text will not linger on how characters manage to pay for their various flights from Pittsburg to Paris, from Kansas to Amsterdam, how most of them make their living, or even scrounge up change for that next pint of booze, not to mention make the rent on an apartment in Budapest – another trait Vincent Czyz shares with many of his contemporaries; although, in their conviction that the world's socio-economic specificities are every self's necessarily distinctive background, neither Austen nor Flaubert, Knut Hamsun nor James Joyce, Virginia Woolf nor Henry Miller could have let such an omission by in their successive attempts to delve more and more deeply into some more and more highly foregrounded presentation of the subject. But the clash of micro-class and micro-class, macro-class and macro-class, that makes fiction interesting, or even useful, to the average Joe or Sue (not to mention to the commercial editors riding shotgun on the stopcock of the smoky trickle of confused tales – overplotted, understructured, and as incoherent and mixed in metaphor as the images within these parentheses, outside these dashes – throughout our Barnes & Nobles, onto our Big Name bookstores shelves) are simply not in focus on Czyz's screen. They are bracketed along with all notion of labor.

If you feel art is an enterprise in which, when you have found an artist doing what every other artist is doing, you have necessarily found an artist doing something wrong (yet another story or poem voicing its appeal to aesthetic distance in that artificial and so-easy sign of the literary, the present tense: *Yawn* . . . !), some of the elements – or absences – I've highlighted here, in a book such as this, might give you pause.

What's extraordinary here, however, what recommends and finally makes such work more than commendable, what renders it a small landmark in the sedimentation of new form in fiction, is a quality of language, a surface that signals that the structure of anything and everything that surface evokes beyond it is simply other than what we have grown used to. Finally such a surface signs to the astute that the reductions our first three paragraphs suggest are, in this case, wildly off the mark. (Czyz is not an MFA product.) Such language as we find here projects a particular aesthetic consciousness, rather, it might be more profitable to read as interested in other things, and not as one merely slovenly, unthinking, or ignorant of the tradition.

Nothing is careless about this writing at all.

Poetry is about the self as it is defined in the response to love, death, the changing of the seasons . . . However indirectly, however mutedly, traditional fiction has always been about money. I could speak easily and easily speak honestly – and at length – about how much I admire Czyz's considerable talent, his fictive range, his willingness to plunge naked into the gutter, to leap after stellar contrails, his grasp of how ravenously one body grasps another, or of how his impossible apostrophes out of the night are the necessary utterances that make life possible, confronted with the silences of the day, with the deafness of those who never hear. But this is still a more or less rarefied, a more or less dramatic bit of lit. crit. It only becomes a recognizable "story" when I write that Vincent Czyz is a long-haired, newly-married taxi driver living in New Jersey and has sought my imprimatur – a gay, gray, pudgy professor with income tax problems, who commutes to work in Massachusetts by Peter Pan (cheaper than Amtrak), and who has published thirty books over as many years with various presses, commercial and university . . . But Czyz's are not traditional stories. Indeed, they are part of a counter-fictive tradition that attempts to appropriate precisely the substance of poetry for prose: Novalis's *Heinrich von Ofterdingen,* Rilke's *Die Aufzeichnungen des Malte Laurids Brigge,* Toomer's *Cane,* Keene's *Annotations* . . . Average Joes and Sues are just not Czyz's concern. He's fixed his finger, rather, on yearningly romantic figures who combine rough American – or foreign-tinted – dialect with pristine insight; men and women who, clawing at the evanescent tapestry of perception as it unravels madly from the loom of day, are as concerned with myth and cosmology as they are with moment and the night, and who now and again have more consonants in their names than vowels, many of those names not commencing till the terminal handful of letters flung from the alphabet . . . Though they fixate on indirectly answering just such questions as Czyz here sets aside, not Proust, not Musil, not Ford of *Parades End* or *The Fifth Queen* is "easy reading" either; and finally for much the same surface reasons. Though the sexuality is more or less normal, the poetic method is closer to Genet's – another writer whose novels tends to ignore those grounding questions, unless the characters are pimps (i.e., living off prostitutes of one sex or another) or in jail (i.e., living off the state).

As an appendix to his 1934 collection of essays, *Men Without Art,* Wyndham Lewis proposed "The Taxicab Driver Test" for good fiction. Suggested Lewis: Open the text to any random page and give it to any average cab driver. (Fascist Lewis assumed the driver's first language would, of course, be English; Czyz is conversant in several – besides working as a cab driver, he's taught English as a foreign language in Turkey . . .) Tell him to read it.

Then ask: "Is there anything here that seems strange or unusual or out of the ordinary for a work of fiction?" If he answers "Yes," then you may have some extraordinary fiction. If he answers "No," you don't. Lewis went on to apply his test to, respectively, a Henry James short story and a banal society novel by Aldous Huxley (*Point Counter Point,* which was thought much of back then because it was a roman à clef about the Lawrences and the Murrys – I remember reading it when I was around seventeen. I said, "Huh . . .?"). James certainly wins; Huxley doesn't. (Today, does anyone read anything else he's written other than *Brave New World,* possibly *Island?*) I don't think the Taxi-driver Test is a hundred-percent reliable. Still, it's a good one to keep in mind; and it's a salutary corrective to today's mania for "transparent prose," even (or especially) among our most radical experimenters. I mention it because Czyz's work (as does Melville's, Joyce's, Hemingway's, Woolf's, Faulkner's, Patrick White's, William Gass's . . .) passes the Taxicab Driver test admirably. The work of the vast majority of Czyz's contemporaries does not.

That is to say: Czyz is telling stories many of his contemporaries are trying to tell – and telling them far better!

If you are a reader who can revel in language – in the intricate and intensely interesting "how" language imposes on its "what" – then, however skew his interests are across the fictive field (and how refreshing that skewness!), Czyz is a writers rich in pleasures; it's a pleasure to recommend him.

– New York City, May 1998

ZEE GEE AND THE
BLUE JEAN BABY QUEEN

The heart has its reasons that reason doesn't know.
— Blaise Pascal

Halley's, she said to him once, her hair spilled over the pillow like a silken ruby aura, you're like that.

He didn't understand.

You're far away, someplace I can hardly imagine, but I know you're coming back. She was looking up at the bedroom ceiling, mostly lost in the half dark, hazy as one of those alternate higher planes fortune-tellers talk about. You always do.

She thinks of him during long winter nights silent and clear as a sky full of constellations (he has shown her the place where her sign rises, how his is framed at certain times of the year by her bedroom window). The ice jackets on tree branches, on overgrown grass, shiver and crinkle with the slightest breeze, tinkle like chimes. During the season of changing colors with its misty-breathed mornings, she wonders who is waking up next to him. One of those free-love girls with big tits and too much mascara he likes so much most likely, shaking her can all over the bar he met her in. And on those sweaty Kansas evenings her hair just won't stay, a hot orange moon big over the fields, crickets rub against each other's solitude and she misses him most.

Memory is like a weird city, he said, when you're in it, the street names keep changin, or the signs disappear. You try to find your way back but you're never sure which direction you're goin in.

He did some sleight of hand: Now you see it, now you don't.

In the dream that comes to her most often, she's in an abandoned mine bucked up by railroad-ties, tracks for the coal carts careening off into darkness. No windows down there but she knows it is always winter of nothing growing, no wind, no resin smell of rising sap or cut grass, no whiff of the old barn soaked to the wood's grain in the earthiness of hay, manure, horse sweat reaches her in the cold of uncut diamonds and dull gold. Feeling her way with blue hands (bluer veins hard as marble), mostly numb, trapped beneath the fields in a footsteps-echo-on-the-stone vault of glassy black, the glittering hard eyes studding the rough walls are no light but cold light.

A place memories are put away for safekeeping without the beam of a miner's helmet to set them off, a home for the restless shades of people badly missed – Old Man Varanelli, who was always smoking Toscana cigars even the day he never made it up from the mine when the timbers cracked and gave in, they say it was like God granted him a last request; the Thomas boy who was only 18, taller than Zirque and handsome as all get-out, a wonder to see on the baseball field, electrocuted that rainy night on farm machinery (that's what brought on the early frost that year); poor Pap, only five feet two inches of him, he said the funniest things before he turned up face down, naked as you please, in a flooded drainage ditch.

She hears the sound of their picks clanging clinking digging for something generations of miners failed to turn up, but never catches sight of one, is never anything but alone with the shadows of things that sank – slow as evening falling – out of sight, a fancy spinning lure flashing, then gone in deep waters. Nothing but blue-black dark down there, only a vague remembrance of what orange might be like, of a moon that will rise in the hot sky to watch over her, summertime, when he is not there.

Her voice echoes in the shaft, boomerangs eerily back as if someone else has called him. The picks of the invisible miners fall into silence, but he doesn't hear, and the next scream turns into a fist in her throat. She wakes in a fit of shivering – sometimes with her nose right up against the back of his neck, his body warm with sleep, and mixed in with his smell an odd whiff of the last place he'd been.

Other times there were only the sounds the wind makes.

She's gotten used to reaching in among put-away clothes, pulling a bottle of Cold Duck out of the cedar chest Mamma gave her, sinking into the edge of the bed and drinking herself back to sleep.

My Grandma was Creek, he says by way of explanation, I can't help the way I am.

Creek nothin, Willie liked to cut in, anybody takes a good look can see he's quarter-blood ky-yoat.

All comes out t'the same thing if y'ask me.

Wouldn't you know Earl wasn't above shouting it across the bar?

Didn't matter who was right, the upshot bein Zirque chases what he fancies on a mean horse that bucks him every time, he just gets up and slaps the dust off his jeans.

Could've been a pool hustler, but that was nothing next to being the first country singer out of Pittsburg, Kansas to make a name for himself. Switched saddles and decided to be a rodeo rider, hardly ever winning a thing but having a grand time being tossed into the chewed-up dirt, the crowd holding its breath while he high-tailed it out of there, clowns trying to keep the bull from gutting him, stomping him, marking him permanent. He sang jazz in cramped St. Louie dives where some of the drinkers eyed him the way rodeo bulls stared him down. Moaning blues to anybody within earshot, he wrote songs on candy wrappers, inside matchbook covers even though he can't play a note. When nothing else was going for him, he washed dishes in Chicago. From the front seat of the cab he drove in Kansas City he talked Golden Gloves, that time he got dropped for a five-count, the crowd's roar not as loud as the ocean breaking in his skull, took a standing eight a round later, remembering the hot white lights hazy in the smoke and that stumpy Italian kid with a head like a cinderblock coming out, thick arms up, to get it over with.

He beat me for first, but I finished on my feet.

Quiet times he sold magazines door to door, *Mornin ma'am now hold on just a minute this won't take but a minute and it's painless I promise* because he was always making promises, hardly ever making good but not a person can listen to him and still say no – he'll take in anyone not chained to her better judgment. Somehow or other he always manages to make off with whatever he's set his sights on, getting by on roughed-up good looks, neighborly smiles, words as smooth and pretty as glass. Only Helen Keller is safe.

If life were a pinball game, my name'd be right up next to the tilt for having hit the highest score. He winked.

Oh there are six feet of you Zirque, too much to be a kid anymore. When are you going to stop acting like one? You've about run out of quarters.

He smiled because he could always borrow another, steal it, lease his soul if he had to (fine printed so ownership would revert to him at year's end). But that year costs him. Last time he was missing a tooth. Coke deal gone bad was all he would say. He used that smile (slow as cigarette smoke making itself into a graceful coil) to show off his new space, like he was proud of it. God only knows how he could be glad to be missing a front tooth.

I only do drugs to keep 'em out of the hands of little kids, you know that.

She slapped him in the chest for that, knowing she couldn't be the one who hurt him the way he comes home sometimes. So bad once the hospital had to wire his jaw shut, one of his eyes purpled up, swollen shut, just the lashes sticking out, and his nose – he has such a nice one it could have been on a Greek statue – his nose was twice as wide as it should've been. If something had to get broken though, thank heaven it was his jaw, shut him up for a while. He was an honest-to-God saint the way he took his daily punishment, drinking meals through a straw, hardly moving from the house, reading all day practically, so quiet she kept checking up to make sure he hadn't slipped out.

Five uv 'em Blue Jean. I took out two clean, but one uv 'em got me from behind, and they were still in a world a trouble, I wuzh gonna put a good hurtin on all five only I got cracked with a bottle an it wuzh downhill from there. Got t'admit, my head, hard azh it izh, ain't no match for a bottle a old Number Seven. Glass ain't quite azh fragile azh it'sh cracked up to be.

There were probably two, three just maybe, but he liked to blow things up balloon size, carry you off to Oz or some such place where there were emerald cities and talking scarecrows and Zirque could whip five guys as long as none of them had an empty bottle of Jack Daniels handy.

In the beginning when it was too painful to talk, he wrote little notes. Most she saved and most ended with *You know I love you*. He stayed for a whole year that time. Things were so beautiful she wouldn't mind if he got his jaw busted again.

Most often he comes back just bucked, still slapping at the dust, with nothing but the clothes he's wearing, that jean jacket he'll never let go of with a hundred pockets, she's patched it up at least that many times. Now and again he comes cruising down Broadway (all the buildings lined up to watch) as if he's an astronaut back from the Moon, a car twice as fancy as the mayor's – a cream-colored Continental with spoked tires, a convertible of course, the roof immaculate white when it stretched itself out, rode her all over town, the front end so long she didn't know how he steered it right into a parking spot in front of Toni's Place thinking he could get a kiss out of her just because he bought her all those dresses and that handbag, those fancy two-tone Texas riding boots, just because the money he was carrying around in his pockets was enough to pay his debts ten times over.

You could've done anything you wanted to . . .

They were swaying on the swing seat out back, the acreage level and clear except for a clump of trees in the west, silhouetted in the evening.

Chiaroscuro, he said, Italy has its own light, its own word for it, a thousand painters died never getting it right, but they tried.

The copse of trees blacked out, a break in the west from everything flat else, while the swing he always promised to oil but nearly always forgot went on creaking, forward and back, between now and then, between what was and what could still be...

You could've done anything, she said, anything at all.

This way is better: I don't know exactly what it is I want, might as well see the hand I been dealt before I throw away.

But you'll never catch up with yourself, there's always something ahead of you that goes faster whenever you do, like chasing your own tail.

She knew she was right, but he had this way of putting his arm around her, making the floor tilt and from that off angle, that skewed way of looking at the world, nothing looked impossible, nothing was worth complaining about with her head on his chest and his particular smell coming through an old flannel shirt worn down by a thousand washings. She doubted herself, lost the resolve that had hardened while she looked out a kitchen window, meticulously cutting onions for dinner as if he were going to be home for it. Setting a perfect table for one, but always making a little extra just in case. Everything fresh from Pallucca's Market: the green peppers, the red ones, the tomatoes for making sauce (nothing he likes eating better than Italian or Mexican), the garlic, the red onions for salad, white for the too-sweet tomato pureed by hand, an all-day event making sauce the right way, especially getting caught up cutting green peppers, sometimes taking an hour just to do them because it's good to concentrate on the shapes of the strips. This one looks like a Z, maybe I can spell his name before I throw it into the pot and that'd get him over here, how could he resist? Never powdered seasoning, always the hard teardrop clusters of garlic, though the smell sinks into her skin, *whoof* the smell, but all the Italian women say it's good for you, and olive oil too – only cook with olive oil – and for a cold, a little red wine is best and to settle your stomach after a big meal, red wine and red wine if you're having trouble sleeping. And what is he up to right now when this sauce is just getting to the thickness it's supposed to be, smelling up the whole house, and the bread is about done, too. How far is he from here she wanted to know, could she measure in teaspoons laid end to end? A bell should ring when he comes within a thousand, when he's anywhere in the state, the whole damn country. God knows he doesn't have the courtesy to call, or even to barge in and give her a big kiss and hug hello. He likes to be found, like a dug-up bone, let you show him how much you missed him, probably got his sense of dramatics from his Creek grandma, too. A bell to keep her from getting up all the time, she wouldn't mind at all, just look the floor tiles are worn smooth practically, a direct line from the back door to the stove, her feet did that she knows, but how? She never saw it till one day she noticed the grooves were going out of the linoleum in a whitening trail, a tiny Milky Way on the white floor of her kitchen, hazy undefinable inexplicable, an object of ceaseless wonder but there it was, questions about its origin a source of constant curiosity, she doesn't remember so much back and forth, back and forth looking out the back door again and again, odds against finding him, but once or twice she found him there sitting on the edge of the porch, beat him silly with a rolled-up newspaper for making her wait like that.

In the old days, Pap would come by, too shy to knock for a whole ten minutes sometimes, of course she'd invite him to stay for dinner. He'd limp inside, usually a bottle of red wine in his hands, kee-auntie, a basket covering the bottom, she always saved the bottles for the basket. It was kind of nice, listening to him talk nonstop, lisping kind of because what a shame he's got a harelip besides one leg being shorter than the other. Always a gentleman, never a cuss word, he'd make her laugh gossiping about Earl or Red, their latest bet, Earl was putting up his car against Red's pickup that he'd get that new woman who'd just moved to Pittsburg to marry him by Christmas. Sure you will, Pap said and wanted in on that bet.

Somehow he always seemed to know when she was starting to miss Zirque in a way that company made her feel even more alone, he'd know, say he had to get going, and off he limped. And she'd look at that worn part of the floor and say to herself next time I'll avoid it, take a different way, walk anywhere *but* there, even out the rest of this damn floor, but what was the use with a whole kitchen full of reminders of him? Tiny slant-roofed houses he'd brought from a ceramic shop in Paris, an elegant blue-glass candle holder he'd bought from a wrinkled little man with a gray goatee in Miami (Arizona, not Florida), a Dutch plate he came by in Amsterdam (It's legal for the girls to be right up against the glass, mannequins in lingerie except they wink atchya, wave atchya, tempt you sore), a '40s-style beer glass stolen from the Grand Emporium in Kansas City where there's a neon outline of John Lee Hooker.

She never did make good on that promise to put away his picture, the one she took of him on Locust Street, leaning against the red brick of a building boarded up since Prohibition, standing there in a long, blue-black Navy coat with the collar turned up against the wind. Like a postcard sent to her from one of his trips. *Greetings from Locust Street. Wish you were here.* His dark eyes holding the spark of train wheel on rail, his mouth set like a promise still unkept. A feeling comes and goes too quickly to warm her or even to catch its name.

He's told her what the canals in Venice look like at night, in winter, when there are no tourists, just the lights on the boats and the sound of water slapping against the mossy stone buildings.

Wish you were here.

He's spent his money in sight of the Mediterranean, on islands she's never heard of, probably making the same bad name for himself, taking on the same shady debts on that side of the world. Comes back with fancy words he learned right after *bonjour, comment t'allez vous, hi how are you? Estoy bien, dankeschön,* fine, thanks a wagonload for askin.

Picked up a whole bunch in Germany, along with a fancy beer mug with a silver lid on it. *Weltanshauung.* That one sounds like a big brass bell ringin, don't it?

It's sitting on a shelf in the kitchen losing its shine because beer doesn't suit her. Except for now and then a shot of Kentucky bourbon, it's about all he drinks. Zirque in Germany must have been like a bookworm locked in the library. But he hardly talked about small-town breweries and yeast-bottomed beers when he got back. Instead he said things like German Expressionism isn't just music made with metal-on-metal percussion or distorted faces painted in warring colors, in black and red, it's all over Berlin, in the streets, at the dinner table, in museums.

They're so unhappy they name their kids after it, imagine callin a little fella Max Angst. Cities, he said, are built around it, neon clubs and all.

He doesn't have the slightest idea what cities are built around, he doesn't know what it's like waiting out the turn of the seasons, thinking you recognize the back of his head, only to find the face unfamiliar. What she's really looking at in town are her display-window memories arranged just so, behind glass where dust won't settle, where you can have a look but you can't put a finger on a familiar feel for reassurance. He's not there when she doesn't have the energy to get out of bed and face the day. When she turns on the television for the sound of voices, even a commercial. Anything but the wind chimes. The clock. The summer insects. There are times when swallowing a whole bottle of aspirin with a pint of whiskey doesn't seem a bad idea.

Just once she wants to be dead when he gets home. If she could just time it so he'd be the one to find her. Before the flies really got to work. If not dead, at least gone. It'd be worth the look on his face if she could see it, him climbing in a window and some people living there he doesn't know. Just to know what he looked like when that happened, when he realized she'd sold the place and moved on. And there's no way he can find her. Wouldn't that be something? It doesn't matter the look would only last for a moment, that he'd shake his head and drive off.

She can call the real estate office this afternoon and make the arrangements. She just might do that.

Summer always worse because she doesn't teach aside from riding lessons here and there, her kindergartners aren't around to take her mind off anything, she winds up clip-clopping into town on Baldy, that horse the only thing that keeps her sane sometimes, a quiet ride better than a bottle of Cold Duck any day. Baldy (his head is white as an eagle's) tied up outside, she sits at Carol's Corner Cafe for all-morning breakfasts (Carol's old clock with its fancy Victorian hands is always wrong anyway), talking to Carol's sister Connie who never slept through a night in her life and looks it, wrinkled as an old dollar bill, a cigarette always burning in her hand, green with snaking veins, speckled brown.

Oh the things I seen in this town, honey.

Connie can tell you them all, pink hair rollers in the whole time, cheeks drawn hollow as she smokes, she was there for the 1888 mine disaster, the worst in Crawford County history, the men trapped and their dark-skinned, black-dressed women waiting in the steadily falling snow, hardly a one of them who spoke English, they'd come from Italy for the better life.

If you could have heard what was coming from the mine you'd've thought the center of the earth haunted. Sixty-eight men died that day.

Looking out the window of the Hotel Stilwell where she slept last night, thinking of youth gone beneath the hard autumn frost brings back that college summer, Zirque and Earl pulled up alongside her in Earl's '56 pick-up, doing three miles an hour while Zirque tried to talk her into a ride, what little patience he had snapping like an old rubber band, he hauled her into the back like some kind of oversized bird. Earl gunning the engine the two of them fell, Zirque cracking his knee good, he laughed the whole way to the 1106 Burger Drive-In anyway. She wouldn't eat anything though, not for all their come-on politeness thick as cooking lard.

Ain't you heard poutin is hazardous to my social life?

Seven french fries was all she would go for – and about as many words, Earl winning a coin toss for her burger, Zirque finishing off the fries.

Who can say how she wound up sneaking out of the house in the middle of the night, easing the screen door so it didn't suck itself closed with a slam, the spring softly squealing anyway, the crickets so loud a wonder her parents could sleep with them chirping away. He'd be there in the dark, the warm air sticky with something honey-suckle sweet, what the wind picked up on its travels through southeastern Kansas. She'd reach for his hand without much looking, without much thinking about it, because once he had it, he never let go, she never worried, he could have walked her over water she trusted him so much, but he only took her up the block to his car, past the row of silent front porches, the flickering blue glow of a tv set left on in Mrs. Breddafeld's house coming through the window. She was always there, fast asleep in her pink nightie, her hair a Medusa's nest of curlers, sunk into a huge brown easy chair that seemed ready to swallow her.

A hundred times at least Zirque took her down Cayuga Street to where he'd parked his Chevy Impala, as loud and heavy as a locomotive coming at you, and they drove along the train tracks, the poles lining the rails planted in the darkness, a row of crosses against the sky tapering into the distance. Until they came to their place, where he'd taken her a hundred times, but this time was different, this time she let him unbutton her favorite white blouse, the August breeze cooling against the dampness underneath (it was hot, she couldn't help she'd begun to sweat), let him take her panties down past her knees, over her bare feet, but he wouldn't go any further, wouldn't do one more thing besides kiss with his shirt off, skin pressed against skin, the Moon up there over his shoulder and all the stars in the leather back seat of that old Chevy convertible (tinny blue with rust eating away the back fenders), the leather making her sweat more than she wanted to, more than women ought to, but it didn't bother him slipping over her, his denims rough across the soft white where her panties had been, pulling the hair just a little while she undid his belt buckle, which scratched her once, made her jerk underneath him, he smiled as she tugged at his pants, down to his ankles – whose idea was it that she couldn't stay just like that, her legs wrapped around him couldn't he see how perfectly they fit together, moved together, could live together? She wanted it to be like that always, their first time, why couldn't it always be that way when they were so in love? The Moon a halo behind his head, and her hands pushing against his chest, her head thrown back into the leather of that musty old Impala too noisy to start unless it was a whole block away from her house, her fingers passed right through his skin, tightened on bone and muscle and lodged in both, and somehow she was breathing through him, her lungs feeling grand and cavernous enough for an echo but breathing through his mouth, a tunnel of wind where his mouth met hers, who needed to breathe anyway in the last moment when for the last time she shuddered against him, her fingers digging into his back, her body filled with the beating of tiny wings, softly dusting mothwings everywhere from her feet to inside her skull tingling just under her scalp so lightly feathery barely touching that maybe they never did touch just stirred up the baby's breath she felt, had already carried her to the stillest most unimaginably still place, everything around her absolutely at rest, it had all stopped forever, or maybe was just gone, burned up in a long beautiful fall and drifted away as ash, dust, nothingness, but she knew it hadn't, it was just that the thrumming wings had taken the place of her body, their gentle swarming intimating the shape she'd once filled out with something a lot more clumsy, a human-sized constellation made of the invisible trails moths trace out in their fluttering erratic patterns, the gorgeous easy warm breeze going right through her there's no sensation in the world like the air moving through skin you don't have anymore but you're still solid enough, sweaty enough, pressed tightly enough against him to feel it until at last when her eyes opened again, she realized she couldn't breathe he was so heavy, *Oh please Zirque I love you but please get off me.* His head hanging over her shoulder as if he'd died came up and even in the moonlight she saw the hard lines of his stomach, ran her hands along his flanks, down his narrow hips.

It was years later he called her Blue Jean, smiling down on her in the backseat of a new Cadillac even though she had her own place by then, they went ahead for old times' sake, my Blue Jean Baby Queen he called her from a favorite song.

I wrote it you know, they stole my lyrics.

He was joking when he said it, but only half. There's a song they play on the radio that haunts him because he hadn't known who to show it to and when he did, they put a different name on it, he never got any money or credit. Okay, a teaspoon of angst for that one. She still remembers picking up the matchbook-cover song while dusting, years before it made it to radio, his jaw still healing. She found them all the time – on envelopes the electric bill came in, torn movie tickets (the words so tiny she could hardly read them), the insides of book covers, the corners of newspapers, she saved every word of every song in the making.

Rock on.

Some of the best times were in the Pan Club where you have to buzz just to be let in, they want a look at you first, Willie bartending and Red talking. Red (his hair is about orange) had done time with Zirque in Jeff City and has the shiny white thread of a scar splitting his left eyebrow to prove he was watching out for him.

Red who told her of destiny altered by a drunken sign maker who mistook the sound of the F in Fan for the P in Pan. Rather than rework what had already been cast in neon, he offered to knock a hundred off the price to keep it that way.

Pan's a mischievous, half-pint forest god with the horns and legs of a goat, Zee Gee told Willie, most often sighted chasing beautiful women if Greek fairy tales are to be believed.

Accidents that pan out are signs of God at work, Willie announced, pocketing his good fortune. Willie used up some of it at a county-sized flea market in Texas where he picked up an alabaster likeness, woodsy setting and all, which he kept behind the bar in a forest of gleaming long-necked bottles.

While Pan grinned from the other side of the bar and Red scratched his stubbly chin and smiled, Zee Gee hustled some 19-year-old biker in a pool game, then beat out Willie for 10 bucks.

I been practicin' up for ya Granges, Willie says with a smile clamped on a cigar stub, his cue twisting in blue chalk, a wink at Blue Jean because it's a game they play so Zirque won't feel he has to pay it back.

He plays pool by instinct, he says, which makes her roll her eyes and look away. Maybe Pittsburg U doesn't give out degrees on the topic, but he had to put in his time at Bartelli's Blue Goose Bar before he got to be any good. Leaning on the table's edge (white Tee sleeve pulling back to show his dark-complected skin), he'd line up a shot with a style distilled from the best he'd seen in pool halls up and down the Midwest, watching him play kind of like the fair being in town, listening to him talk himself up, a sideshow act – keep your eye on the ball – sinking a shot in his careless way, smile like it was nothing, counting on luck like it's something to lean against, the brick side of a building that won't let him down short of a California quake.

Then he'd sit down, a good sweat going, put his arm around

her and the floor'd begin to tip to one side, his eyes black volcanic glass while he talked about where he'd been (careful to skip the pages where the names of women are written). Red, Willie, Earl (his over-white dentures the only thing smooth in his craggy face) would be at their table, full beers materialized while the stories flowed and only the question of why it couldn't always be that way went unasked.

One story about a Navajo dance he called Yay Bi Chay (spelling it a mystery right up there with the Trinity) out there in New Mexico, winter, the dusty earth gone cold, smoke from fires headed for the ancient light a stars. The men wore masks, he said, opted for paint steada shirts, and danced all night with a strange little hoo-hoo sound like no animal he ever heard, around and around with the gravity of a planet, pattin down the dry earth with their feet in a longwise circle, a billion bright holes poked in the dark mask a the sky to get a peek at the dancers – why did it seem their feet landed up there too, up in that blacked-over nothin? Fill the nothin with a little dancin is why they did it, hoo-hoo away the silence for a while – you never know, the earth might lose its shape, flatten out without em. Dust settling almost as soon as their short quick-time steps kicked it up, only firelight and a little sky-sparkle to see those Navajos by, they traveled to the curved far end a vision and back, the faces watching shadowy and rigid, one old man with glasses on like a smoldery-eyed demon Zirque didn't know why smoke wasn't comin outta his mouth. The painted dancers – gray and black if he recalled right, like they'd rubbed their bare chests with charcoal and ash – the masked dancers kept up until the stars faded (though the fires still burned) and the sky grew gray-blue. He stayed and watched and drank, passing his bottle around, later picking up a toothless Navajo hitcher who smelled like smoke and beer, both of them with eyes itching and red, running on something the dancers had passed on. Zirque road him near 200 miles home for which he received a blessing in a language he didn't understand.

Jack Hanes interrupted, complaining loudly the painting business was damn well bad enough to make another beer about as hazy a possibility as the Second Coming.

Hope the beer makes it first, Zirque said, taking a swallow of his own before going back to the dance.

It was hypnotic, he said, staring down at something at his feet, like watching the waves roll in over the shore. No matter how many you watch, you can still sit for one more. Felt it about the same place, too, a deep, deliberate pull, like a peek at infinity, and the big surprise is you're part of it.

The dancing painted men in their masks, antlers branching from their heads (he mentioned antlers, didn't he?) got her thinking maybe he's not ... well maybe he's just wearing a mask himself, he'll never die, just change the mask. Right about the time something like that came to mind, he'd put a quarter in the jukebox and play that song and sing to her.

See her shake on the movie screen.

Hollywood doesn't know what it's missing. Tall, shapely, green-eyed as cut glass, hair the color of a two-year-old penny, the shine of a fish cutting away, a flash and gone, still a few shades darker than Red.

Prettiest girl I ever seen.

Red always reminded them, before the night burned softly down to gray ashes they threw to the stars, what a right handsome couple they made. The three of them driving off in a convertible if Zee Gee could manage one, up route 69, on to the place where dawn meets the road.

Zirque the Jerk, Red would say shaking his head when he got stood up for drinks. Red – he has about the most angelic smile you've ever seen and hands wide enough to palm a truck tire –

wouldn't know what to say or do to make her feel there was anything between Kansas and the Moon worth living for.

He'll be back, was the best he could manage.

He's a refrain from a song, she wanted to tell Red, you never know when you'll hear it again, but when you do, you keep hoping the words will be different. They never are. Maybe because everyone's willing to grant forgiveness, she the abused saint of them all.

It makes her wonder if he feels any difference between pain and pleasure, he seems to give them out in equal amounts.

Life is like that theater mask, it's two faced, you know, one face with a big Cheshire Cat grin, the other with that same grin upside down, in reverse.

In college they told her comedy is when everyone at the end of the play marries everybody else. Tragedy is when everybody dies in the last act.

What about utopia, you ever heard a that one? He probably asked to get at some obscure fact, offer it like a pretty shell for her collection.

Sure, I know what it is. It's when your man stays with you all year round and it ends with they lived happily ever after. It's comedy.

C'mon now Blue Jean, a woman as pretty as you to come back to, hair the kind of red likely to singe the naked retina, you ever known me not to come home?

No, but I've never known you to take me with you either.

Well, a few times, okay, the trip to Mexico the one she remembers most. There were pyramids down there that stacked up to the ones in Egypt, he told her, and could have shown her pictures in a library book but he told her to pack a trunk and throw it in the car.

We're going to Meh-Heeco.

She'd never seen so many poor people in all her life, outside of town in plywood shacks, sadly faded colors much too bright in the first place, but maybe it took their minds off walking on dirt floors, off the fact water had to be carried in pails. There were plenty of penniless families in Kansas she knew, but not all in one place.

In town, crowded as church on Sunday morning with no end to the shops and souvenir sellers, he bought her silver jewelry, carna-vollay-colored dresses and blankets from men who stopped them in the streets. He never paid asking price because when he spoke, pesos evaporated.

A thief would offer 2,000 pesos. *Un ladron.*

One thousand.

Madre de Dios! Giving it away would be better.

Be my guest.

He started to walk away, but they wouldn't let him, first giving chase, then giving in.

The first night he sang in Spanish with three little men in colorful ponchos, darker than him, playing tiny guitars and shaking maracas. La Rubia they called her, so air-mosa.

They think you're about as pretty as a sunrise, Zirque said. They'll be wanting to name a drink after you before we leave.

She drank salty margaritas, Zirque playing the big spender, taking shots of tequila, buying for the men who joined in. That night, with mostly table candles for light, she could see he was kin to those people, pure cannibal if he did up his face right. His eyes more squinty than ever but his smile innocent and generous, like her father's. They danced till sun-up, those men making music out of clapping, calling *La Rubia! La Rubia!*

Morning was a beach near Ensenada with sad, half-starved horses. He took her riding anyway and paid the straight-haired boy with big brown eyes twice what he should have, making him promise to get the animals more feed. She'd never ridden on a beach and fell in love with the smell of the sea and the spray kicked up by the hooves, all with bluish mountains dissolving in the gray distance.

They kept driving south, climbing winding badly paved roads through tiny towns where the goats crossed the street in bunches and short men in ponchos and sandals (cut from old tires Zirque told her) looked up inquisitively at the red Cadillac convertible with its fancy tail fins. They passed the religion of the land housed in stained once-white walls and roofed in cracking Spanish tiles as orange as sunbaked clay, brought a long time ago on the armored backs of bearded foreigners along with rusting crosses (now and askew atop steeples), the road empty except for them and the goats, out of place in that moss-green mountain stillness. Zirque drove with one hand on the wheel, the other holding hers, the air getting thinner all the while, the mornings cool enough to make their breath mist.

It's not like those westerns that make you think Mexico is one big desert, is it? He put his arm around her. We're half way to god up here.

Finally they made it to a city so old it was already abandoned, weeds growing through cracks in stone streets by the time the Aztecs got to it. The Indians who'd built it, he said, had become extinct. Sure enough, the wide perfectly straight *Calle de los Muertos* was empty except for the tourists and souvenir sellers. And there – she could hardly believe her eyes – were pyramids, two of them.

Piramide del Sol, he said pointing at the one closer to them, Pyramid of the Sun. And over there's the Moon.

Flatter and wider than the ones in Egypt, settled not in sand, in the desert, but in the green mountains, with steps going to the tops. The Moon Pyramid was smaller but prettier, terraced, not so much the pile of stone the Sun turned out to be, cement holding in place the old broken stones. She tried to imagine what it was like when it was a city ... did they really have sacrifices up here? Thought of herself on her back, stony cold altar underneath her, at the flat peak of the Pyramid of the Sun, a man whose head was wild with feathers – great long ones fanning out like a peacock's tail – standing over her bared chest with a knife –

A flint knife, he told her, no metal back then, not here.

– a strange cry going up from the bird-priest before he plunged the dark blade in the name of the Sun, in the name of the great serpent whose image she'd seen in stone, a dragon more like, with a few feathers around its head, Ketzal-whatever.

Gives me the creeps thinking about it.

They're all gone, long time ago. Come on, let's go to the top.

There must have been a hundred steps to the Sun, and when they got there, a little out of breath, it seemed she could see enough land to cover the whole state of Kansas, except there were mountains grander than anything in Kansas. She'd never seen so far in her whole life – had anyone back in Pittsburg? She knew then where eagles got off looking so arrogant, a view like that an everyday thing for them, up there where gravity lost its grip, the earth a more majestic place than you want to give it credit for when you can only see a little piece at a time.

Beautiful ain't it?

Oh yes, this must be half way to heaven.

But he's left her somewhere on that stairway one too many times. She's not going to take him back again. Not when she's got the card of that real estate woman in her pocket and the one parent God left her on this earth in Joplin, her mamma, who would take in her only daughter, Joplin hardly any distance to speak of. A new place, a new man, a new life. Lord only knows when he'll be back again. Years could be. He can make someone else Mrs. Granges.

She pulls aside the brown drape – heavy enough to have covered a settler's wagon – to look out the third-floor window of the Stilwell Hotel, the oldest building left in Pittsburg, put up around 1889 if she remembers right, where she spent the night with a man who's still asleep. If she can get out of the room without waking him – if she never sees him again – her faith in a guardian angel will be renewed. Younger than her, he was sweet it's true, but stupidity showed on his face like a price tag someone forgot to take off. If it weren't for Zirque, she wouldn't have to go out and whore herself out of spite. To get coke or sleeping pills. Just for company.

Outside, big slow flakes drift in a slant past the glass storefronts – the old Gutteridge Pharmacy with its baseball black-and-whites, Pittsburg's Hardware Company, Carol's Corner Cafe where everyone goes for the breakfast special. And she can hardly believe it, but there he is at a stop light. Sitting in a red Cadillac convertible, the kind with fins. Top down, flakes of snow gathered against his dark hair like lost stars, that Steely Dan in-a-room-with-your-two-timer song on the radio fading as he pulls away.

She really doesn't mean to bother God about all this but, her eyes fixed on his glowing tail lights, she can't help it. Lord in Heaven I couldn't stand to go to the bottom of any mineshaft again even if it is a dream. I don't want to be like that Greek girl he told me about, what's-her-name, who was stolen away, who let herself die a little, turn brown like autumn grass – just for a while – saving herself for better days, waiting for spring. I know he'll be back, he'll bring spring with 'im (nevermind this light snow), Zirque you always do, please Zirque, I want it to be spring, not any mineshaft winter, please can't you be on your way to my house?

OVERHEAD, LIKE ORION

Mid the uneasy wanderings of paleolithic man,
the dead were the first to have a permanent dwelling:
a cavern, a mound marked by a cairn, a collective barrow.
— Lewis Mumford, *The City in History*

The downtown is brick. A sense a permanence in that, some-thin you can lean against after last call. The pitted surface a local history, a mason's hand in all in those neat layers and straight corners showin in the scanty light – mostly from poles overhead, lettered neon thrown in, free floatin in shop windows. Broadway, wide an' two-way, goes off to meet a dark sky. Broadway or Main Street, every town big enough to have a name has one.

A light turns red in quiet enough to hear the metallic click.

From a few hotel stories up, this town don't look like much, a little cross-hatchin a tar streets an' concrete sidewalks on the plains, could be swept away by one a those summer thunder-storms, angry clouds comin in like a dark billowin herd driven by wind riders, winds up takin up the whole sky, lightnin spiderin across a stretch a black big as half the state, but town's still here, the dust a worn out years blowin down Broad, the centerpiece a this place I guess bein the Hotel Stilwell, a fancy one in its time, run down now, what's left around here a the grandness of Old World Europe, quite a sight in its day.

Sometimes Pittsburg seems a Hollywood town almost, all façade, mostly sky an' open field behind. Alleys, streets an' back-sides a buildings don't make much of a maze – no New York or Kansas City – but it ain't the way home that's hard t'find here.

Take a left down 5th Street. Farley's Tavern stands an aged landmark, an anchor for things lost'n uprooted. Slow fans hangin from one a those high fancy tin ceilings. A place bygone travelers would haunt given the chance. Weightless transparent moths flutterin in the mellow light, brushin up against the front window, see-through but impassable.

Here on Broadway the neon Gutteridge Pharmacy sign burnin silently red lets you peak at what's behind the window: antique drug bottles, boxes of imported cigars, black-&-whites a baseball greats like Lou Gherig, Ty Cobb, a tall freckled boy from these parts whose name I don't recall, on his way to bein a major leaguer when he got electrocuted on farm machinery one rainy night. Two greats, one woulda-been, all three gone – the Thomas boy, that's him, a black-cat-crossed path, eyes closed peaceful now, celluloid mask all that's left a him an' the rest. The ghost of an entire world (that lived an' died a billion years before this one) moves inexplicably through me, leaves inside a my ribs the kinda space could take in a mountain range.

After miles an' months, Pittsburg (we got one in Kansas) was a promise kept. I'd had my share a dead ends an' one ways, of un-marked dirt drives without a single lamp to let you know what you were gettin yourself into.

A man gets tired a trackin down the source a the forces that shape his life, that show themselves on rare occasions in unex-pected ways. Cagey as the secret shapes of woman in curves of flame. You grab holda the main circuit, hang on for all you're worth. Makes you feel like a pool ball sent reeling by the cue, makes you glad to have landed in a pocket.

Other times – right now is one of 'em – I need to be movin. Preferably through open country. (Conveniently forgettin those bottomless places only a woman knows how to fill.)

You make do.

Wherever they finally plant my body, I'll always live in Pittsburg, alongside Gutteridge's baseball heroes, the invisible moth-swarm outside Farley's, next to Blue Jean (prettiest girl I ever seen) and the rest of 'em – Red, with that scar like a lightnin bolt through an eyebrow, likely to be drinkin at the Pan Club right about now (Hey, where's your green card? Willie said first time I walked in, Can't serve an illegal. Earl snapped a beer cap at me, both of 'em laughin. Wouldn't it be somethin if one a them drove by right now and gave me a lift outta town?)

Somewhere up in KC, Skunk is cleanin those glass circles he wears on his nose an' complainin the price The Cordoba charges for its girls has gone up. Who knows, maybe Pap's with 'im.

Blue Jean at home earlier this evening, pannin the sky like a prospector for her sign risin, sleepin now, the pillow held tight.

The Earl, silver-haired though he is, married again. Cheatin on his wife, again.

Watch y'up to Earl?

Pickin m'nose an' rubbin m'ass. Earl'd lift his KC Royals cap –covers where he's going bald – settle it back on his head.

The Duke a Pallucca, his short legs carryin his thick body, Branson-bought walkin stick in hand, logs endless miles in Frontenac an' Pittsburg, talkin to Indian ghosts who greet him in dawn-dusk mists an' call 'im Troubled Heart because a virus about shut down his primary pump.

How are ya Duke?

Fair t'middlin.

Me – No Trail, False Trail, Lost His Way – the least likely of all to be tracked down. One a these shoulda been my God-given name.

As a boy it started (called me by my initials, Z.G., even then), never got my fill of empty places, abandoned buildings, mine shafts. Exhaustin things hereabouts I discovered the railroad tracks one winter, desolate but promisin, most a them rustin destinies since the coal mines died out an' the miners had mostly gone to the earth they worked. Ran alongside a train car, jumped it, cold wind squintin my eyes, yankin back my hair, occurred to me borrowin a ride beat payin. Came to the conclusion there're things enough in the world, why add t'the pile? Course, you can do time for borrowin without permission.

Once used a waiter's uniform an' posed as a valet parker at a fancy restaurant in Chicago. By the time the maitre D' came out to see what was goin on, all he got was a good look at the tail lights. Mercedes Benz that time. Shopliftin, bad checks, dope deals. New York, Chicago, California, Oklahoma, Mexico. Places somehow tied to what's been done in them.

There are ways to tell.

First night I sleep in a place somethin that happened there happens again in my dreams. Leaves owners with astonished faces hoverin over steamin breakfast eggs often enough. *Well I'll be.* Somethin sticks to the wooden ribs of a house, stains the Earth like blood from a biblical killin never dried up.

Blamin my restlessness on anythin that can't get up to argue the point, I take the way of greatest desire, whatever the moment dangles before me. A blueprint drawn up by expectation, most often endin in disappointment. Tempered by the Nowherevilles no one's ever heard of but you spend a good part of a lifetime there, not measured by a clock but by what happens to you, how deep it presses into memory.

Half my years it seems rose an' fell in the Duke's half-lit basement. College-educated, sternly Catholic, his face somethin saintly an' weathered, a stone likeness that's been standin an' watchin the archway of a gate since Roman times, ain't much gets past without his noticin. He's like that card in a fortune teller's deck, wavin around a lantern, leanin on a walkin stick when he's on his way somewhere, mostly alone, whether readin from books stacked ceiling-high in his basement or strollin the hazy beginnins of day on Cayuga Street. He can go off on a one-sided conversation like no one I know, every sentence a keeper till you have so many you don't know what to do with 'em. Talks insteada sleeps, right through the night, pullin down a book every now and then for cross-referencin, losing me in funhouse turns till just when I think there's no way back I find familiar ground.

Memories, he says, are handles connected to time.

What he learned from his illness, he said, is the heart ain't a muscle but a place, where you either live, or you don't.

Blue Jean says I broke hers a hundred and fifty times at least. But I always come back. I got a chronic case of claustrophobia that'll turn terminal if I don't get away from time to time. You can't call it id or superego, it's an illness a the spirit around since the time a the ziggurat-builders in Sumer.

Man's always been hollow, since the day a goddess breathed him alive. Just solid enough to build cities. Me, just empty enough for dust storms to kick up. Not somethin to wait out, but somethin that *wants* out. Aren't too many ways either. To pass the time, I useta rope steer, sell door to door (I still do), steal cars (I always will). When I get the chance, I don't mind singin in my half-assed voice, watchin twists a cigarette smoke drift up toward the hot light. The music sounds out the deepest places in you, leaves you alone in them, a disappearing act kinda, turns you for a little while into the answer to the prayer you been prayin all your life. Till the house lights come on, the song ends, the spell's broken.

I do the same things over and over it seems, the place what changes. For some reason, a beer can take on a different taste in a bar you never been to, Mexico maybe. Or Nebraska. Greece if you're the kind who gets around.

There's quite a feelin to be had sittin on a white-stoned veranda overlookin the darkened cone of a volcano – set in the waverin blue shimmer a the Mediterranean – that downed a civilization around 1400 BC. I watched the sun settle behind that blackened rim a disaster, turn the water inta melted bronze while ships dwarfed by distance set out for wherever. And even though I was in a place where ships arrived everyday, a twinge a me wanted to be on one.

It's always that way. In a pocket fulla crumpled, unanswered (or once-answered) desires, we keep a photo of what it is we want (again maybe) an' hold it up to everythin we get. Time after time there's a shakin of the head, a return a the photo.

There's a still of me in Blue Jean's kitchen, standin alongside the reddish pillars at Knossos, the labyrinth island a Crete. Inventors a the flush toilet, keepers a the sacred bull rites, of the bullbeast with a man's body. Lost at night in the dark cobblestone alleys, adrift in streets, in half-lit stone-walled bars fulla men with heavy heads an' thick black mustaches, there's an invisibly thin thread ties me to her I never lose sight of.

A detour takes me to Delphi under sea winds, not a streamlined Minoan boat with sails but a ferry stinkin a diesel with no sleep for the worn-out on an oil-slick deck, the vibrations a the engine like a star about to explode. Delphi, center of the world an old Greek told me, bald as Telly Savalas, *Evreeteeng at Delphee.*

No, just some ruins an' beautiful mountains, remnants of an oracle.

Used to be, Apollo's priestess was go-between for the god an' questioners. Sometimes great men, sometimes small-timers with great questions. The oracle answered true, but had a likin for curve balls. Some king went there with startin a war on his mind, asked the oracle what would happen if he did. Oracle said a great empire'd fall. The king got excited and headed off, sword in hand. Was his own empire that went to dust.

The whole point bein, like anythin else, even a statement that would hold up in court can lead you astray.

Keen as we are to pick up the hint as to which way things in this world are goin, don't take more than an onion to send us headin off in the wrong direction. Take what Blue Jean said to me while makin dinner one evening. Looked at the onion she was cuttin an' wondered how it got that way, with its layered arrangement – peeled neatly away, or made rings if you sliced it right – and couldn't bring herself to believe the complicated nature a the onion was a chance act. Based on this evidence, she cast her vote for God. Like late-night neon, an onion can say something without meanin to – specially when Blue Jean's the one listenin. Mainly what an onion says to me is come and get it.

I can smell her kitchen a thousand miles away.

Watchin her cook, one a those scratched-up Chet Baker records she borrowed from Pap wearin out the needle a that antique phonograph player used to be her daddy's, the back door open to let in the August breeze and the evenin sun fadin amber while behind the salt an' pepper shakers, winged Eros – painted black on burnt orange – forever offers white-skinned Athena fruit (piece a pottery I managed t'bring back for her by stickin it dead center a the clothes stuffed in my duffle bag). Postcards an' photos on the walls, wine bottles an' porcelain vases arranged with dry flowers on countertops, glass do-dads an' antique what-nots found at second-hand shops in Joplin or front-lawn junkyards, she's got quite a collection goin.

She cooks meticulously, favors oregano, onions, garden-grown green pepper, garlic fresh from Pallucca's Market, parsley an' black pepper. Never measures a thing and never mis-seasons down to a grain of salt. Home never smelled so good. Get your feet off my table, Zirque.

Summer in Kansas brings out the mature lines in her face, reminds me what she'd look like if she lived in a place like New Mexico or Arizona. Her body with the smooth hardness of a reclinin rock.

Sometimes, she says, it's so flat and plain around here I can't stand it.

Sometimes I think exactly that: I can't change it, I can't stand it, I might as well get as far away from it as I can. (Each bootfall takes me farther.)

From time to time I take her with me. Monument Valley, rock formations like gigantic sailin ships stranded in an ocean expanse a desert, oddly masted, too heavy to be carried on a light dry breeze headed for livelier seas. The crown a creation, where the sun wrote its epitaph in afterglow on the dark sandstone. Venus rose in the last a the blue an' the towerin stone became stoic silhouettes, like time still standin.

I bet you could catch sight a the next day from the top a one a those, she said.

First light in Kansas (summertime when school's out an' she doesn't have t'teach) most often finds her in the barn, brushin down Baldy, her favorite horse. On cool mornins toward September, Baldy's flared nostrils steam, an' the wind gets streaked the color of her hair when she rides. She's probably better'n I am but defers to me because a rodeo rings.

This mornin we came to the fence around her land, I wanted to jump it an' keep goin. I looked at her, she looked away, she knew what I was thinkin.

This mornin leavin was right there in the room with me,

holdin the door open, pointin the way. I looked at her, knew I loved her, an' knew another minute would turn love to resentment. The flatness, the fences, even her face – beautiful as it was while she slept – I needed to be somewhere else, anywhere else, with anyone else.

Though dreamin tonight when I left, I know she can hear me. She can hear wheat grow.

Here on the edge a town, lights dimmin, darkness outta focus, Pittsburg's cemetery marks passings. Gray, white, black marble stones for no reason other than life doesn't seem so never was, see-through, over. Lookin over a shoulder, thinkin about backtracking, I see the pattern Blue Jean an' I fell into. She saw the seed of now in what was then same as I did, she didn't accept it is the difference.

Zirque (she was in the middle a the dishes) you think it's true you do to other people what you do to yourself?

What makes you ask?

A shrug. Psychology, she said.

A night course she took to be less small-town.

She put a drippin dish in the rack. If you lie to yourself, it's easier to lie to people you're with. You think so?

Sounds about right.

From a city divided by a common wall, I wondered is she lookin up at the same moon? (There are two Berlins, not east an' west, but one bombed out, lastin only in memory; one built on those vanished foundations.)

No, it's day where she is.

Buildins gone, bricks left, blueprints an' history remain. One Berlin exists only in imagination, the mythic realm a the Hopi on their mesas overlookin the fallin a time like slow dry rain on an earth erodin in desert wind. They still recall the Red City a the South, destroyed like the bustlin 1930s Berlin of old, but both a them still exist, underneath what we're standin on though we can't get t'them anymore, the Place a Dreamin it's called maybe, the place we crawled up out of like ants out of a hill, each passin minute a grain a sand added, the hill goes up an' there's no way back down. So vintage Berlin somehow reaches out to New York an' Paris along jazz wavelengths, reserves a whole dimension for Hollywood (sittin on the U-Bahn subway, a blond German with a duck's ass an' divin-board pompadour, a worn leather jacket, James Dean patch that was just a silk-screen shape no detail to its black ink shadow. James Dean an avatar, the sincerest form a religion bein imitation).

Bridges have caved in but a saxophone goes on squeezin sound from brass, echoes against the stone ruins of *kristalnacht* burned-out synagogue, the temple a window-eyed mask with no face behind. On the Wall, a shadow left in the shape a someone reaching up, shot in the act. *What are you looking at,* in spray-painted German, a translation chalked in, *haven't you ever seen a wall before?* Tremblin shadows cast by searchlights still whisper past on nights, all that's left a the ones scratched onto the wall: 1970 – 12 shot. 1971 – 11 shot. 1972 – 6 shot ... so far. You gotta admire they're givin it a go, gotta admire the one's who made it (where there's a wall, there's a way).

In night clubs just underneath the velvet, the fancy gold trim an' the chandeliers with diamond-shaped crystals big as horse turds, the grayin stained chipped bare cement remains. A crystalline wind-chime hanging in the breezeless ruins, Berlin night clubs like to let you know Viennese grandeur is founded on the same ugliness as everythin else.

Cafe Orianenberg, steel chairs twisted like strung-out entrails only a little more elegant. Everythin tall, elongated, backs a those chairs rise up way past your head, as if gravity were weaker there. An illusion because gravity has pulled them, agonizingly slowly –

as if lookin to prolong time here through space – out of their original shape. Not so much the back of a chair I was restin against as a steel cuneiform tablet made to look like cracked clay, the destiny of a city written on it, a thread of tragedy in the tapestry a history. You expect rain t'be thick as engine oil, corrosive as battery acid, t'smell like asphalt. Even sunlight in those cafes is walled off, shows up in cement-cut squares.

Steel gray light near dawn, lookin at the waterstained pension ceiling – permanent yellowish cloud formation on the dirty white-sigh sky a that faded ceilin – I'da given anything to be with her then. The mornin light comes inta her bedroom on a particular slant I haven't found in any other part a the world, no kitchen has the seasoned smell a hers sunk right into the woodwork, no woman I ever slept with feels the same next to me.

Good mornin Sweetness and Light.

Don't call me that, makes me sound like coffee.

You're the fire in my stove, you know that, right?

Stop it, Zirque.

The light in my window.

You're so ridiculous.

The bulb in my lamp.

I don't know why I put up with you.

Come on, let's head out to the Corner Café, I want everyone to see how good you look in the mornin.

Morning passes by in the steam a coffee, the smoke a bacon grease, paunchy Al sweatin over the grill, Connie goin table to table talkin up a twister *Don't come over here with that cigarette,* she only smokes one, but it never goes out not once did I ever see her light up the second one I swear the first never goes out. Then it's a PiCCO malted, nothin Blue Jean likes better. We used to run into Pap now an' again, gettin one to cure a hangover, *Fanshy meetin you here Granges,* he'd say as if he had high manners.

Leanin against the fender a my car parked in PiCCO's gravel lot, Blue Jean would work so hard on gettin that malt thick as it was through the straw she'd forget me. A gust a wind and the leaves a September came up around us, a whirlin circle, settled back down in fall colors amber bleedin into red dusted with orange this whole town covered in every moment we ever spent together a drift a fall color over Pittsburg and Frontenac, an' every breeze that kicks up we remember while she sits there on the hood a my car wearin my denim jacket the sleeves coverin over her hands just about, every candle lit beneath the stone statue of a saint in the darkness a the old Catholic church on Locust Street gathered right there in her eyes above that malted smile poked through with a red-striped straw, I heard – though he was gone from this earth by then – old Raymond Pallucca, his voice a rusty wheelbarrow *Well hello there Rae Anne how you been don't you look beautiful today you're not in a rush I hope you can stay and say hello to an admirer,* a little girl she looked so happy, the cold sweet malted slush in her cup all it took, a warm kiss against cold lips, her tongue cold too (that's how we know we're walkin breathin warm- blooded fragments a the universe), an' then a little shoppin on Broadway and a greasy burger an' thick fries at the 501 drive-up joint where we catch sight a the Duke a Pallucca an' Millo Farnetti that old mine mule he lived in Italy on and off twenty years got his picture in the World Book Encyclopedia under journalism, an' somehow it's evenin already an' we drive back home to the quiet a the fields don't need a thing besides her on those cool enda-summer evenins, everythin its rightful place feelin without a doubt with her huggin herself to me the way she fits to me the way the two of us fit to the whole sweep a the land – every blade a grass bendin past the porch steps, every blackbird call in the deepenin grayin blue, every strip a cloud an' shred a light the sky has left can't move a thing half an inch right or left (like touchin the water to get at the reflection it'll all disappear) just hold onto her on that backyard swing, a little countrywestern or New Orleans jazz driftin out from the radio in her kitchen I'm never happier than when I'm with her I guess I can only handle so much before I stop appreciatin it wind up sleepin on rocks for a while to remind me how good it'd be t'get back to a feather bed.

A shame, the Duke said, you don't leave anythin behind, any more than a boat marks the water by its passin.

It's no coincidence the constellations're named after mythical beings, those old stories a tunnel – studded with bits a the Milky Way – we travel to reach a place we feel like we belong, we get a part in the stories we tell from cradle to grave, grave an earth cradle meant to hold us once again when we're nothin but leather-skinned bags fulla bones an' withered organs, curled up fetal, head-to-knee the next thousand years.

Never even scratched my name in a desk in Pittsburg Elementary, best I can hope for when I'm gone I guess is somebody'll save my skull like those African primitives do *Where be your tribes now, Granges?* Put it on a shelf somewhere like the one Pap used t'have, paint it a color to match the room maybe, set a beer next to me, I'll catch somma what dries off. Leave off my lower jaw if you don't want me jabberin and keepin you up at night, I'll just sit up there, watch the seasons turn, the light fallin slightly different fall to summer, pale winter light the loneliest for my bones up there on the shelf, keep the fire stoked you'll always have a friend exactly where you left him say hello to when you come home.

In the city where I want to live, desire an' outlet – a pair a one-way streets – run into each other, I want to set up shop on the corner. Might as well try standin at the core of a nuclear reactor, you say. But there is love an' the phenomenon of joined bodies, resonance on another plane. Maybe as close as anyone'll ever get. I hear that's what artists're starvin for. They know existence isn't something you can look up in Websters an' have the vagueness cleared up, but they go on tryin, usually cuttin it down to size so you can take it in at a glance.

Veronique said art's a way of lookin at things that shows you somethin you've never seen before but has always been there. I said, Art's a drunk who drowned one night in a sewer ditch in Crawford County Kansas. She didn't even crack a smile.

All right I said, take an itty bitty piece a nothin weighs nothing with a high-charged name, an electron, gets excited, jumps a gravity groove – no, an orbital – finds itself in a new dimension. Spinnin itself dizzy on the edge, it can't stay forever. When it falls leaves behind a fragment a light. We leave behind writin, a paintin, a song, a dance.

Better, she said.

Better than art Veronique, a subtle shift in emotion made solid, given a cold tongue with the fadin taste a malt, imagine that.

I met her in Paris, Bar Sept, smoky little cave with tables everywhere, dozens a small orangish lights t'give the effect a candles, a collage a magazine photos coverin the walls: sculpted women wearin the latest fashions; bodies a soldiers frozen as if they'd once been flamin wax, hardened, the fire gone out; presidents, politicians makin speeches to admirin crowds. In the crowded bar women with fitted looks, a platinum Warhol wig, darkness made visible by wraparound sunglasses, curiously held cigarettes, voices formin words as smooth as shells worn thin by the sea's relentless rhythm (*Ne me le dit pas. Ce n'est pas possibl*e!) polished lips slipping over glass rims. Stole the bartender's tips t'buy my first drink. A floor down there like a dungeon, steep iron stairs an' moss creeping through furrows in the old stone walls reminds you high civilization's been there for a while.

Soon as I saw her I invited myself to her table.

She looked at me, straight through me, then turned away as

if talkin to the wall. Pale with black hair, sharp cheekbones, uncanny lips which somehow intimated themselves in the shapin a words (you'da been able to see them even in perfect darkness long as you could hear what she was sayin).

Camus and Dean, she said through her French accent, the first real outsiders, modern history begins with them.

How do you mean?

They had – *qu'est-ce que c'est?* – a floating consciousness. In some way above things even while right in the middle of them.

Veronique gave me this theory: You will only meet a certain number of people in your life. You will meet these people again and again whether you try to or not.

Red, the Duke, Pap, Blue Jean, Veronique.

When I came back to Paris, she was her own proof, I ran into her in another bar, went home with her that night, too. We didn't always know where to find each other in Paris but usually did, middle a the night more often than not.

Night intensifies the difference between shadow and light, she wrote to me, that is why I sleep all day.

Blue Jean calls me Rip Van Granges, thinks I slept my life away, coulda been a this, coulda been a that. But you take rodeo riding I never wanted to make a life of it, or anythin else. This place is nobody's friend, never will be, but you carve outta whatever your knife can cut into somethin you can live with, your initials, a grinnin god, a back porch. You surround yourself with things a your own doin, somethin a the way a seein things you've come to call your own. An' you make an uneasy peace with things your blade can't scratch.

You appreciate things more when you've seen a huntin knife as far inside a man as it can sink an' the stare in his eyes as he gets a look at a place he never imagined he'd be going. If vudasia (the Duke's word) is the hauntin suspicion you're some place you never want to be, that has to be the worst case there is.

I've been close enough.

Only sixteen years old, balmy kinda August evenin, ridin a Honda, old box-type-fender, wasn't doin more than 25 miles an hour, enjoyin the mildness a the summer drizzle. Picked up my leg just in time, I woulda lost it cop told me later. All I saw were the headlights before everythin turned black, reached out in the center of an endless darkness only to get a hand on somethin as rough an' cold as buried coal, the bottom a some earth-frozen mineshaft I guess only it felt like the bottom a endless space, this taste like I'd swallowed a mouthful a clay an' I called out with my clay-clogged mouth but there was only my own echo down there in a shaft a pure black carved outta dusty Kansas ore. Took a while before I saw off in the distance a hangin light, one a them old lamps burns oil maybe, a miner come lookin for a fool from way above sea level took a wrong turn, I called to him *Hey, bring that over here, wouldja, help me get my bearings.* The light kept gettin brighter, but the source was gone an' I was surrounded by a thousand suns it seemed only it didn't hurt my eyes, can you figure? I heard a voice, Old Man Varanelli's I would swear it was he'd died years before in one a the mines, heard him say *We're not ready for you yet.* Felt no pain, near floatin in the thick light, that's about what I was, a fleck a dust trapped in a shaft a sunlight, felt as good as those Sunday mornins you get up knowin you don't have to work, the air is real crisp breathin seems more than you could ask for, whaddayou mean you're not ready for me yet?

Next spoken words I heard weren't Old Man Varanelli, *We got him back.* I read in the *Pittsburg Sun* how I bounced off the Caddy that hit me, off another car (the window was open a crack, I broke his glasses in two as I flew by, ripped off a windshield wiper with the back a my neck), then went 65 feet down the road. Front tire a the bike came clean off, the forks were stuck in a tree (couldn't pull that off again if you staged a couple thousand accidents) paper said I was dead for near five minutes.

Dyin's no fun sure but despair's no carnival ride either. That train station in Italy, a depression thick as the heat the greased tracks scorched by the Mediterraneo sun what it smelled like. Futility. Sounds like somethin temporarily outta order, looks like Greek columns standin atop a cliff above the sea, all that's lefta the Temple a Poseidon. Kids' initials carved in the sun-whitened stone, insects makin the same lonely sounds they do in Kansas you might think Classical architecture makes the difference or being in another country. But sometimes you might as well be lookin at a fillin station gone to weeds on a dirt road in Oklahoma, a likelihood temples were as common to the ancients as fillin stations and no less useful.

I recall a grand old cathedral, vaulted ceilins high as heaven, glowin colored glass reminds you holes're poked in the fabric a things, somethin shines through, gold saints an' bishops an' a sad-faced Madonna lookin a lot like the Mona Lisa. Tried prayin in the cavernous darkness, here an' there a few candles like lost souls, felt just like I was talkin into a dial tone, no connection. Prayed Blue Jean'd wait for me, wouldn't be lonely, Red'n Earl'd keep an eye on her. But just as I left somehow in the glow – rare purple outta ancient Tyre, fall-leaf yellow, a green near as strikin as Blue Jean's eyes, red on its way to violet, all in cut-gem kaleidoscope shapes – somehow in that illumined gloom I finally saw the larger pattern, bigger than life, floating up there Jesus in the dark stone wall. Felt not so much a faker but a betrayer, a user, hedgin my bets just in case you're listenin Lord.

A room is all I need Blue Jean. One in your house and one in your heart. Not the run a them, just to know I have a place to come back to, your mouth your tongue cold with a PiCCO malted and the smell in your room early mornin (half your perfume, half what's under it), strands a red hair fallin across the side a your face (no alabaster likeness in any museum could come close) you account for all the sweetness an' light in my life. Alchemists of old thought gold was a chunk a sunlight gone solid, if you believe that Blue Jean then you're a piece a heaven fell t'Earth. Once upon a time with see-through flesh, bones made a brightness, a red-headed kachina with green stars for eyes, come all this way from a home out where Halley's Comet could get lost the sun's so small you can hardly see it you landed in Pittsburg Kansas real as the rest of us I watch your breath on clear cold mornings hopin you'll keep me warm keep me company keep me here with you one day I'll be home to stay.

After death finally does us part, I can't say I'd mind bein stretched out overhead like Orion. A man can't ask for much more than that at the end, t'be made into a constellation, to be pointed at by young lovers in their parked convertible, a signpost to restless travelers, always a part of the ongoing clockwork starshifts in the sky, what makes it familiar like the old compadre you want it to be. You can't live forever, but you can become a universal signpost.

I remember you on our back porch Rae Anne, not far from rustin tracks going nowhere now, blue evening tied around your waist an' the season's last sheen grown coppery on your hair. You watch for the things that go arm-in-arm with night and I think: what was once (Knossos, Farley's Tavern, my love for you) has always been. And everything, I can't but believe, is still to come.

CADA EDAD TIENE SU ENCANTO

Some time around dawn on September 16, 1810, in the Mexican Village of Dolores, Padre Miguel Hidalgo uttered his cry for freedom from Spanish rule. The famous call to rebellion has since become known as El Grito de Dolores.

Here, Eduardo will tell you, is the magic: When he wasn't looking, two weeks were turned into 12 years. *Abracadabra.* He will hold out his black bowler (a magnificently round fit atop his bald head) to show it is as empty and echoing as the plundered tomb of a Mayan king. Then he will laugh.

Twelve years in a hotel room! Who would have believed it?

No less than the Hotel Nacional, which you will see listed in your travel guide – if you have brought one – as one of the cheapest in Mexico City.

Most likely you will have been lured by the limping manager (El General, Eduardo calls him with a salute), who hawks rooms in the tireless voice of a carnival caller, *This way, this way. The bath water is running is always hot, the rooms are quiet comfortable cheap, the site historic. Here, page 15 of your Baedekers, this is us,* El Nacional, *built during the reign of Maximillian.*

Most likely you will have been doubtful, barely able to see through the evening haze thick with diesel fumes, to where the brushstrokes of grays and smears of browns, the soot-streaked stone and grimy windows materialized into El Nacional, now squeezed between buildings equally faded, worn, abstract.

Don't be fooled, El General will have said, this was once *un gran edificio*, the Versailles of hotels, its foundation stones taken from a ruined Aztec temple or two by Los Montez, a family on intimate terms with Emperor Maximillian, the ill-fated Viennese gentlemen who danced to music fluted by Napoleon III.

Yes, Eduardo will say when you mention the aging manager's extravagant claims, I know you carried all that luggage to the room by yourself – El General's leg was years ago crushed when a beam fell on it during an earthquake – but formerly there was a full retinue of servants (all Indians, all scandalously underpaid, it is true). And such was the power, the prestige of the Church in those once-upon-a-time days that clergymen stayed the night for free.

You will try, but you will not be able to reconcile the velvet-lined memories of El Nacional – stately oil paintings of Mexican *personajes* such as Vicente Guerrero, Benito Juarez, General Santa Anna (of Alamo fame) stolen to the last; hand-carved chairs with legs bowed as if unable to support the weight of overstuffed emerald-green cushions; candelabra chandeliers – you will not be able to place them next to the buffet in need of refinishing in Eduardo's slightly tilted room.

The city is built upon an old lake bed, Eduardo will inform you, it would not hold still even when Madero rode in triumphant to end the dictatorship of Porfirio Diaz, streets shook, buildings cracked, roofs tumbled.

You will not be able, even in the pliable realm of imagination, to restore the balding carpets in the hallway, the dulled paint (unevenly done in the first place) in need of dusting and a fresh coat, the water-stained ceilings, the bare-bulb lighting, the brownish tapwater (the Victorian clock with wrought-iron hands has stopped in the lobby but rust marches on in the pipes). Time is a measureless matter of daylight filtering though the exhaust-fume sky through yellowish shades brittle as old newspaper.

It's a wonder the rain is not black, Eduardo will say.

On his lopsided buffet, a miracle of warping and water stains that had once floated several city blocks in a flood – on that buffet indescribable via Euclidean geometry, admirable to anyone with van Gogh's eye for disproportions, you will notice, neatly stacked, five or six boxes of Earl Grey Tea.

I would give up Mexico's current form of government, the Republic, Eduardo will say, and live under a restored monarchy to obtain a year's supply.

Then he will smile disarmingly, his teeth yellowed from proximity to too much smoldering tobacco.

A monarchy is rather dashing after all. Not the silliness Iturbide attempted, appointing himself king – where is the divine providence in that? – or Santa Anna and his ill-mannered clownish followers, no, something with dignity.

No doubt you ran into Eduardo in the hotel lobby which, no matter how musty or poorly lighted, is as securely linked by telephone wire to Cairo, Bangladesh, Jerusalem, Passaic, N.J. as to Mexico itself. You were amused by the pompous air of the manager whom you overheard exclaiming that he will breathe his last breath in the service of his guests.

Viva los turistas!

There, while trying to place a long-distance call – your Spanish is not very good – Eduardo probably took the opportunity to introduce himself and offer his services as translator.

Technology, he likes to say, has a way of dangling the improbable before you only to confound you with an insurmountable detail – language for example.

Anomalous Eduardo Lerma, as old as Mexico City permits men to be, will speak English with an Oxford accent, carry a long umbrella and don his bowler as would any gentleman who has grown accustomed to London's fog. At Oxford University, he will not have failed to inform you, he was another in the long legacy of nobility, possessing a scholar's instinct for well-worded truth, a rogue's predilection for women fragrant with the perfume of willingness.

Of all the things he learned there, the one he would take with him if forced to choose – Let us say the planet were coming to an end in a week – is etiquette.

No matter when apocalypse strikes, one must be properly dressed for the occasion and be sure to utter words that will be remembered.

Resting his creaky back against a chair in the lobby, Eduardo must have directed a comment at the aging manager who steps from past to present, past to present and loses a frame of motion, the continuity, in between –

Digame General, como está la pierna hoy? Que tiempo pronostica para la semana que viene?

– before inviting you to his room to sip tequila with him.

It is not the best brand, he surely will have apologized, leading the way up a staircase so dim, so humid with years, so badly lit, you will imagine for an instant you are in the catacomb stillness of the temple of Quetzalcoatl in Chichenitza, ascending the breathing wet stone steps that take you to the tiny red idol of a jaguar god, somehow lit in that ancient moss-lined darkness by a single bare bulb.

In any event, tequila is just to make do.

Eduardo would rather a few bottles of a thick Jamaican rum

of a color and consistency not unlike maple syrup, an island warmth left in the pit of his stomach.

Yes, rather than repossess all the land taken during the war of the Alamo, I would rather several bottles of this very wonderful rum.

Eduardo will empty his glass with the forlorn grace of a butterfly swept out to sea by mischievous winds.

Oxford, he will say, was a grand experience.

He will pour himself another.

But it was nothing compared to traveling half the length of a country, from Texas to Mexico City, on horseback.

I was a true *caballero*.

He will talk of the 20,000 pounds sterling – Quite something in those days – he had with him with which to finish his education. But the first lady who caught his eye on return to Mexico (Ah, she had the cheekbones of an Aztec princess) was gracious enough to allow him to reduce that sum by a thousand.

There were other women in other cities – Gaudalajara, Chicago, Vera Cruz, New York, Los Angeles – who were just as eager to eat in the finest restaurants and mingle with the sons and daughters of bankers, industrial tycoons, politicians.

Never the same woman for more than a week or two, no matter how beautiful. They all had to have their turn, don't you see?

He will recall nights spent dancing in domed clubs, twice running into Tommy Dorsey's band and once managing, with a flourish, to get an autograph from Glenn Miller for Louise who bore a striking resemblance to Patty, the prettiest of the Andrews Sisters. The music in full swing, he and Louise danced, two art deco silhouettes pressed against the vault of heaven, the stars wheeling overhead, outdone only by the sequin sparkle of her dress. The world was wondrous unending unbelievable through a glass of red wine.

What does it matter that 20,000 pounds, enough to last a wise man a lifetime, had bought only six months?

Ah, yes, there was *mi padre*.

A hard man locked in another era, enamored of the flint knives of Aztec priests and the hearts bared to them as offerings to the Sun.

Sacrifice, Eduardo, there is nothing that more ennobles the human spirit.

Although Padre was descended of a wealthy Spanish family, olive-skinned, his thin mustache perfectly trimmed always, a suit and tie even at the breakfast table, he was the kind of man who could live in a hut with an earthen floor if circumstances demanded, eat corn tortillas for breakfast and again for supper, working in the fields from sunup till sundown, the whole time sprinkling the earth with the salt of his sweat.

Discipline, Padre often said, is what separates man from beast, and I respect no man who lacks it. A man must conquer his urges Eduardo. No one is fat against his will.

No, no, Father, I beg to differ. A sip of Earl Grey tea at one's leisure is what separates man from our four-footed friends. Wasn't it Shakespeare, he will turn to you and ask, who said even a beggar is in the poorest thing superfluous?

Disinherited, Eduardo did not take well to routine.

What is a man if he cannot take a nap in the sun when the mood so strikes him?

He will admit that even as a child he was too old to change. There was never a time when I would permit myself to be anything other than what I was. Though now I must admit that I have become like the descendant of an Aztec ruler: when we dig subways nowadays, we come across the remains of my empire, I cannot help being reminded. But so many years have gone by that now they come to only so many old stones. And I must live on top of them.

Certain regrets are acquired tastes, sipped at now and again despite their bitterness.

Sometimes (he will rub his brow with thumb and middle finger) my head hurts all the way to God.

You will see him then as he sees himself, leaning over the faucet in the morning for what one day shall prove to be the last time. Like El General, the manager, he too has lost most of his hair, is not oblivious to the strange smell that is his own, is a sourness that no amount of soaping or perfuming can rid him of, the smell of age, the smell he remembers from his grandmother's sweaters when she crushed his child's face to her great stomach, it belongs to him now, is something he can never take off, and no matter how many times he sees the sag in cheeks he keeps meticulously shaven, he will be surprised at how unfaithful his memory has been to the image in the shiny metal. If he were not so thin – yes, he will think, his chest is birdlike, is mostly ribs so how did that paunch, a round bloated *piñata*, get there? – he would have jowls.

You will see him wandering the halls early in those mornings, steeped in the settled darkness, what seeps through the imperfect joining of night and day, through the ill-fitting walls of the hotel, exposing a body that is a pear in shape, sagging over the elastic waist of his baggy boxer shorts, a clownish sight he would be embarrassed to know you can so easily imagine.

You will see him hesitate outside one of the rooms, hearing as he always does the gunshot he never heard in the first place. He will enter that room, searching the peeling wallpaper of faded flowers until he finds the place – to this day you can see the poor job of spackling they did – where one of the bullets disappeared.

I was a child then, the horse more popular than the car, the Nacional was still quite a place, its owner a meek, spiritually minded vegetarian who got ill at the sight of uncooked meat. A wealthy man with a yellowish complexion, he was very popular with the servants, having doubled their wages, infuriating his wife, Olga Luz who, as it turned out, wanted nothing to do with sallow-faced Frederico and sent her lover to kill the poor man in his sleep. Frederico awoke, several shots were fired, and he was killed anyway. Olga Luz and the lover disappeared for all time.

Leaving their children to war among themselves for ownership. The youngest child, Magdalena the Silken Voiced (and that is not all that was rumored to be silken), the daughter of the Olga Luz, was half sister to Wilfredo and Santiago, brothers born of a different mother. She carried on scandalously with Wilfredo, only to leave him for an unhappy American oil man who spent most of his days drinking tequila and most of his nights staring out at the darkness as if Mexico City were at the bottom of the long-vanished lake, as if he were a body adrift in a tide of unhappy memories. The relationship lasted long enough for her to embezzle to her heart's content and divorce him, cleverly having gotten him to keep the hotel in her name.

By then the Nacional had begun to fall into disrepair. Spending the money not on upkeep but on her own frivolities – perfumes at a servant's yearly salary per ounce, dresses adorned with the luster scraped from Africa's deepest mines, men she fancied as she aged whom she attracted with her status and wealth – she found herself alienated from her family, dying at last within the wrapping of her satin sheets, sheltered beneath her canopied bed whose lace coverings were endless looping hours of work for patient Indian women and their tireless fingers. Magdalena left behind a genuine will proven false –

A bit of legal magic, Eduardo will say bitterly, that would have made a young man who was no Montez owner of El Nacional.

It was not long after Magdalena ascended like the evil saint she was that the first presidential suite was cut up as part of a scheme to create more revenue with more rooms rented out more often. This process went on over the years as the neighborhood grew more crowded, until one morning you woke up to see clothes hanging in that imprecise zone between two buildings and within a week's time several families had squeezed themselves in, diapers were hanging on cords tied to snapped-off broom handles stuck into the ground, to iron fencing, to a sapling struggling in a patch of unpaved earth.

On the city's perimeter, entire villages spring up overnight – *abracadabra* – the new inhabitants praying to the Indian Virgin of Guadalupe to keep the police from evicting them from the harsh land they have claimed, from their rows of shacks leaning, lop-sided, unevenly joined. No straight edges, Mexico is a country without reliable geometry. Stakes and ropes hold things from flying off, tarpaper keeps the rain out, the lucky ones with cloudy plastic windows flapping in the breeze, blankets or no windows at all for the rest. No sewers, electricity, running water, heat, they pray that the diseases of overpopulation do not take their children who play in the dust of the dirt roads and mark their faces with their own filthy hands, who would not be admitted to the city hospitals without a few pesos to get some orderly's attention. Others live in the city dump, in caves dug into the slopes of piled trash, eyes peering out at you like night creatures caught in the glare of headlights.

Oh these Mexicans are brilliant at improvising, Eduardo will say with a sparkling mixture of condemnation and envy. Look out the window, down on the street, there is the ten-year-old fire-eater Little Lopez, who is discolored from the time he was careless with the fluid, who nearly died when he inhaled. He has gathered something of a collection of thrown pesos over the years, he is better off than Carlos the streetwalker, the wino, who picks through garbage, warming himself in winters at one of the bonfires made of truck tires, burning in the last of the vacant lots – a lucky thing there is so much rising smoke, the gods can't see what has become of their people.

I, I am a perfect Christian, Eduardo will tell you. It is an accident I am here. The Spanish would never have come here if not for empty coffers. They cared nothing for calendars with a different measure of time, nor for a mountainous terrain inhabited by a fierce dark people whose religion revolved around the sun.

What can be expected of me, living in a country founded on a haunting rumor passing from conquistador to conquistador, whispering of an Indian emperor who had not been crowned but coated in a fine layer of gold instead, who plunged into a lake to wash the glittering excess of royalty from him, sent it to grace the murky bottom, who presided over a city that blinded from a distance so that you must never look straight at it, but always out of the corner of your eye? Whose streets turned up gold on the bottoms of sandals? Whose people are like children, blissfully unaware of the value of what they play with day to day?

These conquistadors came with a strange fever, a sickness induced by the lack of a cold yellow metal, it is an accident they stayed.

Can you blame me for wanting a home in Barcelona – I do miss the sea from time to time – a servant or two, and a small but impressive collection of Picassos?

Instead of Picassos, there were wives – no less beautiful though much more trouble – five of them in all.

My first, Isabella, always thought my father would eventually soften his disposition and reinstate me as heir. She had the name of a queen and the shrewdness of a sewer rat. As the years went by, Padre showed no signs of weakening and she left me for another man.

It was all just as well. At the time I was having an affair with Concepcion, my second wife-to-be. Her voice could shatter glass as easily as her looks ruined hearts. I would go to any length to avoid an argument with her. I remember her so well there is no photograph that could be more faithful, a woman of Spanish aristocracy with henna-colored hair and her eyes, ah her eyes were the kind could induce men to point revolvers at one another. It is a shame our love was the crystalline variety – beautiful to the eye, but rather impractical, nothing you could dig a ditch with. One day she gave such a yell it went to a thousand pieces. I was still on my way to another part of Mexico when the echoes died away.

Immaculada accepted me for what I was: a man of simple means with rather extravagant tastes. I met her as she threw seeds to the pigeons outside the Catedral Nacional, its stone the color of bad weather, too monumental to be anything but alienating, God's will done on Earth, the masses cannot be fed why not the pigeons? Why should everything go hungry? A doorway to her heart opened during this act, I stepped in, took off my hat, and there I stayed for a good many years. There I still am sometimes. I cannot say exactly why I left her, but she is the reason I put myself up at the Nacional.

He will laugh so strangely you will be sure at that moment – with nothing of supernatural proportions in sight, no sail of an ancient mariner's lost ship – he has broken with the familiar reality in which forks, knives, trolley buses, television sets are commonplace, and we all agree on their uses.

What fantastic irony, he will say, and the steadiness of his voice will lift you out of the fear of that pit into which you thought you had descended, what fantastic irony that I put myself up here and not one of the thousand other tawdry hotels in this city.

Because you will not understand, he will remind you of Magdalena of the Silken Voice, the Byronic woman who had carried on with a half brother, whose extravagant tastes and frivolous values began the downfall of the Nacional.

She was among those whom I had enchanted while squandering my Oxford tuition. She was of course, much older than I, but even so, the ruins of empires – Rome, Greece, Egypt, Tenochtitlan – have their own sort of beauty. We were perfectly matched, both well bred, knowing we would never end up in marriage, I using her for her social position, she using me for my youth. She took an extraordinary liking to me, she actually – as far as was possible for her – fell in love with me I flatter myself to think, this queen of an already eroding glorious past.

He will shake his head and smile sadly because you still do not understand.

I am the young man she willed this place to, only to have her half brothers, Wilfredo and Santiago – nearly dead of old age – arrive on the scene with an army of lawyers and disprove the validity of a perfectly valid will. So I was no better off than Mexico with the broken promise of wealth brought by oil, the fool's gold of no new empire.

Here he will dig in the top drawer of the warped buffet and produce a handful of carefully ribboned letters and lavender envelopes, an age of his life meticulously bound, and hold them up as proof.

All in her hand, all signed. It may be these would have swayed the jury in my favor, or perhaps these too would have been discredited, but I withheld them … out of naive faith in justice, out of useless reverence for the unscrupulous dead, out of what is left of *mi padre's* sense of honor – I can't say.

Returning the letters to their wooden vault lined with silence, he will take out another handful of papers, wave them around with his back to you while searching out more papers.

These are how I make my living...

He will produce articles typed in English, which one of the city's newspaper pays him a pittance to translate into Spanish.

Without my Oxford English I would be standing next to Carlos smelling of burned rubber during the long winters.

To lighten the mood, he will hold up his faceted tumbler in toast (any excuse to drink more) and bring up the young American from Kansas – a great flat state I am told – and his pretty redheaded wife. He, Eduardo will tell you, his tone taking a shift, was from the land of the strong dollar, he was like those conquistadores who first came here, armor gleaming, and saw opportunity spread out before them like another ocean. He had his entire life ahead of him and a beautiful woman who loved him, who would take him by the hand and lead him into it.

Ah, she was so much my Concepcion all over again, her hair more coppery, her eyes as innocent as wide as one of those harmless nocturnal creatures we have in our deep forests. She could not accept the fact that pyramids aren't the exclusive property of Egypt, she could not get over the subway ruins whose ancient stones at night are lit up red-yellow-green for the *touristas*, are unearthly even to those of us who have seen them like that for a decade, she could not fathom that Tenochtitlan, the throne of the Aztec civilization, is buried beneath the world's largest city.

Don't fool yourself, I said to her, don't bewail too much this ignominious end, the Aztecs were no Senores Simpaticos, they overran their neighbors, exacted tribute, made slaves of captives and sacrificed their own people – they occupy a prominent place in Mexico's history of oppressors.

She and her husband, who spent his money quite freely, took me to dinner, bought me a bottle of Jamaican rum, adopted me into their hearts only to leave with a promise to write. I am ashamed to admit I've since lost the postcards of the great American Midwest and Christmas greetings sent to me over the years. They belong to someone else, to another lifetime. They are gone like coins to the bottom of a dark fountain.

You will realize then what a rare occurrence you are, that the visitors in Eduardo's tiny room are stirrings out of the past, barely brushing aside the curtains as they come and go. You will feel, inexplicably, a degree of the awful stiffness morning brings to Eduardo (an intimation of what it is like to be trapped in a body trying to return to the inanimate stockpile from which it came), the futility of afternoons checking the empty mailbox, the evening remembrances (eyes closed and tequila fumes beginning to efface perception) of friends whose funerals Eduardo has attended – Alberto Gutierrez who struggled through Oxford with Eduardo night after night in the library and went on to become a respected politician, a portrait of him in his small round glasses now hanging in an administrative building in Guadalajara; Pablo Ribalta, El Torito, the Baby Bull, who had *cojones* the size of grapefruits and rode with Pancho Villa when he was 12, no bottle of tequila could withstand his onslaught, what a demon he looked in the meager light of a bar or a brothel – his favorite places to be – with his great long mustaches wet with liquor and sweat pouring down his face, his huge white grin in his dark face, strong as a pack mule but his heart finally burst, all that strength but he too is gone; and most of all Vicente Gonzales, a handsomer kinder more open-hearted man never breathed, nor does he any longer his casket having been laid open by candlelight the old way in the house not in some parlor, his best suit, his bow tie perfectly tied and *Madre de Dios* even dead he looked better than the tear-glistening faces bending over him. Like Eduardo, you will vainly salute young lovers arm in arm on the sidewalk below who cannot see you, you will invite hotel guests (who always seem to have an excuse ready) to share the bottle. And then you will light a cigarette in Eduardo's honor in spite of the surgeon general's warning, instead of a candle.

Did I tell you this city sinks close to a foot on a good year? he will ask, hoping to keep your interest. The only steady bit of ground is, miraculously, under the famous Angel Statue, if you didn't know better, it would seem to be slowly ascending to the place it came from.

Yes, this country, once thought to bleed gold when wounded, has proven a dream of dust, far from a source of water now, sitting upon an old lake bed, cut off from the rest of the world now by stern-faced mountains (the Sun is hazy on the hottest of days because the fumes create their own weather, their own sky).

And yet they still come, you should see their faces, the *campesinos*, the farmers wearing sandals cut from old tires, bewildered as they step from the bus, used to the emerald green of mountains and the fertile fields they've left, the lowlands and jungles, entirely lost. Benito Juarez should never have shown them what was possible. Now every Oaxacan, every Indian who comes to Mexico City wants to become president, transformed by the crush of city life into a diamond shining through history's darkest moments.

With innocent reverence they gaze up at the handiwork of our artists who have managed to record Mexico's moments of glory, to turn tragedy into wall murals, events into colors – banana yellow, gunshot-wound red, overgrown green, peasant-earth brown, peon white – they turn blood into paint, their oils dry with the faint smell of rusting iron, and the plastered stone wall that had meant nothing a moment ago – other than you will have to go around it – becomes the wailing wall of a country in agony.

The world will never end – look how much it has endured already without even coming close, wishful thinking an apocalypse. The only mouth we know is the mouth twisted in pain, the mouth gasping for justice – Orozco and Rivera ... ah, pain is all we know, the loaded rifle all we respect – Emiliano Zapata taught us that. The painted figures shout like vainglorious Santa Anna who lost his leg to a French cannonball and never let the Mexican people forget his unwilling sacrifice, exclaiming as he asked to be crowned that his last drop of blood would be bled in the service of his country.

So now you have seen the New World the Europeans set out for. But which is new? The one of the Mayans or the Aztecs? The Zapotecs or the Olmecs? The Toltecs or the Tarahumara? All older by millennia – not years but another kind of time, more nebulous, harder to measure – than Europe. This is the land of the guttural tongue, the great dead stone cities, the legend that has begun to lift itself out of the ruins like those surreal paintings in which the images are raising themselves off the canvas, emerging from flat two-dimensional art into the four- or five- or 22- dimensioned actuality we cannot keep track of anymore even if we read the latest scientific magazines.

But in truth, these are things for someone of greater stature to worry about, the next Benito Juarez who may be getting off the bus coming from Oaxaca today. If I confine myself to my own worries, my own complaints, Eduardo will say, well, they can be counted on one hand.

Aside from a shortage of import items, he will mention a knee which has never been the same since a fall from a particularly unruly horse. He will cite the Nacional's infamously infrequent hot water (one day I threw open a window and hollered *El Grito del Eduardo* for a steaming shower). At predictable times of the year, he has strange dreams he is certain are somehow linked to what is going on in the mountains, to what does not belong to the city.

A loud uncle with grandiose manners once told me of an Aztec practice – particularly savage in its imagery – in which once every 52 years (one year for every week of the solar year) a fire is turned loose in the chest cavity of a sacrificial victim and all the pots are smashed, all the used vessels, an out-with-the-old-in-the-new kind of thing, a resurrection. (I wonder what kind of coincidence it is that the Pemex building, the seat of the government oil monopoly, is 52 stories high, a monument to air pollution.

Think of how the terraces of the old temples built in tiers reflected the Mayan conception of heaven as a place of levels, Dante would have been proud.)

A miscellaneous warning, like a stray gunshot, he will point out the window and say: Out there you must be careful of coyotes, the kind without fur.

But it will not be these coyotes he sees in the sunless hours before dawn, it will be the Aztec ritual haunting his poor eyesight. He will be drawn by what is burning, by the hot orange light, the face of sacrificed human gazing indifferently at the equally indifferent heavens, the two glassy eyes earthbound stars with the red gleam of flame in the pit of their black-hole pupils.

Eduardo will straighten his back against the bedboard, he will choose his words with the careful desire to be remembered, those things he would say as the clock strikes, sounding the demise of the world that will not end.

There is a great fire burning in Mexico, he will say, beginning with the tiny ones dowsing the streets in woodsmoke, the cooking fires tended by women in colorful serapes who carry styrofoam begging cups, Carlos and black-smoke-billowing truck tires, the oil out of the earth's plundered insides, the fire roaring inside a hollowed-out human chest – a fire whose source is at the center of our existence, and the smoke – we pour ourselves into the fire but it is the smoke that will choke us off in the end, a day as black as the eruption of a fabled volcano that brought about the extinction of some forgotten civilization.

What we need in Mexico is 20,000 years of solitude at least, and no cars or cutting down jungle for farmland and why not a few dinosaurs – the allosaurus, the brontosaurus, the triceratops – to liven things up? No foreigners in the rich plant-infested heat (a heat and humidity rivaling those of a woman's erogenous zone), no boats larger than reed-bundle canoes to take away from the distraction of lazy winding rivers in the Yucatan.

For my own part, I would be able to bear the unheard-of inflation of the peso if only I could afford a fine Jamaican rum to go with my Earl Grey tea. What does it matter, eh? We dedicate ourselves to immortality – there is a little Ozymandias in all of us – but we cannot stick around to bask in it, so who is crazy? If you want to build a monument, pile up the things you have done, a grand and determined accumulation of the women you have loved, the dawns you have greeted with reverence in your heart, the times you swam the Caribbean and had the salt washed from you by the sweet downpour of a violent thunderstorm. Yes, if life were made of colors mine would arc across the sky after a good thunderstorm.

Still (he will breathe a sigh laden with cheap tequila) one goes on wishing.

By the time his chin has dropped toward his chest, he will have lost himself in a vanishing city where on every street corner, graced by a stately wrought-iron gas lamp, is a woman in a sequined dress, the slitted pupils and jade green eyes of a jaguar, a beauty he had once danced with, now a ghost of memory made of shifting light standing silently beside the post with its hissing lamp. You will sense that Eduardo has gone off quietly, his stare into the pristine past a portal to the place where his lover Magdalena awaits, but he will break the spell by turning to you suddenly.

Ah amigo, Eduardo's eyes will hold the dull glow of the sinister fire burning in Mexico, c*ada edad tiene su encanto.* Every age, he will repeat with a finger raised for emphasis, has its enchantment.

Ages in history or ages in a man's life, he will leave you this final mystery to remember him by.

THE NIGHT CRAWLER

A ring around the moon is said to be a sure sign of bad weather –
usually rain or snow. You can tell how many days will
elapse before the storm by counting the number
of stars inside the circle; if there are no stars in the ring,
the storm is less than twenty-four hours away.
– Vance Randolph, *Ozark Magic and Folklore*

She's seen somethin, he was thinking, got a good look at it I
bet is what fogged her eyes over like that.

Rain tomorrow night, she said, her dark face thin and drawn,
a sweep of badlands, all ravines and wind-worn crags, two blind
niches gouged out for eyes, a jagged rut you had to figure for her
mouth. Don't be out in it.

Whaduzzat mean? He shifted in the chair, stirred a memory
out of the dry wood that sounded like a creak. Am I shupposed
to melt or shomethin?

Lord, she laughed, I guess it's You I have t'thank for puttin me
down here in the middle a these farmers an' fishers an' drunks who
decide winter's comin on by the color of a caterpillar.

The drunk, that'd be him. Left out the harelip and clubfoot – harelip wasn't all the way fixed and makes his esses come out wrong. The clubfoot, he bobs instead of walks. Hardly taller than some a the kids around here, five-foot-two, *but I ain't blue,* he sang when he was drunk enough standing up was a chore, *I ain't runnin. With a six-pack downed, the world can drown, long as there's another beer comin.*

She looked at him with eyes frosted over, two windows in the dead of winter. Don't be out in no rain. Fact is, you juss might melt.

Wiry hair pulled back tight to her head, the sheen of a beetle shell. Blind as a bat but she had a sixth sense for light, kept the shades in the house down all the time. A musty wood smell in her kitchen, not many the breeze that blew through the window, lifted a corner of the blue-and-white tablecloth, a stillness in there you'd think the clock up on the wall in the shape of a tea kettle had stopped – the hands moved all right but you knew they weren't in step with rest of Frontenac. She couldn't see it anyway, what was the point?

Shtay inshide, is that what you're shaying?

Stay outta the rain.

Well what the hell, inshide, outta the rain – what's the differensh?

Don't be out in no rain.

Don't go out t'night?

Tonight.

On account of a little rain? Geez but you're talkin strange t'day ... shtay outta the rain ... 'bout as meaningful as don't spill shalt on the table cuz it'll bring on a piece a bad luck ... or don't watch a friend outta sight – might never see him again. He rubbed his chin, stubbly, blondish brown.

Art Papish, she said, shaking her head at a schoolboy who

wouldn't listen. What is anyone goin t'do with you? Slowly – might've been it took most of her strength to do it – she shook her head again. I guess that's enough for today.

Well, here's what you wanted . . . Art stuck his hand into a rustling paper bag, pulling them out one by one. A bottle a rum, he said, and turkey gizzards fresh from Pallucca's Market. That oughta square us for the next couple months.

That's fine. She reached out, put a shriveled hand on the smooth glass of the bottle. You don't sound so good today, you had a drink?

Not a one, he said.

She knows about the dark circles under his eyes, his eyes trying to edge back from the light, sandy hair a nest of curls he hadn't bothered to comb out. Somehow, right through the dusty air of the kitchen she felt all the nastiness from last night seeping out his pores. Whatever it was Marano shot him up with, it felt like he was missing his liver, the rest of his insides sliding around in the extra room, his head buzzing all the time, a little dizzy, joints weak as an eighty-year-old's. He'd've loved to heave it all up, but he was afraid of what would come out, ugly as an owl pellet – pieces of mice, wadded-up beer labels peeled from warm bottles, snake scales, ten years' worth of baloney sandwiches from the Texaco 7-11, chewed cigar stubs, bird beaks, blue pills, green capsules, white powder that burned like the sulphur rained down on those sinner cities back in Time Immemorial, a rat tail, a chicken foot, a cicada with those cellophane wings twice the length of their fat bodies (downed with a shot riding on the bet), wads of fur – every wrong thing he ever took into his body over the years compressed into a rough ball, booze probably the least of the evils.

You can help yourself to that rum if you want, she said.

Now Risa, you know if I get shtarted on that bottle I won't leave here till I finish.

I guess you'll be goin now.

I guessh I will.

He got up, careful to look at her sideways, avoid those whited-over eyes, nothin left a the irises but a ribbon here an' there, couple a swirls a brown, like those glass marbles kids play with, he wished she'd take the trouble to put on some dark glasses.

Glad as hell to be in the open air, her kitchen dusty as a tomb, things incubating under those linoleum tiles. Made him feel better to be under sky, plenty of clouds but all white, not a thunderhead among them.

Shtay outta the rain. He shook his head. Rot's shettin' in on the boards she's standin on I think.

Walking, bobbing more like, no car to get him around, it was sitting in his gravel drive, a rusting monument to 1962, a green Ford Rambler splattered with huge birdshit rain drops, white and dried-up, the money his sister sent every month wasn't enough to get it fixed, not the way he drank.

Doesn't matter, he thought, I could be in an endless field, my feet know how many steps to take down Broadway before the right onto Fifth Street, hit the Washington Tobacco Store for a couple games a pool, a right out the door, head to PiCCO for the best malted world's ever tasted, peg-leggin all over Pittsburg all day, follow me and you gotta map a downtown.

Might as well gimp on past the Duke's house, see what he's up to. Maybe hitch out to Rae Anne's place later on, or just keep walkin, see if I can run into her by luck of luck.

Just the way she moved, her walk down Broadway was enough to stop your blood, he wished she'd turn his way, look at him dead on, a full turn of her head, a stretch a two or three seconds is all, a real heartbreaker she got it all over the other women in town.

Used t'follow her into the theater before he knew her, neither a them with anyone t'go to the movie with, watched her more than the movie, the best place for it – hard to pin down as a dragonfly most times, hardly more than a ripple in the air, a wonder when it finally lands, looks at you with enormous eyes, a shine to their green-blue no painter can touch, eyes big as the whole head, a clump a gems carryin around on see-through wings a vision a the world no one can guess at. Nothin so beautiful as the blue light on her face, the curve a her nose – it ends kinda sharp – a blue angel in the dark, green eyes gone violet, the movin silvery light a heaven on the screen, she'd wonder with a box a popcorn in her lap how to get back, how she got tossed out into the rough-carpeted seat with everyone else in the first place when she'd had a life up there, 70 mm wide to fit her an Zirque both, but he was off again an she'd gone back to drawin, mostly made-up things – horses with wings, winged dragons, birds you never saw before in your life, all of em with a better place they could get to, didn't have t'call TWA or PanAm for a reservation, just up up an away. To those floatin cities she liked to sketch. If you could find your way up there with someone like her, no reason ever to leave.

When she went to Carol's Corner Cafe, he'd watch her from a hall window up there in the Stilwell, perch on the ledge like a gargoyle, the Clubfoot of the Hotel Stilwell.

Wings're what I'm misshin, he thought out loud. Ugly enough I guessh, sit shtill enough sometimes too, no I ain't shtone, but my hangover face'd turn a pretty woman to a pile a quartz, your average ol' nothin-shpecial lady to a slab a gray shale, and her – you can shee jush by lookin can't yuh? turn her into a sea collection of emerald an' ruby an' diamond, shilver shkin and bronze hair.

Sitting was good enough, up there on the sill, about as likely to move as a granite block, watching, her name in his mouth, weightless where he was granite, her name unpronounced, he wouldn't let it go or it would be gone from him forever no matter how he reached for it back . . .

No, he could never touch er, not with hands like his, get the shakes sometimes, too big for the wrists they're hangin offa, fulla wiry brassy-colored hair, too much a that too, he couldn't imagine touchin her the way Zirque did, nothin more than a hug she'd send his way now'n again, left a metal taste in his mouth, a tinglin under his scalp, under his skin, a thousand ants crawlin all over him as if he weren't altogether solid anymore, a good wind might scatter his insides like dead leaves out a scarecrow's unbuttoned shirt. Even in his own dreams, the most he does is fall asleep cradled up with her, the way he'd most love to let go a this world, with her arms around him so he wouldn't feel anythin but her. Find him like that a thousand years later, fetal, like those bones in that Italian city Millo talks about, covered over by a volcano, their bones tangled up with one another all those centuries, settled on a bed a soft gray ash, still holdin onto each other for a thousand years, they died anyway, but there they were, bones comfortably forever settled in ash, all that love comes to in the end.

If he could always see her it would be enough, always be around her, watch her do anything she does, the way she lets her head tilt back when she laughs, her tarnished-copper hair falling long and wavy, the way her smile takes over her whole face, makes you feel like the stadium lights been turned on for you, there you are in the center of everything, the night backpedaling so fast it's about to fall over, that'd be enough.

He brought her things as an excuse to come over, little glass ma-bobs and porcelain do-dads she liked, showed up for dinner knowing she always set for two, her and Zirque in case he showed. He'd sit on the front porch with her and she was glad for the company, he knew, but still a salty bitterness in her mouth because he wasn't Zirque. Never stayed too long, just sat across from her watching her while she talked, rocked herself on the swing seat, scouring the fields with her eyes maybe she'd spot Zirque, like he'd always been there she just hadn't noticed. Other times Pap caught up with her in the Corner Cafe while Carol's sister had Blue Jean's wrist caught in her old woman's hand (tireless as a coon trap), it was all Pap could do to get a few words in under the table, weasel a cup of coffee out of Carol, sip and listen to them from the booth behind, turned around in his seat, leaning over the back of it, his elbows out like a kid with no manners.

Pap, up at dawn this morning – it was cold as the barrel of a gun in winter, stick to your skin if you touch it bare – knew it was too early for her to be at Carol's, needed a couple glasses of old Number 7 whiskey to get the blood moving.

Lookin out the window, the light growin, he spotted a pale moon, cold round rock up there, white and frostbitten, a high school-age god hurled himself an iceball through space. A new meaning to cold if he could be up there to feel it, him and his pot-belly stove, everything on the whole miniature planet (misshapen like him, only done half way, s'posed to be a planet but look what happened, got shortchanged in a big way, only gets away with bein so ugly 'cause it gives off a shine), him and his pot-belly stove'd be all the warmth in that corner a the universe, any other life up there'd come shuffling over to the beacon light, Pap Prometheus and his Amazin Woodburnin Stove.

The skull on a bookshelf, Yorick he called him after a famous skull the Duke told him about, Yorick said, You'd run out of wood soon enough (bein the smart-ass pile a calcium he was), and it's doubtful moon rocks burn.

Just my good luck I'm an earthlin, got this shausage from Pallucca's t'throw in the pan.

They stuff it by hand over at Pallucca's, he cooks it by hand, fingers shiny with hot fat, no spatula or fork, he liked his hands to smell that way.

Nothin like shausage on an autumn mornin, Yorick. Season a rustlin, nothin shtays shtill, shaddest time a year to go past a cemetery, nothin shleepin peaceful anymore, dead leaves blowin around, wind findin every hollow there is, makin em sing like haunted flutes, whistlin right up through your backbone, always a wind like a shtorm comin, sweepin over family an' friends. We put em in leadlined boxes, marble slabs on top, where do we think they're goin? Probably should've hung em out on lines, bone chimes, couldn't do a slow dance if they wanted to in those boxes, scratch marks an' broken nails I bet if you dug em up, tryin t'get t'each other, should bury the dead naked, let em spread out under the earth, let roots lodge between ribs, rainwater pool in the sockets where there used t'be eyes, fingers disappearin one at a time in search a the earth's long-ago, faraway center, might be shome parts that come back up t'the light, feel the autumn wind, it shounds like a half-sigh through the burned-out church on Locust Shtreet.

Autumn time you feel the gapin hole in the roof a the church shomewhere in your shide – if you shtill had one – makes you pull up your shirt an have a look, make sure no one speared you when you had your head turned. And those really cold mornins like this one you don't even wanna go out, just fire up the wood shtove, get shausage goin on the cookin shtove, warm your hands an watch light come inta the sky through the window over the sink curtained pale blue, they float on the breeze in summer, the shapes somehow calling her to mind, twistin in that slow way, a blue lady in the pale curtains.

Yeah-up, nothin but time an' shausage grease on my hands it's no wonder I need t'sit around an' think a things t'do t'take my mind off spendin all my time waitin, just you and me Yorick, y'-think she'll come by today?

Doubt it, Pap.

Yer jusht a shkull anyway, whaddayou know?

A real one, too, not one a those Hollywood fakes, somehow Yorick still managed to yap an jabber. Up there on the bookcase Granpap built with pottery Zirque brought him back from Gallup, New Mexico, Zooni or somethin, white clay, painted-black design with a couple a insect-lookin figures except they had two legs instead a six, humpbacked fluteplayers, Zirque said.

Clubfoot, harelip, a touch of scoliosis, humpback is one thing he missed out on.

Yorick and Zuni pottery, a couple of half-melted candles, a beer bottle with its own porcelain-and-rubber cork wired to it brought back from Amsterdam when Zirque talked him into that, a photo of all three of them on Blue Jean's front porch happy as could be, next to the brass kaleidoscope Granpap put together, mirrors made the clustered crystals at the end grind together, new colors, odd shifting shapes, the same old memories getting mixed up, but only so much they can change, the faces and people and places pretty much the same, but the order a things like furniture in a room somehow got rearranged.

Was Zirque there with us that time? I thought it was just us two. Way I remember it, I been around a lot more than him, kept after you in the silver-blue light a shadowy theaters, that brass tube into memories grindin together, Gramps that's some kinda magic, howd'ya do it?

One-eyed Oscar sleeps on toppa your shelf, that cat'd rather sleep there than a feather pillow. Time to time he'll look at you an' you'll shee shomething older than you're used to smolderin behind his one green eye, somethin straight from the moon they hunt under, the other just a wrinkled pinkish-yellow socket.

Oshcar whaddayou think? Don't just sit there lickin your paws, come clean. Am I gonna shee her today, are you throwin in with Yorick or what? You ain't even lishenin you dumb cat.

What's the shense a askin a cat ain't smart enough to have two eyes who I'm gonna run into today?

I sure do wonder, he said, rockin forward with each step, on his way to the Duke's house, the afternoon warmed up considerable from mornin, if I'll run into er today. If not when he got home he'd pull out that T-shirt he'd gotten hold of, slipped off with it one night, kept it in a drawer and somehow never lost her smell, that old cotton trying just as hard to hang onto anything she'd let go. Born again from just a whiff, as clean and innocent and stupid as the first day he looked up at his mamma with a wide-open wailing mouth. A season in the smell of that shirt, her own, balmier than spring, prettier than fall. When street lights were just beginning to catch slow fire along Mckay Street where the Duke lived and gnats crowded the Texaco 7-11 sign on 69 in a little cloud of swarming specks and the last of the sun was about gone from the fields out where she lived, he'd've given anything to be coming home to her.

Littlest things get her excited, Chianti in a straw basket – not the pot-bellied bottle so much, but the basket.

Art, she said, that is adorable it reminds me of Italy I've never been there but I've seen pictures in magazines, Zirque promised we'll go one day.

She saved it (you're wrong if you thought it was empty). Some people use a camera, she gets by with pretty glass bottles. All by herself, those insects swarmin around the sign, me in some bar gettin drunk waitin for who-knows-what, she's pourin into an empty glass from one of her bottles the dinner the three of us had out on the front porch one night.

Zirque dragged the kitchen table out there for the occasion, she'd cooked Italian, made polenta an a fancy flat round onion-bread no bakery had the recipe for, craysha they say it around here though if old Millo came by he would go off in an Italiano accent.

Pap brought three bottles of Chianti so they could get drunk and laugh at Zirque when he started talking about *chiaroscuro* those words he brings back from his trips no one's ever heard, thinks he's so smart . . .

She was alone pouring that for herself, the last light of the fields a halo around the bottle, no it ain't right, Pap would be the first to admit, but look here Rae Anne it's worse for me.

Alone even when he is with her and Zirque, he was the only one who had to leave after dinner. He could stand it while it lasted, being near her was enough, knowing she loved what he'd brought, that she loved hearing Zirque tell his stories even though he'd left her two months to go out and get them, Pap's stomach feeling like an overfilled water balloon it was all so damn good he just kept eating, the wine warm and deep in his guts. It was only after they'd worked the self-timer on that fancy camera Zirque stole or conned or won on a bet, after it got dark, past midnight maybe, all the wine gone the evening gone the night fallen like winter though it was warm, the end always came no matter how good the story, and Pap went off, turning down a ride from Zirque because then Rae Anne would be the one alone, he said he'd hitch, felt like a walk in the balmy night air, the crickets filling up the silence stretched out inside him with their lonely calling t'each other across the dark fields, he needed something like that, like the fireflies had, light himself up, make a constant scraping prayer – wing to wish – like the crickets, send up a signal *Hey over here, gimme a lift into town wouldja? I sure could use one.*

Nighttime when Zirque was gone, he'd seen her walking Broadway, the street near empty as the bottles in her collection, breath become mist, a fog out of her mouth, somethin an angel dreams of bein able to do on a cold day. Somewhere Zirque was missing her enough that he felt it too, as mysterious as what held the moon in place, and the rest of this mess which ought to all have flown off in every direction. Love the same, couldn't see how it held them together, but no matter where Zirque went off to, he always came back.

I wish he wouldn't sometimes, let her get on with it, but she goes on waitin, can't help herself. I can't either, I keep an eye on er, wingless an ugly she hardly knows I'm alive.

Damn him but sometimes his heart's nothin more'n a chunk a moonglow, pale'n see-through, you'd think it'd warm you up a little, but what it does, it gives you the shivers. I know there's somethin more solid center of it, but it's easy t'lose sight the way he treats her sometimes.

Some nights in drizzle more like drifting mist Pap saw her, long red hair shimmery with it, smeared with light from the street-lamps, and up a block a couple arm in arm, and in some other city maybe Zee Gee was thinking of her, the falling mist in her was pain. No shape, it found its way everywhere, seeped through her, rubbed off on you when you took her hand, want and need and sadness that smelled of her.

And there Pap was like something sinister watching, but wasn't him that was a hole waiting to swallow you, was something coiled underneath Pittsburg's streets, under the sewers, traveling through them you could almost feel it when you sat still enough, somewhere around two or three in the morning, that strange way things had of going against you, but wouldn't let you close your hand on what it was, and he wondered what was older, the darkness or those beat-up brick storefronts.

Bricks pressed outta darkness, maybe they're the same age, condensed out of it, old partners, no wonder the walls don't hold off anything like they're sh'posed to. Doesn't even gather itself, that creepin fog under the street, never takes on a shape, a hairy slouchin, somethin you can take a shot at with your double barrel, it's wily all right, like a coyote Zirque'll tell you, a trickster, a shape-shifter the way Indian gods can be, you need t'tune your ears in keener than a dog, catch things that don't make a sound. The whole time you feel tattooed, marked, singled out, ain't no wall thick enough to hide behind it always knows where to find you.

The Duke of Pallucca, another famous walker, stick in hand, saw Pap on the side of the road, passed out on his feet, bent over, about to pitch forward likely, started throwing rocks at Pap. Pap spun around in the street looking for where they were coming from. Coughin real bad, really hackin, staggered so much he lost his balance, fell into a ditch on the side of the road.

Pap what'sa matter?

Papish rolled around some before he stopped and sat up.

I was at a party lash night, me an Marano. He was meltin pills in a jar and shootin people up with em. He asht me if I wanted to go uptown'r downtown. I shaid shurprise me. I don't know what the hell he shot me up with, but he fucked up my week. Pap pulled a flask out of his pocket. Shhhh, don't tell anybody.

What the hell you doin t'your boot?

Got a piece a cardboard stuffed in this hole t'keep the rain out.

You don't give a goddamn about anything except gettin loaded, do ya?

That an cheap whores.

Come on Pap, walk me home.

The Duke with his favorite walking stick, a branch, a little crooked with an old man's bearded face carved at top, the Duke – he could stand to lose 40 or 50 pounds – leanin on the old timer's head the whole time.

Had a disconcertin dream, Pap, a tooth fell out. Makes Italian widows cross themselves if you tell em about it.

Think it'll rain tonight? Risa says I shouldn't go out in the rain.

Don't need a fortune teller to figure that out.

Folks around here got her pegged for a witch.

If she were, she'd turn em into toads. Buncha idiots. They don't compliment you too much either. That skull a yours and your one-eyed cat, you wanderin around burnt-out churches at night, you sure are a prime candidate for devil worship.

Pap made a noise like spitting out a chewed-off nail. Worst he did was up and down the street beating drainpipes with a stick to sound out the hollows in Pittsburg, get a feel for the emptiness around him, wake up the whole damn town, let them know what they were sleepin on, right under them, navigatin the sewers quiet as fog. They took the rope off the bells in the church on Locust to keep him and mischievous kids from ringing em at off hours but couldn't do anything about the drainpipes.

Couple thousand years ago, the Duke said, Chinese used t'bang pots and pans, sticks – probably their own skulls too – when there was an eclipse.

What for?

Tryin to scare off the dragon that swallowed the sun. Always worked too.

Scare off the darknessh, now that's a good one. I ain't got what Risa got, God-given built-in sonar pings off past lives, off events ain't even happened yet, things that ain't solid. Me, I'm just bangin away at the pipes, a crossh between Paul Revere an' an ancient Chinaman.

Hey, saw Cara today.

Now there's a girl knows how t'shuck the poison outta you. Don't charge all that much either.

Guess you'd be the one to know.

Well take a good look at me, I ain't no Clark Gable, why waste my time?

Most everyone is crippled somehow or other, Pap, just happens to show up on you where you can see it.

Pap started hacking again till he spit something up, heavy from the sound of it.

Shtick to whores I'm tellin ya, Pap said, the ones like Blue Jean are taken no matter how bad Zirque treats her. You an' me don't got a shot at them anyway, we can talk an act shweet as can be, buy boxes a roses, we might as well be chasin a feather in a twister. Now whores at leasht you get what you're payin for, no almosts, ifs, I-could-haves – it's a done deal and you don't feel left outta the game, you took a turn, an' if nothing else comes your way ever again at least there's that, you don't have t'go t'your grave miserable about misshin out.

A deep-sea moon last night, the way the clouds covered it, blurred it, striped it uneven, Risa's eye in reverse, glowing white iris up there, swirls and stripes of clouds floating across it, a full moon, kind of a halo around it, made Pap think of those fish that glow in deep ocean.

Makes you wonder: what was nature thinkin when she put god up to that? Fish that glow? Insects like a cloud a stars adrift in the evenin? Forty-watt worms in caves – no one there to see em, what for? Why all the trouble? An' tiny squid, a few inches long, Zirque said he's never seen one but he's read about em, somewhere off the coast a Japan, light up like a pinball tilt, a real scratch on the retina, Zirque said. Teeny little reflectors an' lenses on em – can you believe? They put em in tanks, study em, but the lights fade an' a little while later, no one knows why, they're litterin the bottom. Never live more'n a few hours in a tank, a mystery no biologist can figure – maybe we oughta tank a few a them and see how long they last.

An' what's the big deal about light anyway? Ain't nothin when you screw in a bulb, nobody sits around t'gawk an' ooh and ahh, it's the background really. Nobody'd give a damn about a star if it weren't that the rest a the sky is black, the universe is 99 percent black dark empty. It's the ocean mysteries lit, it's the background that makes the light.

The black is the waitin I guessh, a great sheet've unbroken waitin trapped in this body alone with yourself an' no good woman t'ease the loneliness, I can't understand Zirque at all leavin her like he does. Sure I can see how a trip here an' there, a place like Amersterdam makes a star kind of in all the waitin, somethin to look back on. Happens here, too though, that time the three of us took our picture on the back porch, I was happiest, ain't never going to be no happier, the three biggest bright-eyed smiles you ever saw, should've died right then and there, keeled over and kicked right in front a the camera.

Feels like you're waitin for shomethin to happen but you don't know what it is, like it's just about to come if you hang on long enough, but it never shows up an you don't know what you're waitin for anyway. Wind up passin the time by drinkin – who knows, might need to be drunk when you run into it.

Seems like you ought to be in a bar because it might happen there, it's not happenin at home. You can keep company with everybody else who's waitin. Could be a person. Could be a moment different from the last thousand'n one that went by. An understandin. Of why those squid die after a few hours in the tank. Why I don't die in mine.

Somethin's bound t'show up make it all worthwhile, that's what I'm waitin for, that's why I ain't died yet. This can't be the whole story. If this is all she wrote, she's the worst author I ever read. You keep turnin the pages because there has to be more – ohhh-oh, so that's what it is, I get it now. That's half the reason we bother lookin up at the sky, expecting something t'drop out, same with every time the bar door opens, lookin up thinkin today, maybe, today.

The Duke talking about it one night (Pap could only see one eye through the cloud of cigar smoke) in Bartelli's Blue Goose Bar, draught beers out of mugs so heavy could've chained one to a convict's leg. Zirque there that night, complaining he heard Ozzie was going to close the bar down, going back and forth with the Duke, they didn't always lose Pap, sometimes he managed to hang on, one foot in the stirrup, Zirque and the Duke ahead, going full gallop.

Hamlet was the first modern hero, Duke was saying, caged in his own contemplativeness, first one who had t'use his own mind t'deal with his own mind – no stars, no religion, no landmarks, no other way t'navigate.

It's enough to make anybody talk to a skull. Pap finished his beer to the foam, his gnome's face mostly blocked out by the thick glass bottom, a halo of curly brown hair around it, he looked like some kind of weird flower.

Half our mistakes, the Duke kept up, takin the figurative for the literal, the literal for the symbolic. Course there was no garden somewhere in the Land Between the Rivers, no Gabriel with a hot blade, no apple, no tree. Eden, nirvana, a neverending feast of friends is just the warm moist blanket of the unconscious we were wrapped in, an' when mornin came, the blanket got pulled off. Thought rubbed the sleep out of its eyes, looked at itself, an' we lost the language a the trees, the spheres, the animals, the insects. We separated out, different, somethin that fell outta the sky, landed here. Death hadn't suddenly been let into the world but now we knew what was at the end a the rainbow an' we looked up at where we thought we might've come from – where somethin might've hidden itself – an asked for a heart strong enough to bear it all, asked to go home again. Click, click, click.

Zirque waved away the Duke's cigar smoke. Where we live is a state a mind is what you're sayin...

Then whaddo I owe taxes for? Pap wanted to know.

If you want to find the garden again, the Duke kept up, don't bother with a Rand-McNally, use the compass in here. The Duke thumped his chest. Not so much a tireless muscle as a place where you either live or you don't.

There was a strange silence between songs on the jukebox, their voices drifted free, seemed to come from another conversation, Pap fancied he heard the squeaking of the ceiling fan, a regularity to it, before a rainy sea-wracked Doors song overtook the fan and its overhead time-keeping.

Zirque got the Duke talking about the Grendel beastie, Beowulf tangled with him without sword or shield, got naked, and you might think well that's a stupid way to face an ogre, but he'd stripped himself, was trying to be only what he was, nothing more, face the hairy man-killer that way, wrestle this thing we're trapped in. When he dropped his sword, there went all the meditations of the Viking Descartes, whoever that was. Armored breastplate tossed aside and there went Odin, Thor, the rest of the gods he could've asked to lend an immortal hand. Beowulf was looking to bear the brunt without strength or protection didn't come from himself. Skin to hair, hand to claw, head to horn, find out which of them really had more right to walk the Earth.

When they'd about exhausted that vein, the three of them getting up to leave, Pap mentioned the tiny squid. They live in blackness.

We all do, the Duke said.

They live in the blacknessh, Pap said whipping his horse up

faster, legs snug in place now, an' maybe all they're waitin for is a peek at the light, up there, not their own, light outshide a themselves, not their own, bigger endlessh daylight. Only when they get hauled up there, when they meet the light made them in its image they die, nobody told em sometimes the thing you're waitin for kills you. Shoulda waited for a messhenger – you know like the poshtman – someone from the light come down to them, take a gander at 'em, bring back a fair deshcription t'his drinkin buddies who're up there in the lethal light, a world an' a half away from all that watery night. The basement a this world, that's where they live, unlit except for here an' there a flash, a line a light traced out faded disappeared, shomethin you remember in your eye, just enough so you can't argue shomethin' came an was there an' is gone.

Out of Bartelli's by then, walking west out of Frontenac, a road turned to gravel, sky clear as could be.

All those stars up there pavin the Milky Way, Zirque said, that's the spirit trail you take when you walk on outta this world.

Good way to go, Pap said looking up.

Look at those telephone wires, Zirque was saying, swaying, drunk, they go all the way t' Egypt.

Jusht who the hell'd you want to talk to in Egypt anyway? Pap was still trying to get a fix on where exactly you could pick up the trail that'd lead you above the sky.

You know in Amsterdam it's legal to have the girls right up against the glass, like mannequins in lingerie only they smile at you. A few Dutch dollars is all you need.

A city's value is directly proportional to its relationship to every other place in the world, Duke was sayin, lookin strange in the streetlight his hair back in neat little rows, in waves as if a wind were blowin or the light was wind, but it was just the way his hair was, in stiff waves, his round face angelic under a lamp on Mckay Street.

Israfel, Pap called him out of an old rhyme, one to remember well.

Died after a three-day drunk, old Edgar Allan, didn'ee?

Hell do I know? I don't much pay attention to writers still puttin out books, why'm I gonna go fact findin about a dead one?

The infamous Zirque Granges won a few thousand in a card game way back when, talked Pap into Amsterdam. Got whores you can go window-shoppin for.

Most a Pap's time in Frontenac got spent watchin her, waitin, or takin his mind off waitin. Drinkin sometimes the same as flippin through magazines in a doctor's office. Talked to himself because he always listened.

What the hell? You're payin, I'm goin.

Zirque made Pap tire himself out in a museum first thing, tellin him it didn't matter what he knew about paintin, whatever he liked was fine.

One or two weren't bad, couple a bowls a fruit, jugs a wine on the table – hangin one a those'd be a lot classier than wax apples and bananas on the table, couldn't drink the wine outta that dusty bottle though no matter how close t'real it looked.

Picked up from a painting done about 1770 that Amsterdam ain't changed in 200 years you take away the parked cars an electric lights.

Almosht as many canals as shtreets, he said to ZeeGee, ain't this shomethin? I never knew.

Red Light District was the big to-do, looked like postcards a Las Vegas, lights an' casinos, bars on every corner, and the ladies in their full-length windows, red-lit over the top as if you didn't know, standing there as evening came on, the sun's orange-red light sinking into the cobblestone streets like the blood of a bull butchered in the middle a town.

Stores with toys no kid plays with, plastic dickies all sizes and shapes, things Pap'd never heard of, French ticklers, love bumps, ribbed, ridged, rubber blow-ups, chains, handcuffs and whatnot, enough of it to about make him sick.

Sure I like a whore now an' then but who wants to be tied down an pisshed on?

Come on –

Went to a coffeehouse was what they called it, dope den was more like it. Cathedral-height ceiling with beams the size a railroad ties, walls painted yellowish orange with black tiger stripes. Jimi Hendrix, Jim Morrison, Janis Joplin – all Js might've been the trick or maybe all dead – painted bigger than life over the mirror behind the bar. Windows facing the street big enough to hold a vision of Christ in stained glass, but it was just the plain clear kind, hash haze drifting across them from the little round tables, islands in the sea fog of smoke, tiny tables arranged so that a crowd could fit around them, rolling papers right there in bowls on the tables.

Lightheaded, relaxed, things going in and out of the smoke in Pap's head like a game of hide and seek.

Time to visit a lady in glass. Zirque pushin him toward the door. Zirque swept a hand along the perspective of the street. Pick a girl, any girl.

A blonde behind a glass door, the kinda beauty could break your heart over her pretty knee, tall as Zirque or close to it.

Go on in Pap.

Pap watched some guy in a class with him – needed a shower a shave a haircut had teeth like a donkey – walk up to her, a woman who shouldn't have t'put up with so much as a look from either one a them, next thing he knew, the talkin donkey had gone through the glass door between the side where people live and the side where there're things outta fairy tales, went into the magic castle through the transparent doorway and the curtain closed.

Pap finally picked one out, a redhead more than half way to gorgeous. Why not? They're just whores. We make up the rest, just stupid daydreamin as if there were still knights runnin around on horses.

Afterwards, when it was good and dark, he and Zirque sent glimmering arcs over the side of one of those canals. Nothin like a good pissh outdoors. Listening to the stream hit, thinking, Not so easy t'crawl home in Amsterdam, might wind up in one these canals, it'd be a swim or a drown.

Pap left the Duke on his front porch, decided to swing by Bartelli's, do a little waitin, you never know she might come by. Ought to give Yorick a call at home see what he has to say. Tie one on while waitin, buy a few, sip outta the old flask here and there, save a couple a bucks.

Pap, you keep up the pace you're goin at, you're liable to be bellyin home in a drainage ditch tonight.

Wouldn't be the firsht time.

Crawlin through drainage ditches, countin side roads, more than one way to navigate.

Earl walked in some time before Pap fell off his stool, last of his money gone, nothin left in his flask, dust off the floor on the side of his face.

Pap, you all right?

Old Earl, 13 years on death row, mighta killed somebody'r other who probably deserved it, but he was pardoned by the governor an' no matter what he mighta done way back when, he was always good to his friends. To everyone else he's the walkin cosmos kinda, don't know if he's gonna shit on you or make you president.

They're lookin for Granges, he said.

Won some money again, did ee?

Yeah-up. Fair an square way I heard it. But they want it back. Earl didn't stay long, just looking for Zirque he said.

After Earl left, Pap got worried. What if . . . maybe they'll try to get hold a her because Zirque's too hard t'find. Couldn't be nothin worse than that. She's got to know, that's all, maybe get her t'shtay at my place where they won't think t'look, least till mornin, then head over t'see the Duke, he'll know what t'do.

You gonna make it home t'night Pap?

Where thrzz a drainage ditch, Pap nodded, thrzz a way...

Night Pap.

Cold outside, enough to see his breath, but he felt warm, warm an' lightheaded, street wouldn't stay put, wouldn't be still.

Risa was wrong. Ain't rain, just a half drizzle.

Drunk as he was, what with a clubfoot an' all, Pap fell over. Not much sense in getting up again either, might as well crawl on home, ain't but half a mile.

Get home, sober up, hitch on over to her place. Not real likely to get a ride at this hour, maybe shoulda called from Bartelli's . . . nah, wouldn't want her to hear the new language I speak when I'm drinkin like this, wouldn't want her to see me now.

An' Jesus but here comes the rain. Fuck it, I'm hot anyway. Hell wit' this shirt I'm wearin, it's comin off. Howzzat? An' the pants next for good measure. Who gives a goddamn? Ain't no money in that wallet anyway, come back for it in the mornin if it don't get washed away, naked as you please, like cold sandpaper against my gut this muddy grit, but I ain't sweatin no more an' don't really care who comes along long as it ain't her. Piece a luck if Earl'd come scoutin the ditches. We could ride out t'get her after he gets over the shock a seein me bare ass. Who'da known it'd come down to a drunk like me t'keep her from harm's way? Duke's dream musta been about her, they're sure to come after her. Wish I could crawl faster, half wish I had my pants'n shirt on again, ain't no fun hittin rocks with my elbows, little stones diggin into m'knees, goddam wet this old sewer ditch with this stream a goddam muddy water only a half-inch deep but jesus god cold and nasty, got me lookin like some kinda muddy thing just climbed out an ancient sea, tryin t'get around on land not havin an easy time've it.

Truth is, thinkin a her accounts for the warmth in this part a the world, hell don't need any clothes after all. Let the whole damn sky come down, one long downpour over me, I'll bear up, don't need anybody's help don't need a car, crawl all the way t'her place, make it by sunup, rather do it on m'own, all that hair I got on my body finally comin in handy.

Too bad I don't give off a glow to see by, dark is dark can't do nothin about it, I ain't no deepshea Japanese shquid, no lightnin bug, can't see any better than Risa sometimes she's got some kinda light she follows that ain't a fair comparison. Yeah-up, even under the ocean, tons'n tons a water, endless dark'n cold, even under all that I could leave a trail just like one a them fish, a trail a clothes'n a trail a light, darkness crushed to black grit, crush the light too, mix em together, a light-dark dark-light, like you melted down a section a the nighttime sky. I'd be a distant flickerin splinter a starglow in that pompeii nightdark slag flowin under the world through the sewers, catch you up unawares, preserve you for all time in the strangest position you ain't careful, make you the talk a the Corner Cafe one mornin.

Man if I could be wonna those fish, they'd find me still lit up, why can't I leave a thousand-watt corpse for her? Squid ain't no looker, but it'll draw oohs and ahhs, a regular garden slug even, if it's got its own halo. Neon Pap they'd call me. Don't want to be no lifeless boneless lump a tentacles, pair a eyes starin outta it no grace a'tall t'that. I want t'be still alight when they find me. One-eyed Oshcar tryin t'tell me shomethin all along the way he looked at me outta his good eye, y'get t'flare up green-yellow all right but you're in a sewer ditch, no one near but half-drowned earthworms gonna be impressed, leaves you the shapeless lump you didn't want anyone to see.

Fact is I don't much care long as I leave this world in a heap a green an yellow makes you squint, long as it ain't the harelip they remember, the clubfoot, long as they say, Pap, he was a night crawler for sure, sewer rat in a way, a gutter ball kinda, a ditch navigator, but he walked the edge a the Milky Way for a while there, left a lightnin trail, couldn'ta missed him on his way outta this world.

SLOW DIVE

Not inhabited, not reincarnated – I don't believe in these things – not occupying the same place at the same time (physics argues well enough against this); more like two things humming at exactly the same pitch, adrift in a similar underwater reverie, standing on the same numbered square in a game of hopscotch covering all of Paris, Europe, making it even as far as the Dorothy-and-Toto state in America where he comes from.

What does it mean to stand and gawk, reel with *deja vu*, to feel guided, inspired, reborn? And for hundreds of years to blame it on muses or karma or a collective unconscious or something equally implausible? Just this: there is something in need of explaining.

And these musings, do they echo in this city's moss-grown sewers? Or dissolve into the silence out of which everything came (and if you are overcome by the dramatics of a closed universe, back to which it will all one day crawl)?

Here the stillness has taken on the color of deepening evening, a floating gray on top of the failing light – so dense a feather, a metro ticket, *l'addition au restaurant* could be suspended in it.

Yes, even my own body.

Pinned for days on this unmade bed, not like the great-shouldered Greek under the cumbersome bulk of a foolish planet, but by my own marble weight.

Bien. Ca suffit.

Here is the razor, the flame of the candle cold along its edge. A cheap blade stamped out with no love for steel, one of a hundred-thousand others entirely identical to it, yet this is the one that has been chosen for this game of destiny. It's not death I am interested in – though that is one ending to this story – it's just a way

(The blade sinks in with less effort than I had imagined, draws a rise of warm red out of me, the blood is cold by the time it begins to drip from my elbow.)

to force a move. Who knows but I will lose my nerve, call the paramedics before consciousness runs out. Perhaps the police will choose the right moment to kick in the door and interrogate me for what they already suspect. Or Zabere, upstairs, will come knocking for sugar and, finding the door open, will enter. If I do not lift a hand, if circumstances arrange *themselves,* well then I will have to admit –

Through this tiny opening, ah what a lovely gash in the living stuff of things. Your soul leaks out (can you imagine anything so fragile?), hovers over the bed looking at you – you, a wineskin emptied of wine – sniffs at your foolishness, at premature eviction, moves on. (I must remember to send a cup of this O positive vintage to Sunday's mass.)

Less pain than the insidious sensation of tearing – no matter how neat, how clean the razor cuts, the feeling of skin being peeled, of being undressed to the bone.

Ah yes, things have begun to move. As they have not for two? three? how many days? Have begun to flow in the manner of time (you do not move through it, it moves through you), and – how did he say it? – time isn't measured by clocks, but by what happens between ticks and tocks, the marks left on the surface of the heart, the contours taken on by memory.

Together he and I do the slow dance of iron-cored planets revolving around a dull blue sun, a Kansas-to-Paris call away from one another but never close enough to touch except on those rare occasions when our trajectories meet, and for a week, perhaps two, a month even, we pull ever so slowly apart – the longer it takes us to pull apart the longer again before we see each other. This is the equation describing our movement.

I refuse to come to L'America because that is where she has her strength, a bull rooted to the earth. I am one of those transparent sea animals which loses its grace once out of the water, collapses in a bulbous heap upon itself; what would I do in cowboy boots? Let her come here, under my influence. From the photo I have seen, we three – oh what a conjunction of heavenly bodies, who can say what would happen under its jurisdiction? Yes, I have asked him many times to bring her, but she is not like that, territorial, ready to bury her head in the entrails of the nearest trespasser.

She waits patiently for her long-suffering man, but I have walked hand in hand with him down the darkest passages of his longing, left him tired of wallowing in his own semen, sickened by his own voraciousness, full of me, full of wine, worn out by the dream of paradise that enters through the unsuspecting vein, sick of this apartment, which in my vampire existence, I leave only at night, which smells of a cave – bat droppings, human sweat, scavenger leavings, leftover *croque monsieur* sandwiches, smoke and cigarette ashes, long nights of reverent fucking. Locked inside closed windows, wrapped in dark moods and pulled shades, fermenting in the humidity of the old steam radiator, it must reek to the uninitiated nose, only someone with a bleeding craving would enter.

He knows why he comes to me, though we rarely speak of it, except to ravel it in the sodom-and-gomorrah of myth, mummify the truth that he is here to sink, to smolder, to be sacrificed on the effigy of a primitive god, his steaming insides coiled on the cold stone. I am the woman he forces to swallow his semen, whose face shines with it. He loves with such force it closes in on pain, pushing deeper as a way to rid himself of some ancient curse. Wouldn't he like to die in the moment he comes, every nerve flaring at once, bone blackened from the inside out, a carbon copy of existence for an eternal instant – gone in the same flash that set everything in motion, nothing remaining but the ghostly blue lines he had once traced out, little enough for a mild breeze to carry off, a flimsy negative of everything in him that responded to the calling of his name, of everything he once mirrored.

Instead he has managed some sleight of hand, it is I who have become his sacrifice, impaled on the sharp heat of his desire, he begs to wear my skin after he is done, the rest bitten off, chewed, swallowed to feed his glowing hunger. An Aztec returning to the Sun the blood it has lost by killing me, giving flesh back to the stars, sending me to that heaven of strange shapes, broken forms, the unguessed-at sensation, pressing me beneath the deep violet liquid weight of nirvana. Jellyfish forms undulate, wave, repeat themselves in sensuous curves. In the shapes of the jellyfish angels, a symbol, a sinusoidal tattoo that appears on the face of your lover where there was never before any such thing, on your pale ceiling, in the bright magma of the lava lamp, violet and orange and amber and blue the only colors left to the spectrum.

He wants me but only if he can choose where to put it, almost as often as not above the place nature intended. *Bien,* so long as he uses a part of him – no broom handles, no trick-shop trinkets, nothing battery run or electric, nothing made of rubber or plastic or wood. Living his own perversion – yes we should, why not?

Anything to get that feeling of being plugged into this half-filled vacuum that is nothing more than charged particles forever in motion, an invisible spiraling dance of infinite creation balanced against endless destruction – a Vedic god presiding over the fleeting existences – barely time enough to leave more than a lipstick trace on a drink glass, to ask who was she?

And I wonder when I will cross the line from waking to sleeping, from sleeping to unconscious. When my neck will become a curious kind of warm rubber that is as relaxed as water but does not spill. And from unconscious to never-again conscious, how thin that line, the body dead while the mind floats strangely on, running on exhaust fumes, a new sense of space perhaps, spreading over unfamiliar territory, flashes of electrochemical reactions here and there, ever more distant – an expanding universe of lonely bits of fleeing light – less frequent because the lungs have stopped, the heart is – for the first time since it began its monotonous hammering – at rest, the blood lies in waiting – like the silence of this stagnant room – for the hardening, stiffening, fossilizing that will make it into something else.

I look to the fluid-amber light of the lava lamp – sitting on a round night table – red globs boiling up, blurbing along, swelling and contracting, rising and sinking back, huge ruby pearls in honey. They would speak, offer a little friendly advice, if only I hadn't already taken the last of my windowpane.

Near the lamp, a flat-headed stone idol he brought from Mexico, a reclining god, holds a circle of flattened stone, a circle of darkness over its stomach for the deposit of my lover's soft organs. A *chac mool*, one of my beaded necklaces hung over him to make him hold up his end of living in my apartment.

Around the *chac*, half-melted candles in colorful puddles of hardened wax, on the floor unemptied ashtrays, books lying open or stacked; magazines, letters, notes; papers from the world of pink slips, insurance numbers, valid driver's licenses to satisfy one-digit-following-another demands. The walls are no better, a collage of photographs and postcards, coffeestained van Goghs and Gauguins and Monets – badly reproduced in the first place – advertisements and leggy models, a fresh cut-out of pensive Betty Blue pasted over a woman whose face I am tired of seeing.

There is the smell of something old, the sweat of summer nights taken into the plaster, a staleness rising in the old pipes, a fine coat of dust over the wine-cellar dampness, over the peeling coats of green and white paint mostly covered by my incessant collecting of images and words, bits of newspaper articles and pages out of books.

The centerpiece in my room, at the foot of my bed beside a white wicker chair, an easel with a blank canvas. To coax me into getting started on something.

Ma mere was a great fan of Steinlen and Toulouse-Lautrec, the 1880s night life of a Paris she had never lived in but never wanted to leave, a cabaret on every Montmartre corner, Le Chat Noir, Le Mirliton, La Claire de Lune, smoke obscuring the Gypsy singers, the artists hunched over their glasses of absinthe. But Marseilles is where I was born, port city of comings and goings, the oldest in France, who would admit it was founded by Greeks? Massalia's great export to the Gauls – still in animal-hide tunics – wine, which they drank without water, to the astonishment and revulsion of the Greeks.

What was given to me in this city while you lived over a bar where I began as a swelling in your stomach? What filtered through from downstairs, from squeaking bedsprings that kept you awake the nights you were not working (oh the things that go on behind the wall, and all it takes is this wall for them to go on), the smells that sifted under the door, the Corsican band in the bar downstairs playing a mix of the jazz of American loneliness in its coldly lit cities; island drum sounds that invade the body like a *loa* (the body does not need to dress in Sunday best and invade the church); dry North African wind instruments made to blend with the scraping of the simoom across the sand; mournful French songs which have never gotten over the tragedy of death but must make it beautiful – how did all of this scratch itself on the malleable unconscious of your unborn child? Who can say?

You tried to lie, *bonne mere*, about being a whore in Marseilles (look at me, I am hardly any better, selling hallucinations and the promise of happiness through the needle), but you cannot lie to me, who has inherited your curved talons, your infinite capacity for sinking yourself into things and drawing out, in the midst of pain and blood, the truth. I knew when I was 14 you had only a vague idea who my father was – possibly the brooding one who lived half his life in France, half in Tangier, among the minarets and wild bird shrieks before dawn to honor Allah, unable to decide to whom he belonged. The Australian sailor, about whom you knew nothing, not even a name. O Nameless Father who art in Australia, hallowed be thy namelessness. And the Corsican, a regular at the bar downstairs, in and out of the band, who began to think about me when I was barely 15, coming up late one night while you were out and except for the buzzer old Jacques had hooked up, would have made me his. What a brawl that was, down the stairs, across the bar, out in the street.

What luck to have an adopted *grand-pere* who was related to me by nothing at all but I was the shine in his eye as he wiped the bar down at one in the morning. (Perhaps the rumor that he had lost a schoolgirl daughter to a rare blood disease was true.) He would not even sleep with you those months the rent went unpaid, a cruel kindness, forcing you to bed down with unbathed men reeking of cheap wine and vomit to do Jacques the honor of meeting the bill. Bull-chested Jacques with his furry gray beard and huge forearms, his legendary temper, he told the most riveting unbelievable stories ever concocted in the warmest voice imaginable. He sat me on the bar, his hand in love with my straight black hair (the same as yours) and yours also, thick lips good for pouting, with one pout Jacques would let me have my way, *voilá,* the complete works of Hugo, Zola, Flaubert in gilt leather-bound editions as if I were his own granddaughter.

Ah, would the planets have trembled in their orbits, the Moon come up a different color if my father – whom you suspect is actually the one – had lain his hands on me? Often I wonder, a man I had never known (Jacques, I never saw him again after you tried to kill him with your great heavy hands, we never shared a full moment of intimacy), would it have been so bad? Only the knowledge of who he was would have made it evil, nothing else. It might have happened naturally, years later, in another part of France, a night-long event when I was feeling partial to musicians or older men missing their teeth, intriguingly tattooed over their whole bodies to mirror the movements of the Zodiac.

There you are, he pointed, on my thigh, a scorpion, when he was in my room and wanted to take down his pants to show me.

No, it is only when we know and persist in our perverseness that we end up with a god angry enough to lift entire cities off the earth and return them to it as a slow black rain of hot ash. Even then, who can say it is justified?

What does He know of the human weakness for the perverse or the place evil appetites have in the marriage of a riddle-answerer who killed his father, the death of Hamlet the elder, the sojourns of Zirque Granges in Paris?

It is the Corsican's wind-burned face (ritually scarred with strange sweeping marks like Arabic writing) I see at night, *de temps en temps.* Exiled from his mild-weathered island to this sea of bitter-cold waters, I cannot help wondering about him. I remember the Freud-type who told me I have confused intimacy with sex. He is right. The words are entirely linked in my mind, cannot be pulled apart without doing irreparable damage. To be intimate, to know, means to have sex for an entire night with him or her, the matter is almost none at all, an entire night, so I do not care to know just anyone, and you cannot know me until you have slept with me. It was living over that bar, I think, that somehow ruined me in this way.

Left me to sit in the stillness of my room, unable to get out of the dark out of which I was born, my blood running into the sheets, mesmerized by the spreading shape, a thing forming as I watch I cannot help this slow dive through the dense graininess of a badly developed photograph tinted violet, bottom an unfounded rumor.

There was too much Basque in you *Maman*, you passed on the stubbornness to me as surely as these severe cheekbones. A race deposited in the Pyrenees, one of those pools left to dry while the sea retreated ever farther until it was a distant memory, a place like the garden where the first happy hours of humankind are supposed to have been spent. And this pool of salt water retains the ways of a sea long gone, is no good for drinking, does not fit in, does not want to.

And what is that little flat-headed idol doing over there, on the other side of the bed when I left it next to that volcanic lamp of mine? Its face a little blurry, now there's a shapeless lump on the smooth stone platter it is holding. And why is that lamp a smeared glow, the light a receding spark that has no effect on the cold underwater blackness surrounding it? Don't those terribly deep-sea fish have lights dangling from their ugly wide-mouthed heads to attract other fish, like the sinking smeared glow calling to me to follow? Ah, never breathe the name of the dead, it distracts them, calls them back, tethers them to this place they would do better to forget.

This slow thing is a slow dive, the deeper the colder the darker. *Ma mere,* how did you let this happen to your daughter? This slow dive, the way I lived, an endless sinking at three in the morning beneath the streets and sewers of Paris, the trickling water echoes as it drips, mingles with the moldering dead buried in Pere Lachaise. One thing chained to another and all anchored at the nonexistent nadir of an abyss – heroin and oblivion, the waters of the womb and the oceanic darkness of unremembered places where nothing can ever be more than intimated – night of the weeping demons of the soul where you cannot help but wonder why the stars wanted so badly to see themselves (vanity, all is vanity) they spawned an entire race out of dust and opened up a thousand ways to return it to the dust. Why make us prone to disease and the decrepitude of age, why imbue us with a love for needles and the hot white powder in whose glow you see you are just a cage of bone and sinew somehow trapping something of the eternal, which childish pre-Renaissance painters tried to show with a halo? The toothless, choleric, redheaded painter who pointed this out also spoke of traveling to the stars as one takes the train to Tarascon or Rouen, but the locomotive is death. If tuberculosis is a first class car to Aldeberan and old age is the light-years-long walk all the way to Rigel (the shining flank of sprawled-out-overhead Orion), heroin must be a slow boat to Sirius.

The coughing whistle of steam from the radiator warns of rising heat, but no outside warming will save me. The radiator is blind and does its blind work like all of what is visible to the eye it operates on a set of principles since the Beginning blind to us *aussi.*

So there is my proof, there was no need to stick myself with a razor, experiment with the tenuous links to what surrounds us, I needed only to think of myself as a corpse and the heat coming up regardless.

Then again, there is the matter of Bar Sept where I met Zirque Granges and he doubted me when I told him – as I had told everyone that night – that my name was Sophie. I cocked my head and tried again.

How about Therese?

Could be, he said.

Veronique?

Sounds more like the glass slipper but from the look on your face, I guess I'm wrong again.

Whichever one you like I said, and one night in bed he turned to me and whispered, Whatever your name is, Veronique is the one I've fallen for.

I did not bother to tell him in truth I have three names, one name from each possible father, how else can I know who I am?

He puts me on his arm but knows enough to wear a falconer's glove. Then sets me loose on the circling winged fears he has and for a moment, an hour, a day, a reprieve. After I've ripped their hearts through their feathered breasts and brought the bloody lumps back to him as proof (until they rise again and again no matter how he tries to outrun them). And she, the Queen of Blue Jean Babies, the one who takes me from his arm, putting the hood over my head first, the drug which counteracts the side effects of the harsh cure he has found.

He wants to keep us separate, I and his Rae Anne, church and state, business and pleasure, good and so-very-irresistibly bad, he who lives like a member of some tribe his life is so unplanned so perfectly a mess that you cannot shake the suspicion something divine has had a hand in it. And the fingerprints of this invisible, where do they show up?

He told me about a drunk in Kansas who used to make it home on his worst nights by falling into a drainage ditch and crawling, sliding along the edge of near-dawn until it brought him to the creaking wooden steps – the paint nearly all worn away – of his front porch, except the night he'd collapsed in the ditch and a flood brought him to the foreign field of a neighbor who, astonished at what had washed up on a Sunday morning, shook his head and said it was bound to happen one day.

But when? Pinpoint for us that. The moment when sleep becomes unconscious becomes never going to move, never going to convulse in the throes of an orgasm never going to eat, never going to laugh, never going to squat in an alley at three in the morning and piss out too much beer splattering on the cobblestone and on otherwise perfectly good shoes, never going to *une fois plus* feel the warmth of a man's body against you beneath an avalanche of blankets heaped up against the winter cold in this wood-and coal- and gas-and-oil- and-memory-burning city.

How much heat do they give off, these memories that are your only evidence of a life lived, tossed into the furnace in the basement, where they flare up for a second pffFFFT – *fini?* Less substantial than a cigarette, not an ash left, *au revoir.*

They have worked their way – they won't let themselves be anything so useful as petroleum – into the blood. See, in the shape spreading across the sheet now, clearly the face of my whore-loving father. This doesn't count, you will say, the Corsican may not have been the one, there are no photographs to corroborate my mother, a shadow of the memory of a forgotten existence.

I fall back to the certainty of the time ZeeGee had come to Paris, his third or fourth visit, we met under the Pont de Neully, gazing stupidly at one another, sodomy and gonorrhea, a pigeon hiding under the bridge where I had also gone to get out of the rain. His face chipped flint, a neolithic spearpoint, dozens of facets all tending toward a characteristic hardness, wet sealskin hair as glossy as his dark eyes, that missing tooth the space for forgiveness in your smile. You walk sideways around your own life, scavenging claw to mouth as you go, never wondering what this twisted bit of driftwood you poke under is doing there – never realizing you are looking at yourself bleaching in the sun.

In the café in Montmartre with four windows (one for each direction, season, Eliot's Quartets) – famous for having never seated Hemingway or Eliot or any other *ecrivain celebre* – cleaned up, insides warmed with clam soup and escargot, fingers shiny with garlic butter, arguing with three old men about Foucault and Hamlet and Kafka, looking to me to translate, telling your stories of the wino-philosopher Lloyd Cruise who, asked by the cops how old he was, said *99 or 66 dependin on ha ya look at it,* and the Earl of Deathrow, the Polish Kansan, who said *bein ain't no different from nothinness when you been sittin in solitary confinement for a few years.* Who appended onto Nietzsche *what doesn't kill me only makes me stronger, less a course it leaves me stuck in a wheelchair for the rest a my natural days.*

Only the stubborn one with white hair and a black beret refused to smile. Who was confused and grudgingly listened to what happened to you that day you were in Gallup, what used to be nothing more than a railroad stopover in that dustbin part of New Mexico and you came out of a theater, captivated by a procession of telephone poles heading crookedly off into the sunset, leaning different ways as if trapped in motion, the streetlights and red-glare Colonial Motel sign, the white fluorescence of the Big O Tire shop strange echoes of the fading glow stretched across the horizon. The bowing poles connected by their cables seemed a line of Apache crown dancers or Hopi katsinas, branching head-dresses made by the double crosses, the smooth silent orange of sunset in place of the twisting and spitting of a bonfire.

But that was just a stand-in for a stand-in, you said. You see these dances and you know you're only lookin at a few bones a the world which brought this performance on in the first place, an you try to imagine the whole beast, what it musta been like to inspire those masks, grinnin pop-eyed grotesques somma them, all of em harder to read than Chinese runes.

You are saying we live in an empire of signs, Black Beret offered, knocking his little walking stick on the white tiled floor, and the Eiffel Tower is just another mountain aiming too high like the ziggurat in time-obliterated Uruk.

I don't know, you said, but there's a nebulous tide risin an fallin in the subterranean mind an certain things get you to look inside yourself for somethin gone a long time ago, somethin you don't much have time to think about while lunch is bein bagged at McDonald's.

Paris will never have one, Black Beret snorted.

The boons a progress are ubiquitous. You smiled.

Yes, I agreed, so is bad taste.

But I was thinking about Artur, the night crawler, how we are all like him, following the grooves of our habits, our routines and never realizing the very things we trust the most we will one day be buried in. Afraid like no one I know of death, ZeeGee's hopscotching around the planet maybe is his way of staying a square ahead of it. One day it will be his luck that gives out, yes what katsinas are rumored to bring besides rain, it will be a rotted plank between buildings to which he's trusted his weight and destiny which will give out, the *finis* for ZeeGee.

And who do I stand in for? And you Monsieur Granges, are you also nothing more to me? Trace that to its source if you are not afraid, if you do not mind that the answer will bring on darkness at noon, eclipse the Sun for all time, if you will not jump off that evil brink, if you will not plunge the nearest cactus needle or sharp stick into your eyes when you discover the answer.

We came home late from *Cafe Quatre Vents* and I would have suggested to him a soothing cigarette, but he is afraid of the taste of ashes in his mouth, like the mortality he feels in southwestern winters, New Mexico and Arizona when he smells woodsmoke, a sign to him that it is all burning down – imagine fearing something as formless and hardly conceivable as entropy instead of taking comfort in the cozy triteness of warming his feet by the fireplace and placidly smoking a pipe while reading a good book.

As for his bad sleeping, maybe it is only that he cannot find a comfortable bed. He stands looking out my window which here on the third floor looks down at the bistro across the street, the little Tarot card shop where Zabere tells wonderful lies about the future for 100 francs –

What are you thinking?

– tells us such fascinating lies about ourselves we believe them even when they are true. He makes Zirque laugh with silver stardust eyeshadow on his brown skin and silly come-ons. Zabere, if you only knew he could be summoned up during one of your seances if he were only sleeping, never anchored to anything, no not really, except to Pittsburg, that little town he says has as many forgotten pasts as yards of rusting railroad tracks where he is the only one who would risk starvation in Paris to avoid dying of boredom in Kansas and cannot sleep tonight –

What, I asked him, his face street-lit reddish orange, are you afraid of now? What do you see in the telephone poles this time?

– lying in bed with a sleeping bag for a blanket. I know why he prefers to sleep on his clothes and you might think a hamster has better instincts, but it is the dog he imitates, the dog who has taught a pile of rags to conform exactly to his curled body, a transformation so complete the rags have taken on his musty smell.

I know that the woman waiting for him in Kansas is a bed in the shape of his dreams of sleep.

To sleep, to rest, this simple mystery of opiates in the brain, for everyone but him. Maybe inspired-inhabited (an unwilling medium Zabere would envy), is what kept him up writing on matchbooks, on envelopes already postmarked, keeping me awake also, mechanically eating one *petit ecolier* after another, wondering who else in this world had just such an addiction to cookies covered with dark chocolate, what is she like, how will I find her (perhaps him?), how old is she, has she ever given a thought at this moment to my existence?

If you trace the lines as we go from addiction to addiction and plot the points of intersection where our cravings are held at bay, the angry fix an American Poet called it, what you have will be as beautifully formed as the angles in a crystal, as the natural engineering of a spiderweb or the criss-cross of telephone and electrical wires and clotheslines between tenements roping off a bit of alleyway sky.

Heaven has left a wind tunnel in our hearts and the always-trying-to-fill-it, the always-looking-to-get-there is what leaves us face-down beside the curb or stretched out naked on the floor, the cigarette burning down to the filter between our fingers, the candle a hardening reddish puddle waiting for our failure to be pressed onto it.

We need an instrument to study the telemetry of our prayers, we worshipers from afar, in time, in distance measured (by that same instrument) from the angel realm to earth, from sunny pleasure domes and a cloud signed and numbered like a limited-edition print, to Pantisocrasy and the Commune of 1871. What can we drop from there to here and what can we take with us and what will be waiting for us there?

And what is to be done with those of us who have an aching for a myth to support our lives, a backbone, an yggdrasil whose roots curl like a fist around our troubled hearts, whose leafy branches disappear in the strange horizon where vision blends with the sky lording over it, the pale moon and occasional lumps of burning rock-iron-copper angels who fall through it, gather at our feet as dust that has traveled light years to be stepped on and forgotten except for that one phosphorescent moment when we knew to make a wish before it was already too late. And maybe that is what you are doing up late at night, inventing one, crawling up the backbone as you add vertebra to vertebra, Jacques and the beanstalk, where does it lead and who is the giant waiting at the top? And how heavy are those golden eggs anyway? If we don't want the trouble of using ligament attachments as rungs of a ladder, if we allow it to be watered down (afraid of heights) we paint in oil, we pastel, we draw angels in the air, stamp them out of plastic, print them on comforting cards to send to one another, put them on the tops of Christmas trees, make them in the snow, in mashed potatoes, and compose music to mimic the sound of their wings beating from heaven to heaven.

For a moment music is your salvation, you feel a certain way hearing it, and you want to own it, possess it, bottle it, so that you have cornered this feeling and the needle of your life remembers to follow the grooves – this is what you hope, but those times the music refuses to cooperate, fails, you turn to another needle, something stronger. You wander out into the street, tortured hysterical naked, and start to feel how the laughing gargoyles of Notre Dame, a starry sky, the crazy Dutchman's celestial night, a rain-shined street can sink into you, fossilize in the sedentary mind, and how what refuses to crystallize, what remains hallucinogenic, kaleidoscopic and unformed – though governed by unseeable, unknowable rules – is the deepest of all patterns, this I, this me, this peculiar understanding of the sense (or absurdity) of things.

Shall we agree that it is all neither absurd nor meaningful, neither this nor that, that it is merely a matter of here it is? That it was merely a matter of time before America fell to worshiping coca-cola cans and Warhol restaurant menus, the most easily reproducible, the manufacturable, let itself be led around by a platinum-wigged *pede* whose only form of intimacy is a passion for drawing *les dangs* of men whom he admires?

Man's inanity is heaven's lens.

My favorite dear-departed painter would be scandalized.

In the stone wall around his tiny cottage, he saw an epic struggle against chaos. In the twists of tree branches, the desperate desire to live (I lie here, mocking it). He was certain of the exact color to express the sound of the spoon tapping against a coffee cup, but *quel domage*, he turned fate on himself, only thirty-seven. Syphilitic deep-suffering redheaded drinker of absinthe, loneliness surrounded him like winter.

Are you moved to tears? And the stars, what would move them, colossal sources of infinite light and heat, what scene of human tragedy would cause a flaming bit of starstuff to fall?

The smallest and the most trivial, the nearest *clochard*, gray-haired Albert the seller of old magazines, face-down in his own vomit. The old woman downstairs who lost her husband in the French Resistance and two sons in Indochina. But not viewed from a distance as Albert is by passing bourgeoisie who are worried about getting their patent leather soiled with pinkish half-digested wine and bread, rather from a button on the sleeve of his coat, with him through all those years, from fortune to misfortune, and what a story of lost family, the betrayal of his own sons – Albert, you used to be so handsome – and the steal-ing of his wife by an embezzling business partner – who cares? Not even Albert – that he has come to this end, only the button which bids the star look closer and you too will cry.

Look now, who should be at my empty easel but the mad Dutchman (those are starry nights that were his eyes), a blank canvas attracts him the way a living body attracts love, the rod in metallic silvery voice calls to it the lightning, Ouija boards attract the mute ghosts killed in the French Revolution, my adolescent body attracted one of my fathers, this city (the cooking smells in Rae Anne's kitchen) attract my American lover (whose soul was born in a lost Middle Eastern city lying in infamy and dust).

Where are you now?

Under the Pont de Neully maybe.

And even if I had the strength to get up and look for you there, no doubt you would be on your way here by one of your roundabout routes through the Arab Quarter. A Shirley Temple movie. Ah, they've just missed one another in their sleighs, grandfather going up the street she was just on. And so will be my death, no one here, not even Charlie Chaplain Keystone Kops to bumble my experiment.

The judge of all undersea life with a goat's face, his infernal spreading horns twisted like stretched entrails, seaweed beard waving, laughs.

I offer him the stare of the retarded, the idiot savant, my fingertips grown as heavy as lumps of iron, this cold leaving them hard to move clumsy useless, my lips locked in a kiss with a gargoyle carved out of ice, his frigid weight making breathing difficult. Wings of crystalline darkness, of glittering cold enfold me, pins-and-needles pricking my arms, my thighs, the fringes of consciousness – can the bottom be so much farther off?

The crazed Dutchman's hair is no longer red, his face is tattooed in the flowing mystery of Arabic. *Pere,* what are you doing here now with those strange popeyed fish hovering above your head, above the lava lamp whose red has coagulated in such a way as to show my adopted grandfather's anguished trapped cry, your mouth stretching out of all proportion as you rise (ah, such agony, why is there no sound?), Jacques I cannot hear you, the eels like thoughts coil inside me. I am surrounded by a thousand slimy things and I am one of them.

Where is ZeeGee? The inset in my life, a smaller photo within a photo, exiled to a corner, an overlap, nothing so clear-cut as yin within yang, love within lust within sex within sodomy. What bridge in what part of the world on what locust street in Pittsburg, Kansas (there is a Paris, Texas, so I have heard) is he leaning against a building boarded up since Prohibition and wishing for a yeast-clouded beer in a Berlin café where we will be close enough to exchange nightmares? There is more good in him than he realizes and more evil in me than he cares to admit (maybe too in that other woman addicted to *petit ecoliers*; has she even been born yet? she who also lives in a city split by a river, I imagine – the odds are not zero, it's bound to happen). It is a wonder he doesn't feel the clawed grip when I hold him, smell the acrid sulfurous burning.

Who has opened the door of my refrigerator and let in that rush of cold? Oh it is Zabere, the apartment door, Zabere screaming at such a pitch I cannot make out through the thick violet filling my mouth my eyes my ears the words. Did I make an appointment for today? *Zeut alors* I forgot. how can you remember a fraction of an hour when the days have slid one into another, a gray slush nightless sunless dayless timeless and now I see it is unconsciously possible I planned this and my answer of course is given in ambiguity, a definite maybe, I should have known.

C'est trop tard! he is screaming, *Trop tard!* Too much blood is lost, I am too blue, what is to be done? He is bandaging me with torn sheets, look at the definition in his skynny lyttle arms, who would have thought all that strength could come out of them?

Through closed lids I hear him, frantic on the phone, but I can no longer understand what he is saying, his voice is moving away from me, and the room has dissolved.

Oui, oui, y knew it all along, a defynite maybe. but why can't I keep my eyes open, why ys it ympossible not to sleep, and what ys that

coming toward me, no, not a dream, something else, a whyspering iry-
descence as I fall into an abyss y could never have ymagyned yawned
below thys world, a whypsering scattered edge of lyght that can only be
the soul's desyre to softly burn.

BUDAPEST BLUE

I could have told you of photographs I kept locked away in a drawer, black-and-whites of you though we had never met, though I had never seen you, so then not you – but yes, you.

Sleep as distant as the memory of childhood, I'm no better off than a dead leaf, a discarded snapshot curling at the corners, swept end-over-end down deserted streets, cities even continents apart always the same near dawn – scattered bird twitters, shadows turning their slow pirouette into brick and stone, the same cold blue-of-drowned-lips appearing in the sky – and I wonder what, besides the brooding shape of Budapest, is silhouetted against reddish amber.

What if I had shown you the photos and you had seen yourself (not you, but variations ... a woman with your dark unforgiving eyes, another with the natural arrogance of your downturned mouth, still a third with the inquisitive abrasiveness of your glare), would you understand who you are? Or why you were locked in a stranger's drawer?

Haunted by photographic memories, something in me is like

film, and having been exposed is left with only the afterimage.

Of you at the Viennese Cafe where we first agreed to meet.

The last time leaving me with a demand: Three glasses of water, you said, in the evening, before it is dark. In a row.

What good will that do?

It will get rid of them.

You never finished, leaving me on the wrong side of a river, bridgeless, wondering how to cross. Get rid of what?

Looking down at the round marble table, the wrought-iron stem holding up its flat petrified bloom, you smoothed the polished surface with your hand. The dreams.

It was no use asking about the dreams, you wouldn't say anything else, I knew.

Promise, you said, three glasses.

You looked at me then, your iris dark enough, liquid enough, to dissolve your pupils.

Tomorrow, I said.

Good.

Your pronunciation more like *gude*.

Standing up, a flip of long black hair, like a sweep of history – horses and dark-skinned foreigners atop them, destined to change everything – and you were gone, coffee still steaming.

You let me catch up with you later, evening flowing into black. Looking into the Danube atop the chain-link bridge with its stone arches and dormant lions, your lips pursed to spit olive pits, you watched the bats chase them before they silently disappeared into the water, the bats never fooled the whole way.

It's not my fault you are no different than a sultry orange moon floating full and huge over the summer evenings, over the Gothic spires of the castle quarter, a moon arisen out of the strange east of this city's origins. No, it's not your fault I was left to burn softly through the night, waking to the faint reek of singed dreams and exhaust fumes sifting through the screen with the morning air.

I saw you first, unable to keep from staring. You pulled closer to the man you were with, bending to the porcelain figurines in a shop window, oblivious to me. I smiled at you while you kept walking, your arm linked to his, staring back.

I slept even less that night, walking the city's paved quiet, hardly noticing anti-communist slogans sprayed on alley walls, a film running through my mind, image by image, your face most of all. I abandoned my apartment in that run-down quarter of Pest, climbed to the roof, and projected my film on the vacuum of the sky for anyone to see, for anyone to take to bed as a blanket, though it would hold off a chill evening no better than a stretch of cellophane, though it was no more real than the faded ghost of a heart outlined in white paint (the names inside too faint to read) on a wall near Andrussy Street, the brick scarred by bullets fired forty years ago.

You will recognize every film I make by the invisible violence worked on the souls we thought we did not have.

Sleepless through morning, I stepped out of my own film – rough, grainy, its colors skewed to the violets of the spectrum – into the streets of Budapest, which had become the black-and-white of newspaper events, had taken on the jagged porcelain clarity of a shattered coffee cup, and saw you at the Viennese Cafe. Alone.

You let me sit down (my hands on my knees where you wouldn't see how unreliable they'd become), but did not look up from the book you were reading.

I don't like Americans. You turned a page.

I couldn't answer, sat at the bottom of a tree waiting for another apple to fall (thinking about the impossible odds of looking at one at the precise moment it has at last grown too heavy, the stem too weak, and falls). Afraid to shake the tree, of violating something, I waited in the black-and-white stillness, waited for color – even the yellow of old newspapers – to bleed into a corner of the frame.

What are you doing in Hungary?

I'm a film student.

Oh. Yes, how interesting. Americans know better than anyone how to spend money on movies.

America is a big country. The grand scale is the only one we know.

You looked up, this time with an entirely different motive, a different expectation. Why are you in Budapest?

Tempering my American-ness.

Hm. A snort. Compromise might be worse.

You took a sip of coffee, a bite of a chocolate-covered Grandoletti, offered me the box (I shook my head) and read to me from your book:

What does it mean that there is a star always in the north? That it has pulled us along throughout the thousands of years of fear and demonic uncertainties? That it burned silently in its perfection of place, unaltering, unfailing?

You looked at me, your face – as pale as the morning – flecked with ephemeral freckles, and asked, Where is mine? The one I can use when the sky is clouded over, when my eyes are closed, when there is nothing to see?

I saw you again at Golgotha, the bar sitting in the middle of a once-Communist street, the name since taken down, known now by rumor as Nagy Street, a good joke on tourists who are like the blind after furniture in the apartment has been moved.

The streets always change their names, you have to know the street not to be fooled, know it on its way into the heart of Budapest, past the other river which still flows, carrying Nazis, Romans, Huns downstream to their final resting place, running past the cathedrals with their vaulted ceilings buttressing belief against the infinite unknown overhead.

The night is a place where you can commit crimes, go crazy, be ruined. You laughed hysterically for effect. What am I doing here in this black hole of a bar with you?

I've written you into the script.

Gude, why not?

To you I was one more invader, another Roman, a Mongolian, a Turk, a German, a Russian. The history of Hungary built on the threat of dissolution, the ruined walls of fortresses and rule by foreigners, a country that is a peasant woman of such enduring marble strength that although shattered a thousand times, some strange gravity keeps the fragments within reach – a smooth straight jaw here, there an entire arm braced against annihilation, an eye joined by a single curve to the stubbornly intact nose with the background of a starry night behind. A country whose form is nonexistent yet discernible, an abstract of its Magyar past, the green and white and red of its flag, the brown of sunstained farmers' hands, the rich crimson of the fired-upon students who stood in every square before the stern bronze face of a national hero and defied the Russians that October night in 1956. They sit and stand around us, draped in thick sweaters, faded denims sent from overseas (one with blue eyes behind round glasses like those Imre Nagy wore), lift beers to Nagy and the October night the red star above Parliament first went out. Or drink something as strong as absinthe, what wells up from under the city and makes you lose not memory but all sense of time, blowing it up tumorously, so that tanks and chariots rumble along wheel by mechanical gear, and the side of night bulges in an unheard-of direction.

There, standing at a 45-degree angle between the bare brick wall and the floor, nothing relating to anything else the way it should, you told me about one of your favorite musicians who sang that there is a part of us that is too quick flowing too bright too elusive be at home on the Earth we have hollowed out and shafted for dusty coal, have sidewalked for the afternoon crowds. And it is this we call angel, our grounded longing unfolding the wings, abandoning what cannot escape gravity's pull.

Yes, I've heard angels have wings, I said, so you must be one of us.

Isn't that sweet, you said, too casually to mean it.

We drank without reserve and spoke as if that bar – badly lit with blue, hung with posters of old movies: *Casablanca, From Here To Eternity, The Maltese Falcon, Hiroshima Mon Amour* – had been built on hallowed ground and nothing could touch us for our sins or trespasses or be turned against us. We talked of how I would set my only friend's soul on fire if it would light one unknown corner of the universe long enough to take a clear photograph. How you fear more than anything else waking up in a country where no one speaks the strange language of the Magyars, where you cannot make one word out of your mouth understood or find your way home. Of the unforgiven older brother who will spend two eternities in the First Circle for repeating when you were 18 what he had done to you when you were nine. I admitted that notes I had written to a girl through two years of high school had been passed out to the entire cafeteria (I heard my own tokens of everlasting devotion quoted to me by football players for weeks after) as a way of killing the foolishness I felt for her, but whatever it was that died back then, I can't say for sure.

We refused to go home, dragging a bottle of wine by the neck, winding up under the lion-guarded bridge whose lamps cast over it a faded green, using the long pea coat I picked up at a pawn shop in South Dakota to cover the cold asphalt. You taught me that prayer is more than whispered demands and hands pressed together, that it requires more than one person. I learned how it is possible for a tongue to be an Our Father, for hands to restore a soul blackened by its own faithlessness, for the place where our bodies joined to be all of Ecclesiastes. You became a river rushing through my mouth, running into the sea, and what was under the Sun didn't matter to us under the Moon, under the shadow of that bridge where a generation could have passed quietly away without altering the rhythm of our breathing.

Almost asleep, your mouth warm against my ear, I felt you lift your head, wave. To whom? I had to sit up, turn around. The old man who'd watched from a balcony of the bridge, the same one I had seen the other day who'd asked me if I planned to urinate into the Danube, and if so, to do it from *atop* a bridge, not from the banks, preferably at midnight when the voices at the bottom have begun their incessant muttering. *Do you believe that?* No, of course not, it's just the tinkling of bones you hear, rattling over one another, clamoring restlessly, tongues long ago rotted out of those heads, twin voids instead of eyes that wanted nothing more than to see grandmothers, lovers, Papa, sons, daughters, wives, drinking companions, the streetcar conductor again. Then he asked me if my fasz was large or small, if it fit well into women. And there he was, long coat and black bowler, waving back.

In the stillness before the sun has broken the horizon, when you can scent the pureness of an uncreated moment in the cool air, when it is easy to waver between being and nonbeing – a flame about to go out – you shifted your weight on the satin lining of my Navy coat, looking down at it suddenly as if you recognized the previous owner (a musician I tend to think who drank a lot of bourbon, I never did before the night I walked into a bar in drafty snow-drifted New York City and ordered one to warm me up), as if you could shake out of its folds dusty songs, torn movie tickets, phone numbers of ex-lovers ... you shifted your weight and turned to me.

There are rare elements, you said, which exist only briefly –

the memory of the man who wore your coat – and even then only under difficult conditions (at the core of the planet, you know?). It would be easy to think that something warming has formed between us. But I am afraid that there will be no heat when I stand beside it. Arching like a cat, I will not be able to rub my ache against you, I will come up against emptiness. I think I am better off with Gabor.

Really? I kissed you then, I didn't believe you.

He is not like you, you said, he touches me where I am solid, when I want to be a tree rooted to the floor of my apartment, to a place surrounded by my things – I feel for a moment where I belong. You are the dangerous one, I have no idea what I will become around you.

Yes you do. And every time you cross this bridge, every time you see the river, you will remember.

You turned away, whipping your long black hair in half a witches' circle.

Yes, this is what I become, someone who jumps up from the wooden bench in church in the middle of the sermon because she has discovered she does not care for a religion anymore unless she can dress the part.

How could you not be enamored of Italy and the Indian Americas where they dance through the piazzas, the plazas, inseparable from their own shadows grown to gothic dimensions and attract other winged dancers in gowns and masks and capes? You wanted to become the mystery even for a wingbeat, otherwise what is the point? (In the beginning there was no neon, no warmth of cat, no reason for prayer. And yet without our asking, every day a new sun – not yesterday's, not last week's – flares into life in the endlessness of endless space.) You wanted to wade into the Danube, waist-high in the river, a Hindu, arms upraised, but I held onto your wrist, afraid of the deceptive calm of the river's surface.

Three glasses of water to wash color from your dreams, you said.

With no way to film the film I did not stop seeing, I settled for the haiku of photos, evenings mostly, the luxury of soon-to-be-gone twilight, the acquired taste of bitter foreknowledge. A whole roll with you standing on the Roman wall on Castle Hill, in the weak light falling from a rain-gray sky.

You attract the black cat, though you prefer the free-swimming porpoise, imagining them to have quicksilver running through their veins, their high-pitched calls for you.

You shook your head at me when I insisted on cat. You have no sense of porpoise.

I knew then that yes we looked at the same thing and saw differently, our hands reaching for each other had proven ghostly, had passed through each other. And though the word porpoise was in your mouth, you charmed a stray to sit at your feet on that tiny cobblestone street washed with moonlight, to hold perfectly still for the camera.

In your apartment in Obuda, the weathered stone-block buildings so heavy the streets sagged around them, I saw your portrait of Gabor.

Even before I was swallowed by the cavernous mouth of your building, I knew you lived on the third floor. Three of the balconies bare, the only color from roofgutter to foundation – maybe in that whole quarter if you didn't count the yellow street cars – was the red of whatever you'd planted blooming over the railing of the third-floor balcony. Too small really to stand on, you had to lean out a window to get to it, and I knew the first time I stood below it if it wasn't your balcony you'd gotten it on loan.

The stairway, even going up, felt like a descent. Damp and stony, there should have been moss on the walls instead of a patchwork of hand-made flyers selling cars, advertising student movies, renting out apartments, flapping against their staples in the open-door draft. You were at the end of six flights, cross-legged on the age-soaked wooden floor amid the reek of oil paint and turpentine, surrounded by canvases. People I had never met peered back at me (the craggy old woman upstairs whose deeply rutted face holds a vale of tears), places I knew in Buda and Pest, winding alleys and cafes in a white city I seemed to recognize but could not name. More than anything, self portraits: one of you in the alley of that white city using nothing but shades of blue, your hair pinned up, a stare that would keep a century from turning.

I saw Gabor's portrait, looking as though it has been painted on a surface of water, the tiniest details – no more noticeable than a stray hair – floating in the light, yes, more than enough light.

So your style is ... this, I said.

You didn't look up from your sketch pad, a dozen album covers scattered nearby – Robert Johnson, fedora cocked, posing with his guitar; Chet Baker, sleeves rolled up, bent over a piano; Billie Holliday, head thrown back as if the huge microphone in front of her were a serpent that had entered her body. Lead Belly Ledbetter, Bukka White, Mississippi John Hurt, Charlie Musselwhite.

It is a style I decided on for him. You waved a hand at Gabor's portrait but still did not look up. You need to know him to understand.

When I see him again, we'll be like old friends, I said, but wanted to know how to have my painting on the easel where his sat mute still helpless.

You snorted.

I tried to place the voice coming through the speakers, a scratched-up basement recording, the voice grinding the words as they came out, no syllable left unmarked.

Blind Willie Johnson, you said. His step-mother threw acid in his face when he was seven years old. It hurts me in a strange way to listen to him, strange because I still like listening.

When you paint?

Yes.

Blind Willie singing as if nothing had been taken away, sometimes humming, sometimes wailing into dark and solitude as if to break them from the inside out, leave them in ragged fragments. Heaven spread evenly out of reach from where Blind Willie stood, no up or down, directions obsolete, but that didn't send so much as a tremor through his faith.

Blind Willie went on singing, you went on shading with your piece of charcoal, only stopping to reach for a Grandoletti, your most trivial addiction.

Long as theyz a man, I said, roughening my voice, long as theyz a woman, they'll be the blues.

You stopped what you were doing and looked up at me, skepticism and surprise mixing in your expression, a new color.

I smiled.

The charcoal began tracing lines, inscribing the blankness of the paper with the face of someone who could find no other release.

Wrapped in the oily incense of paint, cocooned away in your balconied apartment with the sawed-off voices of American singers, lost to the cry of the infant abandoned on a sloping Taygetus of garbage, to the incessant muttering of thickset waistless old Ildiko upstairs who lost a husband in World War II (nothing left but his hat covering a nail in the wall and a photograph in a cheap gold frame) and two sons to the October uprising. Her coffee – heated on the chipped white stove she lights with a match – is too thick too bitter to be anything but the boiled-down marrow of the dead but it is all she has to warm her in winter. You know almost as well as she, looking out your third floor window, what falls in this rain. How scratches in the flaking plaster covering the outside brick inscribe Ildiko's memories. And you've grown your crimson flowers to spite the bitter drops, each alone in its fall from a place too gray to be anything like heaven, each as alone as a sonless widow before the final strike against a cracked wall, the sidewalk, your flower bed.

How many times have you looked up at monuments or stood before the men wearing helmets, carrying swords, mounted on great stallions, their stoic expressions streaked with green, and asked the corroding metal or smoothed stone, was it worth it? Ask Blind Willie Johnson. Ask Ildiko who prays in the living room, whose knees have worn two bald spots in the throw rug in front of a weeping Madonna. Mary's painted face in a precious Byzantine shroud of gold and silver like braille to the hands of the faithful, framed and hung on the wall above a tiny tv with rabbit-ear antennae that almost reach this image of mourning enfolded in cold metal, this face which stares back at her own. It is only one son she lost not two, not her husband too – crucified by the Nazis – and they've put her in churches, she's a saint because of who her son was but a mother is a mother no matter who her son, the eyes don't lie about what they've seen and even with that flat painting of Mary in the eyes you know.

Sketching me (was it me, all along?) while I stood there, telling me about painting and pain and happiness, about rain and Ildiko (who said wars have taken her sons, her husband, yes, but Stalin-ism reached inside her and robbed her of something she had always believed would outlive her), you handed me a rectangle of cookie, your eyes more on the paper than on me.

A kind of visual alchemy the only thing painting is good for, you said, changing nothing in substance, altering the form only – sometimes into something more acceptable, familiar, the reason, you reminded me, gods have two legs and eyes and merciful hearts, they are not free-floating energies loose ubiquitously in the ocean of being.

As for happiness it is something out of the corner of your eye, you insisted, you don't go looking for it as if you were years at tunneling a mine for a flashing moment when you could exhale, wipe away sweat and say, ah this is what I was looking for.

You looked from me to the sketch to me to the sketch.

Life is a fever, you said, occupied again with the charcoal, a burning. In this city they are too busy taking the temperature in increasingly minute degrees to be affected by its strange unreproducable beauty. Sometimes the dark sanctity of a winter sky makes you a little giddy, the thought of so much space so seethrough your eyes go straight to the glowing white heart of the Milky Way, and in the cold air you are aware of your own heat. You press your face against a horse stopped with its carriage, the tourists' coachman unsure whether to shoo you with his whip or stand beside you, you join heart to heart with your arms around the horse's neck, your face full of the bristle of its hide, your nose full of its musty animal smell.

Leave him, I said, looking over half in guilt, half in anger at the portrait of Gabor.

Yes, you sighed, yes, I'm going to.

And yes, you did, but I misunderstood.

Putting the pad away, you stood up, your nose hardly an inch from mine.

Look at you in this old coat of yours from the Navy. It was never new was it?

I shook my head. I don't think so.

And the night we went to Golgotha, you were missing a button on your sleeve and you held it there with a ... she tapped her wrist where the missing button had been on my shirt ...

A paper clip.

Yes, a paper clip. Your life is held together with paper clips and the wrong color thread and – what do you say? Glue. My American man is wearing away at the edges, but he refuses to notice. Because he is always busy looking somewhere else, isn't he? Not always.

I tried to see myself as you saw me, but your eyes give nothing back, the opaque brown of an amber-locked impurity, I knew I would lose something to you – was losing something to you – standing there like that, afraid to move forward, cross the endless inch separating us, afraid to pull back, the fear of letting go deeper still.

Did I ever tell you you are the most disgusting eater I have ever met? The way you put it all together – a bite of your sandwich, a spoonful of soup – achhhhh – all at the same time.

I'll only drink around you from now on.

Leaning closer, you kissed me tongue-first, the inch between us nothing to you, the space around you long ago made yours. I stood, my eyes beginning to close while your tongue went over my whole mouth, slowly and deliberately, as if to give it a different shape, then, pushing with your tongue, opening what you had just finished.

We didn't bother with the bed though you could hardly step anywhere without knocking over a pile of books, crunching a cassette, sliding over an album sleeve, squeezing a tube of titanium white or charcoal gray, rolling on a camel-hair brush, smearing a wet palette. We became slippery with color, your oily fingers smearing my chest with more, lines and daubs until I looked like a tribesmen from New Guinea. It wasn't until after you had locked your arms and legs around me from underneath, squeezed so hard it hurt, not until after you forced me to come inside you, your head thrown back and your eyes closed, your hair around you like a dark halo, that we wondered how we were going to get it all off without taking a bath in turpentine.

Later in the day, I ran into Gabor in the university library, my body a fading rainbow underneath my clothes, evidence enough for him to ram a bayonet into my chest, but he had no idea I knew you, and I let the accidental conversation that began continue, and liked him, and liked him all the more because he was a part of your life added to mine, and we ended with a drink, Gabor deferential to America, blaming us only for not sending help in '56 when Eisenhower had the chance, asking me about New York, shaking his head in disbelief he had never been there, a place where all languages are spoken, all cuisines served, all appetites find what they crave if only you look down the right street. When we left, he had the address of a friend of mine in pocket, promised to make his pilgrimage to the shrine of Americanness in Manhattan and shook my hand warmly and firmly, a bond that had nothing to do with you. Yes, he is exactly like your portrait, his curly blondish hair, passive mouth and narrow eyes open to the better humans we can be, and I knew even then I would like him, but would also, as soon as I saw you again, beg you to leave him.

Yes, I am going to, you told me again in the park, late afternoon, the sun warm for early October.

When?

When we run into him and the three of us are together and I have hurt him so badly he cannot stay in Budapest because the pain of everything we've done here is unbearable.

You pulled me by the hand, pushed me against a tree, made me sit down.

I love fall, you said. There is just enough cold to remind us we are animals full of warm blood.

You sat on your knees facing me, pulled my face toward yours with your hands locked at the back of my neck and this time only the statue of King Árpád was watching ... from a distance that embraced the first steps of those horsebacked Magyars out of the eastern steppes and the last shouts of triumph over the Nazis, the beginning of Stalinism and the end, the founding of Hungary and our joined mouths.

Do you realize you said, having kissed me quiet, there is no difference between a galaxy and a tree? A falling leaf, a falling star, each has its season. And don't be stupid, of course I know they're just chunks of iron, big rocks burning up, but stars don't last forever either. Everything that holds the leaves to the tree, makes the tree a – how do you say? A complete ... thing, well it's the same thing that holds together the galaxy, holds together the part of the universe you feel but don't see.

But what we can see is what we're stuck with, the only way to cross the distances inside to outside, back again.

Oh yes, how true.

You kissed me again, the cool taste of a wet autumn morning, your sweater rough against the underside of my jaw.

Do you hear that? The singing?

A man's voice, at a distance, passing the time as he adjusted his cap, walked through that clear October afternoon free of the Soviets.

I like the way men sing, you said, as if they are excited about the world. I think of them collecting things and hunting and disappearing under avalanches of snow.

You ripped up a handful of grass, stuffed it down my sweatshirt, and jumped up. Come on, you called, already running, I want to show you something.

Dizzy, out of breath, my head hot and my ears strangely cold, I finally caught up with you at the tram stop. We got on near an open window, pulling out our collars, heat smelling faintly of shower soap rising past our faces.

At your building you tugged me by the hand up the dark stairway.

There, you flicked your fingers lightly, look.

The portrait was shadowed, only one eye visible, half of me in light as harsh and unsteady as fire, the smileless face gouged out of darkness, the strokes straight, swift, irrevocable.

I don't need people to sit for them, you said. I see them better with my eyes closed.

She lets memory decide, but for me memory is an out-of-focus photograph and no matter how close I get, nothing is any clearer, I am always left with the maddening vagueness that comes of things that can never be known.

How could you let our portraits sit side by side in your apartment, two men who would let you be whatever you wanted but didn't want you to be with someone else? Were you really so much the shivering flame about to go out (or flare into a violet only a combustible angel could match) that you didn't know which of us you wanted, deciding only for the day, only after you had drunk your morning cup of coffee? Were you really so double-sided you could not draw out of Gábor the things you loved in me, draw out of me the things you loved in Gábor? Running through the early-morning streets with your feathered Carnivale mask, you never really let us see your face. Your gown fluttering around you like moth's wings, we never really touched you.

You painted yourself as someone else's memory (who had seen you sitting with your legs cocked like that?) in the alley of a white city you'd never been to (shades of blue the only colors) and you wondered how you could feel so well the warm wind skimming the Moroccan night, how there could be Arabic music in your heart. Or maybe it was the sing-song of arguing Italian farmers who share kitchens with their animals that tipped your glare askance, maybe the taste of the salty Mediterranean farther south where there is a pompeii full of old bones uncovered when you brush blueblack volcanic ash from memory.

In whose mind was the look in your eyes, the one you painted, forever lodged? Whose head did you desecrate – a grave-robber in a king's tomb – to find it? Whose thoughts did you roam, rummage through, to know exactly how he saw you?

Standing with you on the Buda side of the Danube I said, Why don't you go? Go to the city you've painted yourself in?

You Americans, you said. I don't want to be disappointed by a small town, however quaint and beautiful, on an island near Greece or Yugoslavia where I will miss all of my favorite movies and will have to rub elbows in bars with goat-herders. I prefer the way I imagine it.

I didn't know what you were looking for or where between here and the sunken islands of a mythical long-ago there is a white city you've never seen or what the man you will meet there looks like, his name, the smell he will leave on your clothes or what he will whisper to keep you forever.

Oh you stupid, stupid American. You smiled and took my face roughly in your hands. You are that man. I always knew I would meet you, I always knew I would leave you.

Not because of Gábor, you said, you had already exchanged goodbyes with him.

(Another prayer is answered.)

It was not a city you walked out of that night but the underworld you lived in, crossing over the river that flows through it, leaving me on the other side without a single backward glance to make me vanish altogether.

I have gone every place we've ever been together to see which has lost your shape, hoping to find you on the steps that lead into the river, in the mist that follows evening rains, in bars where we lost track of the flow of time and beer and the Milky Way, under the bridge where the old man watched, among the marble tables of the café where we first met, along the Roman wall where I exposed a whole roll of film to you, in the park where we sat through the turn of a season with you as ready as Daphne to trade in your skin for bark, your arms for branches, your hair for the feathery leaves of a mimosa, ready to die each winter and revive each spring in fairytale colors (The Earth, you reminded me, knows when to make a show of what it has).

Just below the statue the Soviets named the Liberation Monument (the Nazis were driven out) – the statue of a woman whose arms stretch above her head, whose back is gracefully arched, whose gown is a bronzed national flag suggesting wind – but which is better known as the Reoccupation Monument (the KGB settled in), you can overlook the city.

It sits under a smoke-stained sky, buildings streaked black with pollution tears, its rhythm starting and stopping to church bells, factory whistles, traffic signals. What I see at this hour are long lines of cars unable to move, exhaust fumes joining a collective exhalation that lasts as long as the light takes to disappear.

It was the cement-drab weight of this place, the abrasive grays you abandoned. I am the somberness of the way you painted me, without light without color only shades of dark – a goodbye I didn't recognize. The immaculate stone of your city scorched white by sun and arranged in airy archways showing sky drew you from the cavernous doorways of Pest, which even in summer are as dank and cold as if they led to the frostbitten roots of a tree anchored in a bitter netherworld.

I understand the dolphin in you now, which is not a gray fish but a silver mammal. I understand why you left me here in the sluggishness of all this land, only the Danube to remind me. At my feet a mask whose plumes sprout a foot, the feline eyes lined with darkness, a mask exposing a mouth that could name an emotion you've never felt rushing through you, the same mouth which holds the runaway river every dead sea lies in wait for.

There is no longer black or white, no longer the shimmery green of bird feathers, the desperate reds and yellows we covered our bodies with on the floor of your apartment, no crimson from your hanging garden, no photographs that are anything but blue – from the indigo iridescence of your witched hair to your horizonless eyes and the drowned blue of lips gone cold in memory. The street I'm on a shade of midnight, I shelter under the arches of your body (running with oily still-life drippings), but you are as far from me as Neptune and its moons. The winter trees, the only color Blind Willie could see, the bridge where I last saw you – all blue.

BRING ON THE NIGHT

Phenomena intersect; to see but one is to see nothing.
– Victor Hugo, *The Toilers of the Sea*

17 Sept. 1:15 a.m. (?)

My skin cold and gloss, metallic in this neither-rain-nor-drizzle hanging mist, the dead-man's feet of this dampness swaying not in the slightest, no breeze. My skin bronze and impenetrable, this Paris midnight is burned at the edges by the lead-blue neon of Cafe La Lo, stained to the red of a mouth accustomed to cinnamon, by the glow of a record shop's name.

Harsher white from overhead pings off my sheen, a cold resonance to it. Zabere the pede with bronze skin. We French also say pedale, homosexuel, tante, de la jacquette flottante – *he whose jacket blows lightly behind him – not much else. It is not the big deal of snow to the Eskimos who have 50 or 60 words for it to distinguish between wet, powdery, crusted, high drifts and so on. Americans must hold most sacred of all the homosexual since they have any number of words and phrases for it – fairy, fag, tinkerbell, queer, three-dollar bill, limp-wrist,*

homo, fruit, pansy, queen, flit – imagine if my English were up to date.
At this hour, les clochards *have emerged from the shadowed hollows of Paris, exhibiting the same regularity as lightning bugs in Provence, that one in a stone doorway with a handsomeness to his white-stubbled face (where did he get his last razor, why didn't he take it to his throat?), a slow drop of rain from forehead through eyebrow, down his nose as if this man – too wet to smoke the cigarette he is gesturing for – is being washed away before my eyes. Albert the Ubiquitous, a seller of old magazines and cheap paperbacks with passionate titles, he inhabits every quarter of this city I've ever been to, he gets around.*
On every corner of this city, a hunchback, a deformity, a quasimodo. Moi aussi, *the faggot, Zabere, with bronze skin. Quasimodo, why weren't you a poet? Ugly enough with your clouded eye, your twisted frog's mouth (a harelip, non?); misshapen enough in slumping movement along the cobblestone streets; cruel enough in circumstances; desperate enough in unrequited emotion, but not vicious enough in temperament, not evil enough in mangled heart to give it back to the world in merciless art. All pent up, it became a fabulous lump on your back, a dragging limp, a burden till the day of death. Who isn't looking for his Esmeralda? I can't have her either, we are forbidden by angels with flaming swords so we look down from our bell towers, human gargoyles shitting on passing heads like the pigeons and twisting our stone faces into ghoulish grins. A plague on you. Hot lead on your heads! Where is our sanctuary? Surely not that cathedral like something a receding tide of time has exposed still standing (to our surprise), an Atlantean artifact, carried forward somehow to the nineteen-seventies, a guardian of a passe order of things, walls whose insides have rotted through, guts and soft organs no more, token of a soul longing to come forth in three dimensions and now, at last, it has fled this astral plane (flying this midnight without its lights) and off to the next.*
Ca suffit. *On to La Lo. Close.*

2:03 a.m.

How strange what separates us from one another is so easily snapped broken breached and yet so rarely. We prefer to go on with our isolation, like dots on a balloon spreading ever farther apart as the space around us keeps getting bigger, more babies are born, more cities are built, fewer loves form over the distances –

No, Veronique says, smaller. Every day the connections are more numerous, deepen, invade your sleep.

Is it that we are not alive at all but simply a gravity that has gathered together these bones and my bronze skin, Veronique's brown eyes and black hair, Sartre's bald overheated head, that woman's ivory-white fingers as she handles the tiny silver spoon in her coffee, in order to act itself out?

Veronique taps her cigarette into the amber glass ashtray and looks at the gray used-up remainder of the original as if they are on a speaking basis.

What if there are no lights at all in the sky, Zabere asks, just glimmers of hopeful expectation? Just as there are no shapes we didn't project out of ourselves – the cubists made up all those cylinders and triangles and squares occurring naturally – the cold light of the unattainable is what we view through the telescope, speeding away from us at thousands of miles per hour.

Veronique blows smoke through the mandala roundness of a mouth leading to lower things, dark and unidentifiable.

There is a separateness that lives within each of us, she says, there is something that exists outside of us, it is true, and wants to go on with or without you – the soul's desire to burn softly eternally on – but without you it is nothing.

And what else does love mean but that you exist? If you walked the planet unloved, if you were buried without mourners, if you howled from the top of Notre Dame at an empty city, did you make a sound?

Thank you so much sweet Zabere for trying to save my soul. (She is rolling the cigarette now between her fingers, a satan with a new recruit, feeling the texture of his sins). If it weren't for you, it's true I would be nothing more than a few photos and what you would have remembered of me. Now stop writing when I'm talking to you.

Just let me finish –

We aim great radio dishes at the sky in the abandoned, most desolate parts of the world, listen to the voice of the Great Beyond for something intelligible and check our mail for the same reason, to see what is out there, aware of us, responding to us, in need of us.

– there.

The pen makes a quiet sound of surrender on the table.

Zabere sips his cappuccino through the foamy milk, runs his eyes lightly over the brick walls hung with reproductions of masterpieces tastelessly framed with thin perimeters of silver or gold, a corner of Monet's "Impression de Levant du Soleil" curling down (the glass never replaced) like a layer of night left to expose the blankness underneath. What the city rests on after all.

Look at Paris, Veronique says, a mall, a row of windows on the ages.

Blowing smoke, narrowing her eyes, she drives away the stare of a young unshaven man seated behind Zabere.

Through one rectangle of plate glass we can still be seen fornicating. In another window we still appreciate the latest in fashion, and in that one, the tattoo artists for thousands of years mark us with what we need in order to know who we are every morning (our bodies may have been switched while our minds wandered the passages of sleep more endless than the sewers and catacombs beneath these streets).

A cubist painting, you can step onto any number of planes intersecting, continuous, simultaneous, contiguous, overlapping, coincidental, parallel, incongruous. Though some never touch, never even know of the existence of each other, they lie in sight if you just lift your head. A cubist existence, the prostitute (bearing a stunning likeness to my mother) who has never even heard of spending half her straddle money on books like some of these Sorbonne students, who would rather bend over for a pack animal than spend her entire day operating a forklift at the Gillaume Warehouse. This whore of ours has never even taken a museum tour. Here in the same place, we all exist at different levels, oui?

Smiling or wincing through a cloud of smoke, she pokes the air with her cigarette. This is your business Zabere my little Tarot reader, navigating between planes for the shortsighted.

Everything is a business, *non?* Zabere looks somewhere past her, at the deep night gathered behind the glass front of the café, locking him on the other side. I could have carried the honorific of shaman Way Back When, a well-respected man about town, they would have left me horses, spears, tobacco, wine, roasted cashews and macadamia nuts and great hanging slabs of Italian cheese I like so well. To have me interpret their dreams or give them a sign for a hunting expedition or maybe a wedding. *Sans doute* the way it is still done in backwardsvilles like Kansas where your boyfriend with the handsome darksome face is growing bored with his life. The penniless rabble there most likely leave a dead fish or maybe fowl in exchange for a reading. Here, I am forced to use a glowing sign, a few painted mystical symbols to give people the appropriate air of the ancient and unknown. And this is why they cannot do it for themselves: they have separated real and imagined, church and state, business and pleasure, work and leisure. Once upon a time there was only living, no word for religion, it was not exiled to Sundays or holidays, it was the gravity that held them to the ground they walked on, stitched their lives together like animal hides, fell with rain on their heads whether they asked for it or not, there was never any collection to take up in its name.

Yes, Veronique says, we keep looking and hoping we will remember.

She crushes the cigarette in the faceted lump of amber where anything could be trapped – her distorted face, an insect two hundred million years old (look closely), a memory, an extinct emotion.

Remember what?

The inside, what it was like on the inside. But all that is left are a few walls and columns – faces like Zirque's with hard angles, wedding frescoes in Pompeii and Herculaneum, masks worn to Carnivale hiding what is beneath. We work from exteriors on down.

Yes, masks, everything in fact...

Everything – you would hardly believe it – wants to speak to you: the table I am sitting at in this cafe (a compass if you take that coffee stain over there for due north), the bright figures wheeling overhead (Orion to the Greeks, a white tiger to the Chinese, seal hunters lost in the ocean to seafaring Vikings), the cracks in the shoulder blades of animals scorched by fire, your body, an onion, the cards, trees and potted plants, your own mind, the angry red scars--even after all these months--on Veronique's wrists...yes, the great desire in everything is to be heard, to get your attention.

I told you not to write when I'm talking to you.

Un moment s'il te plaît.

Oh-la-la, I don't know why I put up with you.

Why can't you wait, exercise more politeness, let a man think –

Is that what you're calling yourself these days?

Oh, enough of that, it's tired, it's old, it isn't you.

Zabere takes a dainty bite of his eclair. Did I tell you I got another call for Andy, the American? He must have a number nearly identical.

Probably.

Or it's some kind of joke Riault is playing on me.

Oh look at that stupid woman with the black beret and the little round glasses, Veronique says, she is probably carrying around a copy of Foucault she has never read. I hate these cardboard cut-out intellectuals.

Veronique, you are too critical, let them have their illusions while they last.

I forgot to mention, didn't I? I heard from Zirque, a postcard of Big Brutus, *the biggest goddamn steam shovel this hemisphere* is what he wrote I think. It wouldn't surprise me to find out he is here, gotten himself lost or picked up like a wet pigeon by a warm-blooded girl with smooth hands, whom he will subject to his didn't-mean-to-sleep-with-you-on-the-first-night-it-just-happened-that-way-we-fit-together-so-well routine.

Et tu Big Brutus?

Yes, he has a big brutus all right and knows how to use it or I wouldn't have much use for him would I?

Oh don't tease me like that. What does he need a woman for anyway?

Blue Jean his love is in her kitchen now or will be soon, cutting vegetables as always, naming them: Veronique in Paris, Sonya in Madrid, Ingrid in Bitburg, scattering the parts over the four corners of her frying pan. She sets her table for him, plates as unmanageable as Stonehenge slabs, arranged with the same meticulous attention to position, the only sympathy here is magic.

Oh I'm a better cook than she is I'm sure. And you never cook for him, always it's eating out--

Yes, I prefer not to cook.

What does she know about the crepe? The pan cannot be too hot is the trick--

Every schoolgirl knows that.

--or it won't come out spongy, it will burn and break. Spread it evenly, quickly and it will hang loosely together, a perfect wonder. But it is the sauce –

Go ahead Zabere, Veronique's grin is impish, why not give in to a good woman. I know one or two in Pigale who'll make you shout the names of the 103 elements, forget your own, you will know for certain you're a man.

Doll, *cheri*, I have, you know that, it's not bad but it's not for me. Think how much you adore *men*, you can sympathize. And I thought there were 104 elements. Didn't the Americans just discover a new one?

Made a new one. It disappeared before they were even sure it was there. Veronique lights up again, waving a hand with three rings gleaming, the extinguished match tracing its path with thin blue smoke.

I wonder about Blue Jean – her real name is Rae Anne, did you know? How does she live through the never-knowing of her man? Never caring, never expecting, never asking like a good Theravada disciple is what I recommend. The grass of those Kansas fields has whispered something to her while she sleeps. About how to be there season after season, how to let herself die a little, turn brown, save herself for a spring of eternal return when she will feel more alive than the first day of creation.

He never takes her with him?

For a second, perhaps less, a dark-haired waitress in a white T-shirt holds a position nearly identical to the painted Toulouse-Lautrec woman in a red dress, her black hat erupting with red plumage (she is painted lifesize on the wall beside one of the cafe's lamps, all of them gas as a quaint lure in the dark to drifting-past late-nighters).

He takes her once in a while, Veronique answers, so he says.

How vicious to be so in need of someone so charming so unreliable so unrepentant.

She can get along without him, no matter how long. He is the one who would wash away – a chalk drawing on the sidewalk – if one day she were not there when he returned. He knows it. He is the one who cannot find the strength for the day-to-day of staying, who is afraid of dying, and of himself and of listening too closely to the things Blue Jean hears.

He is –

He wants the stones and bricks and railroad tracks in his ten-or twelve-stoplight downtown to speak his name. No matter if he is dead. He wants his name spoken always and everywhere he has been.

Merde alors!

What is it? Zabere turns toward the door.

Je ne peux pas le croire. Look who is here and what he has dragged with him all the way from Kansas.

*   *   *   *

Zabere, how can you let him call you that?

Oh it's a thing of affection, really I don't mind, the same way he calls you Blue Jean.

The Creole Queer doesn't sound very affectionate to me. He

135

can be so inconsiderate sometimes.

The brick wall they are passing is rough canvas for a '50s Cadillac convertible, white and immaculate, driving out of an American past. Bright colors of nostalgia swirl in Blue Jean's head, mix with the memory of Route 169 empty at sunset, of the 1106 Burger Drive-In Zirque and Red and Earl took her to summer evenings, the three men like boys harassing everyone within name-calling.

But this is Paris, where she has never been. A crowd will flock to her at the Corner Café – pigeon wings flapping around her – to hear about it. The city where everyone speaks a musically different language and Kansas City isn't hardly big-town set next to it. Only what about that woman with the tight skirt, the black silk stockings and high heels –

Zabere, is that a man?

It is common in this quarter. A weaker woman, I know, would wish for the Pittsburg quarter but she would miss so much that is not the Eiffel Tower, that is not entombed in the Louvre or mentioned in the travel brochures.

I'm happy to be here, I'm just not used to all this.

Ah, you make me feel like Lancelot taking my arm that way. Avaunt knaves and dogs, the fair lady is with me.

Oh Zabere –

You look *magnifique* today, the black of your shirt sets off the copper in your hair so well, and your hair is so lovely around your face, it's complemented I mean by those, those flakes of pale red, how do you say –

Freckles?

Oui! What Renoir wouldn't have given to paint you.

Really Zabere –

This way, down the stairs, yes, I have friends in the lowest of places. Here we are.

The man leaning against the doorway is shirtless, just a black leather vest, his beard ending in twin spikes, one on either side of his chin (his head could pass for some kind of garden tool), dark-complected, slit-eyed, he looks like he could give Zirque or Earl a hard time.

The place is filled with racks of clothes, studded leather belts, shoes, boots that reach the knees, earrings as unwieldy as chandeliers, hats and motorcycle caps, the walls hung with film posters (movies she's never heard of), paintings.

Next to each other, there are two women on separate can-vases, the work of the same hand – angled lines seen at impossible perspectives (a mirror folded at the back of the eye), the brush-strokes deep, the skin of one midnight blue, the other a marble green. Staring back at Blue Jean, regarding her watchfully, they remind her of –

Yes, Veronique posed for those. When she's not selling a pill to kill boredom or a syringe full of the voices of seraphim singing to the veins, she makes a little extra money that way.

You mean she –

Oh look here. Zabere points to a black-and-white xeroxed page. The explosion of a milk drop in water, magnified and placed next to the mushroom cloud of an atomic blast, inverted and shrunk down. Nearly identical in shape, in evolution.

I gave it to them, Zabere says, as a demonstration. Isn't it strange how perfectly congruous they are? Except that one is in-verted, is the far grander of scales.

Don't that beat all? Rae Anne says looking more closely. When I was a little girl I used to do that with milk. In the sink. And pretend the explosions were real.

Everything that happens happens again on different levels, Zabere says. This is a diorama we live in. He winks. That's half the secret to reading a future.

A woman behind the counter with a sphinx cut, black lipstick matching her hair, a gold star on her cheek says I saw someone who looked just like you Zabere, carrying on abominably with a prostitute – Get a room! I shouted.

But did he have silver eyeshadow? Zabere asks tilting his head back to set off his make-up better. Did he have sparkles in his lovely hair so much like black wool?

No he – it couldn't have been you, you wouldn't dress that way – but he looked so much like you.

Oh this dress is so beautiful, where did it come from? Blue Jean says sweeping it in front of her, posing in the mirror. I've never seen anything like it.

Too many colors to name, sheer and flowing with enough layers to make it tasteful.

The girl with the starred cheek beckons with fingers to a green-eyed cat on the counter. I once knew a married couple who owned two cats: one playful and fearless, a little *mechant*, mischievous; the other always in hiding, shy. The couple were exactly the same way.

There, Zabere says to Blue Jean, you see what I mean?

*　　*　　*　　*

Zirque drops her wrist, shakes his head exactly once, as if that is all it will take to shake loose the bad feeling.

Should've known. Probably at the bottom of one a my sleepless nights.

Almost the bottom of the Seine. The cigarette in Veronique's mouth (for no reason Zirque can think of) is unlit.

I had a dream, he says, I tried to show Earl a picture of us together. But when I pulled it out, I couldn't make out your face. She's pretty Earl, I swear it, I kept sayin an' held it up to the light

18 different ways, but your face wouldn't come clear.

What is that you have in your hand?

A bit of paper folded so many times the creases have begun to split, a Bic-and-ink drawing: a snowman, a pine tree, a hardly-more-than-stick woman with long hair and a girlish cuteness to her, looking through one of four quarters of a mullioned window, an X about where the stick-girl's heart would be.

Veronique puts her cold cigarette into an ashtray. What's that doing in your hand? A charm? A bit of garlic around your neck? She smirks. All right, we won't talk of her if it will make you feel better. We will talk about Zirque, trapped being who he is for eternity, tired of being Zirque, distracting himself from himself with a change of scenery.

Slipping the square of paper back in his wallet, he says, Sometimes I feel pressed right up against the glass of an extra dimension to this place, squeezed up against who I could be in it. Somehow we got the heat a the Sun inside us, it wants out but there's no way at all except a couple minutes here, a few minutes there.

A regular Zirque the Dane.

Five thousand years a civilization an' we're standin on the same brink worn smooth by generations a footsteps, no further into chaos or godhead, we are no voyant startin at the horizon where our long-ago grand-kin breathed their last. We're crowded like the Persians against the sea into which the Spartans'll push us – and we won't be comin back.

What we see when we look in the windows is the same, Veronique says, only the shopkeepers have changed.

To shop, or not to shop, that is the question.

Wasn't Hamlet two people at least? Veronique asks. One mad, one sane? One cunning and driven, protecting the other one, the distant hesitant vulnerable one looking down on it all? What character talks to himself more I would like to know?

Aren't there two worlds at least? The way we live, passin the time granted us here in cafés watchin the steam from coffee rise past our faces, watchin it become the white cloud out of a manhole cut into cobblestone, a mandala of passage, this way, the evaporatin whiteness risin across the dead street at this hour like fog from a nether-region.

You belong to one, she to the other.

Can't help the way I love her. She changes the contours a spacetime is what it is.

Yes. And who asked you to?

You told me once I'm not attached t'anythin but it's you, you're the one--

Love remains after the ... after the loved one has vanished, leaving ghost pains, the amputee's complaint. All of our ancient loves, our lost loves, return. Eternally. As pain. As three-in-the-morning mist (you've felt her presence in the stillness of that hour, *non*?). Another person can ... ahh ... What touches us once. The sunken impossibly beautiful island city has always been.

So I've heard.

And what about her leaving you alone with me?

Pretty much permission, he says, though a hard one to figure into the rest a Blue Jean.

It's something between her and me, Veronique says, she's made a gift of you to me, oui? Though of course to bring it up would break all etiquette.

She'll come back here with what she's bought, sayin wait till they see this back in Pittsburg, but she'll be usin the scarf she's modeling or the shirt she's holdin to cover over what she doesn't want to think about. She won't ask.

Well perhaps this time, I would prefer her.

Can I write something in your book? Rae Anne asks.

Oui, bien sur. Zabere hands it to her with a pen.

After death I think you see things differently, I think human beings become sheets of light, ruffled tin kind of, with colors coming off of them, like at the south pole –

What do they call those lights?

– like the aurora borealis, they are light with black spots where they've despaired, when they've lost faith and are ready to die, like sunspots. If you could see it from outer space, the earth would be a sea of lights.

That's what I believe.

Ah, *oui,* Zabere says, looking over the handwriting with its deep loops for g's and f's, a flowing hand, almost spiralling in on itself.

Zabere's corollary to Rae Anne's entry: Like stars these people of light get magnitudes and classifications. There, walking by with his cane, a long-ago-collapsed-and-lost-its-great-internal-fire white dwarf. There is Vincent, a red giant (blue stars are the hottest, I know, but I am overcome by the poetic correctness of the color to match his hair). That anti-homosexual--by the look he is giving me--a shriveled yellow midget. Close.

* * * *

ZG, the letters of our first names together – Z,Z – it's almost *si, si. Oui?*

Jamais, jamais Zabere – not a look not a thought not me.

Ah well, I couldn't help giving it a try. Veronique is up to the same thing exactly with

Blue Jean I'm sure. Would you like a reading?

You got enough coca-cola cans here to build a Boeing 747.

Every morning it is impossible for me to get up without having one. You should see me, squinty-eyed in morning light, no matter how dim. I need one to take the taste out of my mouth, sweeten my disposition, jump-start me. It's not the real thing anymore, just caffeine. I'd like the world to sing in perfect harmony with the invisible order of things.

There is a poster of Marlon Brando – draped over the handlebars of a motorcycle, wearing a puffy biker's hat. Zabere leans against the wall, says I coulda been somebody, I coulda been a contenda, and sounds so much like Brando, Zirque laughs.

My father tried to make a little man out of me, Zabere says, pushed me into the ring to sink or swim when I was ten. I learned how for three years but I didn't like hitting the other boys – you can imagine – such sweet faces. One named Robert, an American, he was the toughest I'd ever seen. Sandy hair and blue eyes and such a handsome face, but oh he had such a right hand.

Sometimes I wonder what my life would have been like if we had stayed on our tropical island. The memory of the place – it must be from a photograph, I was not even two when we came to France – I remember a wood-and-stone city near the coast, whitewashed houses wavering in the heat, crowded open markets in a flat downtown with nothing over two or three stories, the smell of rotting fish and drying mud in the humid hanging air, all of the flash and color and excitement of a city's facade having gone into the red blouses, the dangling golden earrings, the grand smiles, the bright yellow kerchiefs keeping the sun off black heads--a place where you always feel a sense of hello how are you today, belonging.

What made you leave in the first place?

My mother insisted I was possessed — fits of crying lasting entire nights the way she tells it. When she had the dream of a butterfly trapped inside a hideous warted flower, she was afraid for my soul. Though butterfly is Spanish slang for *maricon* and maybe that's what the dream meant, who can tell? They're so unreliable. Anyway, she brought me to my shaman-uncle who exorcised the spirit and got a few bottles of rum for his trouble. Probably I had some bad gas and my uncle is still laughing about it all these years later.

The phone ringing startles them, makes them exchange half a smile each.

Alo? No, there is no Andy here... Yes, that is the number but there is no one named Andrew, I live here alone —

Zabere shrugs as he puts down the phone. She hung up.

*   *   *   *

I hope you don't mind the edge of the bed, the wicker chair is already full of things I am too lazy to put away.

This is strange for me. Her hands on her blue-jeaned knees, her body stiff with trying not to show how uncomfortable she is. I guess I had to sit across from what I've been losing him to all these years.

Of course, it's expected.

I don't know what good it will do to know what you smell like, to know if he has ever brought the scent home. I've hated you an' the rest of them — you especially because you're more than a night's worth of no sleep. I've hated you so often when I was alone in Kansas, but it's so hard now because we're here in person, it's not your fault. I can almost stand it, knowin you. He doesn't even realize after all this time but it's not the unfaithfulness

I mind so much, it's never knowing if one day he'll decide not to come back, if he's found something better, forgotten me an all of us back home.

You shouldn't worry, Veronique says, I look after him, I keep him from worse things. There is nothing between us anywhere but here. I have always wanted to meet you. We are, after all, joined through this silly man so afraid of death he cannot sit still, like a child in church. A spacious smile splits open. Maybe he has told you women appeal to me almost as much as men? You're blushing.

Veronique reaches up slowly, traces the length of Rae Anne's eyebrow with the nail of her thumb, sweeps up a bit of coppery hair, wraps it behind an ear, a vanishing moment, the same in which the leaf of a tree flutters against the window until the breeze dies.

In a way I have always known you, Veronique says, through him, the way he reached out for you but his hand touched me, adjusted himself to the shape of a body he was not used to. Ah, but this kind of talk makes you uncomfortable.

Is that yours? Rae Anne stands up and points at an easel. Do you paint?

Veronique shakes her head. It is set up just in case I ever decide I want to.

I used to draw when I was a little girl. Mostly made-up things – unicorns, trolls, horses with wings, floating islands with crystal cities on them attached to nothing ... She sits back down amid the give and squeal of springs.

Yes, Veronique says, remembering a snowman, a pine tree, a little girl trapped by creases of paper, behind glass, tucked inside a wallet, a woman holding at her heart a child.

I am surprised you didn't draw something for Zabere's journal.

Oh I couldn't draw what I meant. And words – well, Zirque is better at that. Itching I don't know where, he puts his finger on exactly the right spot. In one little sentence he says what's been buildin up in me for years. That's how I got into trouble with him in the first place. Rae Anne laughs. He tells the most ridiculous lies, doesn't he?

He remembers through you, Veronique says, through everything he sends you as a keepsake. She leans over and kisses Rae Anne on the cheek. He loves you like nothing else on this planet.

Tingling in the place where Veronique kissed her – the buzz licking the end of a battery gave her as a little girl. Does he?

Mais bien sur, you cannot tell you are the only thing he cannot leave forever, the only one at all?

*   *   *   *

What about that beating when I was three, when we lived in a stone house with two stories and my window looked out on a huge ancient cherry tree, the strapping my father gave me for no reason I can remember, the one that kept me silent for a week, did something go into hiding? Is there any connection to my penchant for le metro, the catacombs, for dance clubs below street level? Close.

*   *   *   *

She knows you in the moment it takes for you to say something, *non?*

Zabere nods.

She sees the love in him – she is drawn to it – and if it were not for that she would have left him a long time ago, though she goes on thinking she can get the rest around this shining core to change.

It's tempting. Knocking an electron or two off lead makes gold. One little electron.

Or two. She reaches for his hand, lifts it up, noticing something for the first time. She looks at the other one, runs her thumb over the knuckles. What happened to your hand? Did you get into a fight?

The door of Etienne's Citroen, Zabere says. He closed it on me the other night.

But this looks like a toothmark, like you hit someone in the mouth.

But *me*, Veronique? You know best of all I have learned to walk away from even those men who are most deserving of a good drawing and quartering.

*   *   *   *

14 Sept., 3:12 pm
  Faggot, buggerer, cornholer, fudgepacker, mud-rider, fruitcake, polesmoker, buttfucker, Creole Queer...

*   *   *   *

Riault with his crazy red hair said to me – he was wearing his Einstein persona, sparks going off behind his head like Quatorze de Juillet fireworks, he said – I get my inspiration sometimes from a ceiling that has leaked badly over several years – I want to show people there's something going on in a stain.

  No, I told him, it's going on in your head.

  His abstracts are nothing at all recognizable, there is no correspondence to a real object. Yes, a stain blown up large, something spilled over. Where is the line drawn in charcoal, the color sch2eme tracing out a connection we7ve always felt existed between us and what sur5rounds us but had never known exactly how we were joined to it, had never been able to picture, where has it been translat3ed for us into a concrete language we can understand?

Quatre Vents – this is the perfect place for us tonight, *oui?* Veronique's brown eyes shine darkly. A window for each of us. Her smile, meant to be reassuring, rubs Blue Jean ever so snake-scale lightly the wrong way.

I like it here Blue Jean says, ignoring the bare leg slipping alongside hers under the table.

Pittsburg needs one, a real Old World café a little high society.

You'd have to import your customers, Zirque says, running a hand through black hair damp with evening's drizzle.

You don't think it would catch on? Something genuine European in our corner of the world? Most of the mining families in Crawford County come of immigrant stock.

Well, I guess if you cooked up hamhocks'n beans insteada escargot you might pull it off.

How can you eat those things, ew! They look like black garden slugs.

No worse than a prairie oyster. Go on, try one. You'll be hooked. It's just appearances, honey, and a bad reputation in your head.

What's in my head is one thing, what goes in my mouth is another.

Zabere! Veronique smacks his hand. You are incorrigible. Writing even here. On their last night in Paris.

Pardon s'il te plaît. It was what she said, it clicked something off.

What? Blue Jean asks.

This bit about what is in your head. Sex is no different, it's all in the mind, 90 percent or so anyway.

Well then you can stop tryin to talk Zirque into jumping the fence, Zabere, Blue Jean says touching her hair lightly to make sure it's still in place, just close your eyes an you can have the time a your life.

Well, it's not quite –

I know what he means, Zirque says. A man can do a thing're two same as a pretty woman an with your eyes closed who could tell? It's the thought a who's doin it – an who it's bein done with. Usin your own hand t'take an example, ain't no good without a major motion picture goin in your head.

The mind is a bottomless pit, Veronique says. Did you know that some mental disorders are peculiar to men and women who are highly creative? They have unique ways of coping. Mental illnesses are cleverly engineered to protect the mind from the tyrannical father, the rape inflicted by your own brother, from witnessing the death of too many loved ones at too young an age, from never having been shown love. She turns to Zabere. Perhaps *homosexualite* is just such a disorder. You see how many creative people – artists, dancers, writers – fit into this category.

Oh it's not an illness it's something you're born with, like a prick. There it is and most of the world is horrified, but you have the audacity to be proud of it.

Sex is a religious experience, Zirque says, popping a bloated black body shiny with butter, fragrant with garlic, into his mouth. When it's good. Starts in your head, shoots through your body, then frees you a the spacetime continuum altogether.

Not a religious experience, a religion, Veronique corrects. With witless priests attending.

Sex is part of religion, Zabere says.

Religion is part a life, should've never settled out. The heart is the church the temple the synagogue an should've stayed there.

Religion is a device – contrived, devised. A defense against a chaotic universe. So goes a theory posited by Brulliard.

Zirque's head, hung over his plate, pops up. A light in the blackness?

I am the one slipping into blackness, Zabere says, I lost four hours today Veronique, I swear it, I cannot trace back where I was this evening, earlier tonight.

Mythology came first, Veronique says, using superstitions as tent poles to hold it up, to keep out the night. The mind is otherwise naked, malleable, easily deformed, cratered, broken, as easily lost in it as a candle in deep space. Making riddles of the stars, spinning stories to go with how things got to be the way they are, tracing out shapes in the sky with the glowing end of a smoldering stick and getting to know them, hello how are you and be on familiar terms.

Zabere, what do you mean you lost four hours, Blue Jean asks, what happened?

Oh *some*one here listens to me at least. I mean four hours, just gone...

A way to make caves bearable as much as fire and animal hides, Zirque says.

And look … Zabere pushes back in his chair, looks down at his waist. This belt I'm wearing isn't mine, but I found it in my closet. Along with a shirt I never bought – it's not my taste at all. Whom have I brought over? It is either Riault or my memory playing tricks on me.

They settled religion, Zirque is saying, his hand almost as dark as Zabere's against the immaculate background of the white table cloth, over their hairy backs like a rough hide to keep off the cold, the hardness of a rock floor. And their shadows, hunched over an half savage, are thrown on the cave walls at the backs of our minds, by the age-old light of still-burnin beliefs. And once in a while we crouch down –

(Zabere, do you remember the dark-haired waitress at La Lo?)

– and from a distance who could tell?

* * * *

Everything speaks to you … the bathroom walls for example. Faggots of the world unite – so that we can kill you all at once. Silly fag, dicks are for chicks (en anglais). *The only thing I feel when I kill a fag is the recoil – and it feels good.*

* * * *

Riault has gone too far this time. He's found my journal somehow, he's gotten in my apartment ... all right, I am not attentive to security, I've found clothing not mine – has he moved someone in? And in my journal look.

Zabere hands the notebook to Veronique.

Zabere the little faggot whose skin is not bronze at all but more like tissue paper. It's me he's talking about with bronze skin. I'm the one who kept him from being beaten and left for dead by that drunk in the metro. Instead, he was the one bleeding from his mouth and nose, unable to get up. I have to do the hard things while he writes in this journal. I'm the one who is there to take care of him as much as I despise his weakness, his habits, his effeminate taste. Without me he would be worse off still.

It's not my handwriting. It's similar, as if someone were trying to write like me. Why should Riault try to do that? Does he think I cannot tell? This is evil of him, just because I refuse to sleep with him anymore. This is the final straw.

Maybe. Veronique says handing back the journal. Maybe just the penultimate.

* * * *

...while I pin down this problem of lan3guages, yes that's it, these thin4gs speak but not always in ways we can understand and we run into problems of interpr7etation, problems –

* * * *

Veronique, I am possessed it is certain, my mother was right, there is another soul inhabiting my body, it is the source of the blackouts –

Oh don't be so melodramatic, Zabere. Evil spirits have nothing to do with it.

Non?

Veronique shakes her head.

How can you be so sure?

I finally met this lookalike of yours. Last night, at Bar Sept. Veronique doesn't look up from her sketch, working – unbelievably – on the easel which has been in her room unused for Zabere doesn't know how many years.

Zabere completely loses interest in the conversation, looks over Veronique's charcoal drawing, sees something inchoate – is that a head in there? – taking shape out of the swirling lines, and wonders what demon is coming into full-winged bloom.

So you saw him? Does he really look like me?

Your very twin.

* * * *

It's not that all of creation wanted to turn and look full-length at itself – the stars our heavenly counterparts, of magnitudes beyond measuring – it's just a little warmth the stars were after, a firm chest padded with tickly woolliness to rest the weary head, a little something to ward off the cold and the winter of long nights, that's all.

*   *   *   *

The river is not far from here, the Seine of polished black glass, a bit of sky flowing over the Earth – look, you will see the crescent moon wavering in it – dividing the city into left bank and right, this side and the other.

Ah, to be swallowed in shadow, for the four-in-the-morning darkness to close over my head as if I had jumped into the Seine's polluted waters, the stillness unbreakable, a deep long descent into the liquid black, back into inky yolkiness, yes. Like Albert the Ubiquitous, Albert the Barely Conscious, cover me, let day become extinct. Take away the photographic hardness – the blurring of Impressionism is so much more preferable – yes, bring on the night. Zabere Andre Saint-Martin would like to blend in as perfectly as possible, to be a brick in the red-brick midnight, a streetlamp sentry along this rain-washed street. Let me run into the sewers, let me become this city, as easily as a shaman living Way Back When slipped into a bear hide and grew the claws of the grizzly – so I will be no more noticed than a cobblestone being stepped on. Let the glow of the streetlight show nothing more than a deluded shadow, a slippery shapelessness in the night, *oui*, nothing more than that silently following shadow, sent to hover over me on black wings, protect me where I am most vulnerable, the soft whiteness where there is no shell, yes a dark guardian angel sent in my own image, my very twin.

THE NORTHWEST PASSAGE

A Portolano

*"Yes, a power we call Sila ... A strong spirit, the upholder of the
universe, of the weather, in fact all life on Earth – so mighty that
His speech to man comes not through ordinary words but through
storms, snowfall, rain showers, the tempests of the sea, through
all the forces that man fears or through sunshine, calm seas or small,
innocent playing children who understand nothing."*
– Eskimo shaman

There is this place. Not a whole lot to put on a postcard, not
likely to dot any map showing more than the state. Who
knows what arbitrary-imaginary meridian skewers it through? The
Duke of Pallucca, walking stick tapping, heading up Crawford
Street, past Vacca's Bakery – established 1912, whitewashed,
trimmed in red, red-and-white checked curtains in the windows,
it could pass for a house.

November Kansas winds blowin Lyman Kishpaugh's dry
voice around, a muttering from Vacca's, Lyman once found himself a part-time home there among the stone ovens and Old World

smells leavened with semolina. Old Lyman with his Depression cap aslant could lift a ton, they used to say, but couldn't spell it. An awkward face looking like it was havin trouble holding itself together there was something about him made you think he was half angel when he smiled, the kids teased him regular as the whistle of the 1 o'clock on the Santa Fe Line.

Carnival left Lyman behind (some say it was a circus), a 17-year-old idiot boy in the strange playpen of a young man's body. God put the strength of a draught horse into that physique of his but left enough outta his head it was anybody's guess who had more sense, him or the horse.

Time to time on his insomniac walks, the Duke thought about Lyman (an odd-jobber in bib overalls), heard that straw-dry rustle of Lyman's carried on the wind out of the south, but this time it was the memory of a dream that bellied out the Duke's sails, his walking stick for a rudder, sent him drifting up Crawford to take a right at the corner of McKay, down past Pallucca's Market (his cousin's place). Lyman already old and feeble when the Duke was a kid chasing Yankee autographs, never met Lyman, but that's who it was dropped him through the web of a sticky sleep near five in the morning.

Out of Bartelli's Blue Goose Bar, closed many years, its ceiling skeletal, rafters showing through like ribs, a skylight of sorts letting in sun and moon, star and rain, drifting flakes of snow, out of the Blue Goose, Millo Farneti emerged, blinking in the late-afternoon sun like it was the mouth of a coal mine or Erebus itself he'd just put behind him. Hair a wiry tangle of gray and black, he had keys to the abandoned Blue Goose where he'd squirreled away manuscripts documenting the doings of the comers and goers in Frontenac and Pittsburg, a crotchety Italian monk still speaking all-but-buried Latin, mapping who'd been where with whom and said what, the filing cabinet he used for storage the only furniture left inside the sooty bare-brick walls.

"Well, hey Ceppo, hello what – where, where you headed?"

"Why d'you wanna call me that? Makes me sound like one a the Marx Brothers."

"Well you know you're a, you're a blockhead sometimes, same as they were."

"Granite slab of a man is more like it." The Duke slapped his ribs. "Upholdin this itty-bitty fair city of ours."

"Yeah, yeah, awright – "

"What says the Farneti? Your head gettin any lighter with all that stuff you're dumpin in that file cabinet?"

"Well, I – gee-zuss! It hurts sometimes when I take a step the wrong way. I … I tell you, the pain …" Millo gestured with a hand. "It don't just stay here in my hip, it – it grabs the Samsonites an travels down my legs."

"Time's kicked you unfair and unlookin more than once."

"You sure as hell don't say. Wait'll – wait – one day you'll be draggin a load a years behind you."

"I'm draggin around enough as it is." The Duke gave his belly a friendly pat. No more than five and a half feet, he went for two-hundred or better, solid, squarish, deepset eyes and stern eyebrows, only a silvery quickness in the eyes betrayed a forgiving nature, a deep reservoir of calm accumulated over the long walked distances.

Facing east, the Missouri-Kansas line four or five miles off, Millo was looking past the Duke, down the street where (the Duke knew) he saw immigrant miners hanging off the trolley after a long day's journey into the shiny black boniness of stubborn Kansa earth, the ones who lived nearby jumping off into a ditch along the road like grasshoppers, his Pa among them. Never one for diggin any deeper than a finger in his ear, all Millo said was, "Grasshopper Corner."

"In New York they went up, piled it against the sky," the Duke said. "Here we dug down, sank shafts."

"And you, you're still in reverse, tunnelin backwards. Klink, klink. *Nunc pro tunc* that – that's your motto. You wanna trade in pieces of now for bits of then, that's it ain't it?" Millo accused.

The Duke shrugged.

"You know somethin, you – you're lookin a little like an old silver dollar been passed to one hand too many."

The Duke nodded. "Never was much of a sleeper." He stepped into the open door of Bartelli's, early evening dimming to an odd glow inside, the ground-up years, bits of plaster and wood, fallen laughter crunching underfoot, brittle in the pale gold of late fall.

Millo, eyeing the shadow of the Duke's walking stick on the floor, pointed. "There was a Greek in Alexandria, Egypt you know, figured out near 2,000 years before Columbus set sail – he figured out the Earth was round just by payin attention to the slant a shadows. B'lieve that? Got wind of no shadow bein cast on the bottom of a well at noon on summer solstice in some other city in Egypt, knew damn well well bottoms were in shadow where he was. Came up with a fair reckoning of the … he came up with the planet's belt size."

"Couldn't keep much from the old-time Greeks." The Duke rapped the jumble of faded-away music and fallen roof shingles with the heel of his stick, his hand capping the bearded old man's face carved on top.

"Gnomon's his proper name." The Duke lifted the stick and looked into the tiny petrified eyes. "Little on the silent side but a good listener."

The Duke looked out a window painted over instead of taped with cardboard, *Schaeffer's* spelled backwards coming through the beige chaos of strokes. "You know I came across a photo a Lyman Kishpaugh stuck between a stack of unidentifiables in the basement. Black and white, Jim Morey grinnin in the picture with 'im. Thirties or '40s I guess. He's got a smile but it's like he's not used to it, posin with a friend for a snapshot. I gave it a spot on my clipboard there's something about it."

"If it ain't under the Sun, it's in your basement, that's my guess."

"An illness we both got – can't throw anything out."

"You know that, that head a yours got about as much in it as your basement. No tellin what you can call up from the vasty deep a memory. I don't doubt you even know the name a that long-ago Greek – "

"Eratosthenes. But it's strange what 10 minutes' worth of a nap 'bout five in the mornin dredged up, it was him all right – "

"Eratosthenes?"

"Nooooooo." The Duke swatted with his stick. "Lyman. He was pointin, real hard, an squintin. Couldn't speak for some reason … I think Lyman knows somethin he was tryin t'spill."

"Lyman never could – he wasn't a stutterer but, you know, he repeated himself, he couldn't string together more than three sentences straight, you know."

"That right?"

"Yes, an here's something else for you since it's a fact-collectin expedition you're on: the last 13 cantos, you know, the *Divina Commedia,* Alighieri was dead and those unlucky 13 were lost. His *magnus opus* would've – they'da likely never swum up from the depths if the Infernal Italian himself hadn't shown up in his son's dream and given longitude and latitude of hidin place." Millo nodded for emphasis. "That's the truth as I know it. Might be … there might be somethin to this Kishpaugh chimera."

"Whaddayou remember about Lyman?"

"Well Lyman, he – he was the most insulted man in town. We kids we … I regret it now, we threw rocks at him. Called him chief because he considered himself a fireman, chased us off the engine all the time. Useta howl and bark every time we saw him too, I don't remember why anymore, you know – maybe he – maybe he fancied himself some kinda dog catcher, too. He ran

after us a lot, never caught a thing he was chasin I don't think."
The Duke nodded, considering what the slant of Lyman's hat
might've had to say about the depth of his faith or the circumference of his heart. Must've gotten a little thick-skinned after a
while, all the stones and names thrown his way. Remembering
the photo, the Duke decided Lyman's slow-to-spread smile held
no grudges, no bitterness toward the world. Had a pretty good
idea he wasn't goin to get much from it – not smilin half as broad
as Jim Morey – somehow letting on that in the little he knew he
knew the shot was over in the flash a the camera, pretty well understood the most could come of the photo was something to
hang in the bakery where he slept, but okay he was still glad Jim
wanted to be in it with him and hoped he could have it to tape
up over his cot.

Millo headed out the door of the Blue Goose, the Duke following him, the darkening sky leaving the streetlights to catch
slow fire along McKay, took you east-west through downtown
Frontenac, it was lined with telephone poles and streetlamps
leanin according to the unfathomable laws governing such things,
crooked marchers in a still-life procession toward sunset.

"Well, you know goddammit …" Millo snapped the padlock
on the Blue Goose Bar's aimlessly silently swirling dust motes behind the painted-over, cardboarded up windows. "I'm never
gonna get back to the house I was born in, I can't even make it
back to that street I – "

"Don't worry, Millo, the trip to Hades is the same from everywhere."

"I don't care about my body after I'm dead. You don't go up
or down, I know that, but you might go sideways. The point is I
wanna live where I came from, I don't rattle around so much."

Everything unfamiliar a bump that shook Millo up, even

thought the house where he'd lived for many years was just a couple of blocks away –

"Goddammit, I know it's – it's just around the corner, but that, that's where creation opened up an spit me out. I haven't been able to think about anything else. I'd offer the woman who owns it now twice market value, but I know she won't take it, and that's the ... well, you know that place it's – that's the life root."

If Millo could put out a rhizome he'd grow under the streets and come up in the ten-by-ten kitchen with its black iron stove where Ma used to cook for his brothers and sisters and Pa and him –

"You got the home pull," the Duke said, "like a salmon."

"I'm no sale man, I can't even get you to buy what I'm sayin. You know it's that house I ... I always understood that that was home."

"You hear about that dam somewhere in New Jersey?"

"Oh geezuss, the one the water backed up – eliminated a whole goddam town. I couldn't take it – it would always keep me a little off kilter that ever happened here."

Millo the Ptolemy, Frontenac with its coaldust still clouding memory, its abandoned brick shells of good times in a lost heyday, its streetlamps slanting off while the sun sets, more to him than the minarets of mosques shadowed in moonlit Istanbul the once-and-future crucible of empires. Frontenac still the center a the universe for Millo he'd spare no effort on an elaborate scheme a cycles & epicycles & whatnot to describe the motion of everything around this plot of land pitted with mines. How to find the exactness where some internal organ of his body maybe is buried, maybe it was that after being born in that house (hospital too long a haul in those days), Ma buried the placenta and umbilical cord underneath the welcome mat to make sure, like the Navajo do, that he'd come home.

"Wasn't gold the alchemists of old were lookin for," the Duke said, "was the Northwest Passage."

"A little – a little off course aren't you?"

Millo's search for anchorage, for ballast so that he wouldn't wind up a rudderless moth making odd spiral patterns, bouncing off the glass outside Farley's Tavern over in Pittsburg, driven half-mad by the soft light inside. Hardly different from Bartelli's Starlit Bare Brick Inn, empty except for what's locked away in there – the dust swarm, the cigarette-cigarsmoke wafted off to a place beyond the sunset, a permanent haze that clouds the way for the moon or rising stars or shades still dancing to music no one else can hear anymore.

Memory not enough, was what Millo was getting at, not without a person, a place, maybe both, to lend weight, bring the remembered back from a missing continent floating on a sea of distant things, a rumored *terra australis incognita* in the southern hemisphere needed to keep the world from tilting on its axis any farther, though really it was Millo needed a counterweight (up from the mines, one cage always packed with miners; the other, going down, always filled with coal-less shale). He was coming into the fifth season, Millo talked about it sometimes, four already behind him the way he saw it, it might not exist but it should.

October 16, 1762
The company men were generous in their offer and seemed to ask little of the expedition in return. We were simply to provide more extensive mapping of the northerly peninsulas and islands, discover what possibilities of profitable trade among the natives might exist, and essay the populations of animals with valuable pelts. However, had I known the hardships that awaited the crew, I never would have undertaken the voyage.

Vinegar and lemon juice have frozen solid and broken their bottles.

Still harder to conceive, the very mercury of the thermometer has shattered its glass! When crew members open a door leading topside, a dense fog pours down past our feet and gathers on the walls as ice. The crew is never warm. Steam rising from the cook's pots freezes almost immediately. I fear that we did not stock enough fuel for such a venture and am considering returning to port.

I am reminded by these conditions of the reports of those intrepid captains who set out in search of a northwest passage, a search which has vexed mariners since Henry Hudson explored the northernmost reaches of Canada in hopes of finding such a waterway as would join the Atlantic and Pacific oceans. Such a waterway, were it to be found, would provide the much sought after short-cut to the Far East for merchant ships issuing from the harbors of Europe.

Yet since the voyages of Captain Foxe, it seems clear that no such passage exists below the Arctic Circle. Thus, even if one is found, it could be of no commercial value. Foxe himself said that though one were to be discovered, it would be no more than a curiosity. Nonetheless, the passage calls out to be found. It seems to me little more than chasing a phantasm that will never materialize on the cartographer's map.

Far be it from the captain and crew of the Octavius *to entertain such thoughts! God speed to us.*

Farley's Tavern, a hollowed-out, lit-up block of brick and glass on East Fifth, closer to Locust than Broadway, front window a kind of half-mirror holding the transparent reflections of neon from across the street, a telephone pole with wire rigging, the face of anyone trying to peek in. Reaching through at the same time from the other side, light shining off the polished bar and tables set with candles, drinkers hunkered down over their glasses in conversation.

Art Papish peering in, a clubfoot drunk who wasn't there anymore, hardly five-feet-two, marking the vacant stool he used to keep warm, pressing against the glass to be closer to a woman whose loneliness had opened up a whole underworld where her lover had left her stranded. There were others caught outside the glass, as barely there as see-through moth wings dusted with a vague sense of loss, weightless longings drawn from the far corners of the night, brushing up against the glow leaking out onto the sidewalk. Among them an idiot-man didn't know any better than to always look in on things even in life, never knew Zirque Granges or the pretty red-haired woman who was sitting at a table with him *Ain't – ain't she something?* But he'd've bet his job at Vacca's – why he'd, he'd put the whole bakery on the line if it was his – that that man's life revolved around her.

The Duke turned down Fifth, looking forward to a little red wine and conversation (Farley's always waiting for a dropper-by like him to liven things up a bit), felt them fluttering up against the window of the tavern, not even shadows anymore, not so much as swirls of dimness in the mellow light, the only way you knew they were there the odd ghost of a feeling, like the splinter of mourning called up by the dawnlight cry of a dove, these early-evening echoes soon enough to be late-night vanishings.

"Well if it ain't the big Pallucca." Zirque snickered. "Don't much come outta his basement till the Sun's good an' gone. Watchya up to t'night? Out collectin rumors or startin em?"

"'Tis kinda neat," the Duke answered with a half-smile, "when in one line two craft meet."

"Little a both, is that what you're sayin? When it comes to collectin he's like you Blue Jean, gets hold of a little bit of everythin from everywhere."

"Savin it all up for the Big Book. If yer lucky Granges, you'll get a page'r two."

"It'll have to be a big book if you want t'fit me in it."

"What's the Big Book?" Rae Anne asked.

"Millo and I, we're tryin t'keep a record a the shape a things past. A map of sorts. Not a big ol' *mappa mundi* – "

"The Earth's still flat where the Duke comes from."

" – though sure we're tryin t'pick up where others with compass and chart have resorted to pencilin in fantastical-finned sea beasts. Tryin, y'see, t'cut down on the *terra incognita* floatin loose these days."

"Oh you and Millo … moppa moondy." Her voice all sarcasm. "You with your Italian and this one" – she elbowed Zirque – "with those foreign words he learned one at a time and mostly forgot now, you're getting just a little outta hand don't you think?"

"More a portolano," the Duke admitted. "A Crawford County-sized piece a the world's all we're tryina keep up with." He looked at Zirque. "And I ain't so sure it's round either, the world I mean. Labyrinthine is more like it, somma the passages, you take the right combination, they get you back to where you started from, same as Magellan – "

"I heard a him – "

" – but wasn't really a circle brought you roundabout."

"There was an old-time Greek …" Zirque pushed over to make room for the Duke. "Think it was Millo told me about 'im, figured out the circumference a the Earth from his backyard. A clerk or somethin, wasn't he?"

"Stamped library cards in Alexandria the way I heard it."

Blue Jean pushed coppery eyebrows together. "Where's Alexandria?"

"Over by Fort Scott." Zirque got slapped in the shoulder. "He was some geometer – izzat a word? The figure he came up with, he didn't miss by much."

"Not bad for a guy who never left town."

Blue Jean, in a pearl gray turtleneck – dull compared to her green eyes – her red hair done up in a bun, was looking at Zirque, presenting the Duke a profile fit for a Greek temple. "You ought to have taken his example and stayed at home more."

"Go." Zirque a smiled, one of his front teeth missing and somehow it didn't look bad on him. "A destination will follow. That's my motto. Logged enough miles to make it half way to the Moon if dead reckoning ain't too much off. You can know something by figurin or reading but you wanna feel it – "

"You have to put our arms around it." Rae Anne trapped both of Zirque's arms at his sides with a hug. "And you better get yourself a new motto."

"Shoulda been like the Duke." Zirque lifted his chin in the Duke's direction. "Racked up those miles on foot. He's circled the Earth without leavin the county."

"Or you could've taken me with you." Blue Jean squeezed his arm. "One'r the other."

"I don't go anywhere anymore and you know it."

"Only took you twenty-some-odd years to settle down."

"First time I stuck out my thumb only got as far as Arcadia. Not even outta Crawford County. Wasn't but 14 or so. Almost got myself rolled in Indian Country, over there in Arizona cuz I was dressed too nice, they wanted to mess me up some. But I talked those Navajos into believin I was a relation come distant from a small town in Kansas even though quarter Creek's what I am. Had em buyin me beers before I gave em the slip."

The Duke pulled out a stumpy Toscana, kept it in his mouth to let the taste sit there for a few minutes before lighting up.

"Pyramids in Mexico," Rae Anne said. "Now there's one I didn't believe until I saw it."

"And there was that old-timer, what was his name? Eduardo? Came from aristocracy but wound up livin in that run-down hotel – the bubble in you're level'd always be off in that place – the whole center a gravity's crooked in that country, specially the politicians."

"He was so sweet." Rae Anne didn't quite smile. "He had that English accent an all …"

"Thought I was a Mexican, too," Zirque said. "A little on the tall side for the home-grown variety."

"Well, you're dark enough, you could pass for a lotta things."

"Tell you something …" Zirque was waving around a cigarette, a glowing wand that drew disappearing shapes of light in the air. "There are places got no landmarks, no Kilroy was here, no footprints. Only way to get your bearings you got to look up, get yourself a star marker."

Zirque Part-Creek slapping dust off his jeans that could be from the Mojave, could be from the floor of Bartelli's Blue Goose Bar, no telling. Adrift in a vanishing city he'd never reach for long, inheritor of the restlessness this land is full of – you got to figure it's not a hundred years America's been carpeted over with tar and concrete, cities piled up on horizons, what they cover's a thousand thousand years old, civilization just a throw rug by comparison – Zirque's a lightning rod somehow, drawing the unrest that passes unnoticed beneath the high-heeled feet of women peeking in windows along Broadway, the booted men sitting around Carol's Corner Café reading about yesterday in the *Pittsburg Sun* or the *Kansas City Star*, eggs and coffee, steam rising to disappear like the long-ago they were never part of. The corner where two streets cross as arbitrary as can be if you're not Millo the Far-Seeing, and he doesn't see much more than half a century back. Zirque maybe has some kind of extra sense, without knowing anything about miners or grasshoppers, he'd know where they jumped off the trolley, might every now and then think he hears a Creek hootcall but decides it was only an oddball bird.

Earl, his hair white underneath a Kansas City Royals cap, took a chair next to the Duke and pulled a bottle from under his jacket. Hard to tell what was in it, the home-made label – *For Use as a*

Motor Fuel Only! Contains Lead! – no help at all.

"Whaddaya know, Earl?"

"Hadda fight, hadda fuck, an hadda steal yer girl." He took a sly sip out of the bottle so as not to let on to Farley. "You're just lucky you're a friend a mine, Granges. Can't mess with a buddy's girl. But you know if she gave me one go-round, wouldn't nothing be left a you but a bad mem'ry." Two fingers on the visor, he adjusted his baseball cap.

"Oh Earl – "

"If you ain't lookin the part a the Blue Jean Baby Queen t'night, prettiest girl I ever seen …"

"ERR-ull …"

"Wondrous fair." The Duke leaned cigar-first into the table candle snug in its glass bell. Smoke and flame flared up, his wide face looking for a few seconds like it belonged to a being dragged down to Earth for some kind of fire-lit ritual.

"Ain't nothing like a pretty redhead, specially one with green eyes." Earl shook his head. "Yer a lucky man, Granges."

"My luck was holdin out pretty good till you walked in."

"I'm gonna ignore that." Earl pointed an imposing finger, his hands big even for a man six-foot-two or so. "An what're you doin here, Pallucca? Aint you s'posed to be spinnin webs in your basement?"

"Not t'night, Earl."

Leaning closer to the Duke he whispered, "I'm goin t'meet Janice later on, Tommy's outta town."

"Now you just said – "

"Shhhhhhh." The finger he'd just pointed at Zirque made a seam from chin to more-than-once-broken nose (healed a bit crooked but he liked to think it made him look distinguished).

"Tommy's one a your buddies, so how're you gonna do that?"

"I'm not gonna tell im. Are you?"

"No …"

"Well that's how you do it!" Earl slapped him on the shoulder, slugged out of the bottle he was trying to keep hid behind his jacket. "A beautiful night in Palluccaville, ain't it though?"

"S'posed to get rainy an nasty later on, might even snow they said."

"When are we gonna get this place renamed official? I think Skunk's makin up fliers t'get it put to a vote."

"Wherein the hell's Skunk anyway?"

"Mighta left town." Zirque put out his cigarette.

"Don't even talk about leavin …"

"Yeah Granges, all the times you left this pretty gal on her own, you're lucky I gave her a shoulder t'cry on."

"I'm lucky that's all you tried to give er."

"If it weren't for Earl, who knows what woulda happened with that biker in the Pan Club parkin lot," Rae Anne said.

"You are beset from all sides." The Duke grinned at Zirque.

"I kinda noticed – "

"And you deserve it."

"Even Lyman Kishpaugh'd've put two an two together by now," Earl said.

"Amazin sometimes – " The Duke stabbed the air with his cigar – "what streets run parallel. You ever bump into Lyman?"

"Here an there, but never stopped to say hello that I recall. I ain't as old as Millo y'know."

"Got a lot more mileage on your face though, dontcha? Look like you got caught square with everything that ex-gal a yours ever threw at you."

"Granges, you're half as tough as y'think and twice as stupid as you look."

"My mamma knew Lyman." Rae Anne's voice rose at the mention of the name. "She tried to teach him to read but he didn't catch on too well. He always brought her a flower, too. He was kinda sweet on her. Just a big kid is all except he had no mean streak, no mischief in him. He used to lose his way sometimes, just forget I guess, which way Vacca's was – it was Vacca's or the firehouse where he slept, I don't remember which …"

The Duke puffed leisurely while he listened, the smoke unfurling in slow easy shapes – pure capriciousness what likeness they took on – then disappeared as though they'd never been.

"He had a big ring of keys, probably not one of 'em opened anything, but he used to carry 'em all around, Mama said, like he wanted to be a bell-ringer, but all he got to be was a key-jangler. He'd make noise on purpose with them and start fiddlin with them when he got nervous. He carried a book with him all the time – what was it called? *The Happy Valley* or some such – but he couldn't read much more than the first few pages, which is what Mama taught him, that book I think was hangin out of his back pocket the day they found him outside the Poor Farm. He'd wandered off and got locked out in the dead a winter and just froze right there on the front stoop."

"Found the same way he was left," Zirque said.

The Duke, light from the candle cutting deeper the lines in his face, a larger version of the head topping his walking stick, exhaled thoughtfully. "Whaddaya mean?"

"Well he showed up asleep on Vacca's front stoop in the first place, didn't 'ee? Maybe the smell a bakin bread is what took him in, an I guess he finished about the way he started, locked out – only permanent this time."

Lyman Key-Jangler (his Creek name) gone on to Friskel's House of Dust. Was it he was just confused or was he lookin for somethin those times he went wanderin off, his mom or his circus friends, maybe a home he'd had before he got left in Frontenac – ?

"Earl how many times I tell you not to come in here with that bottle?" Fred Farley, eyebrows white as his hair, glared at Earl from behind the bar.

Earl held his hands up. "Honest injun, Fred, you won't see it no more. My buddy Zirque was just gonna buy me a beer anyhow."

"Bring it up here, Earl. You can have it when you leave."

Earl pushed out of his seat. "Come on up t'the bar, Zee Gee, an buy me a beer."

"In the immortal words a Shakespeare, *I don't hafta if I don't wanna.*" Straightening a leg so he didn't have to get out of his chair, Zirque fished a fin out of his pocket, put it in Earl's hand. "Buy what you want. And get Friar Pallucca a glass a dago red while you're up there."

Earl took the five-dollar bill. "Does kinda look like a monk with that bowl cut a his and that cloak-thing he wears." Earl winked at Zee Gee. "You ain't half bad most a the time, Granges."

"Looks like it's getting cold out, don't it?" Rae Anne asked.

The Duke could see the wind ruffling the green awning trimmed in white, leaves fluttering past, spinning, carried off with no say over where they were going, all of it silent beyond the plate-glass window.

"Don't know for sure, but after my glass a wine I think I'm going to up North Broad, see about the waterway connectin *nunc* to *tunc.*

"Back just in time to catch them sellin pure bullshit." Earl put down a glass of red wine in front of the Duke. "Him and Zirque oughta be married the kinda things they cook up between 'em."

"Hope you have better luck than to be stuck in ice for years on end," Zirque said.

Earl scraped his chair forward. "Well, I'll tell you what: why don'tcha wish in one hand, shit in the other, an see which gets full first?"

Rae Anne tilted her head back, flattened a hand against her chest and laughed, a kind of music that could rearrange your insides, sets loose a little dust devil in there that turns everything in circles.

"You ever see somma Pallucca's books?" (Earl had sided with Rae Anne, a way of lawfully drifting a little closer to her, a way to keep the other two from leaving him out of the table talk.) "Make a library look ramshod."

"Ramshackle," Zirque corrected.

"Whatever the fuck – "

"Ramshackle don't make all that much sense either."

"What … the fuck … EVER." Earl pounded the table with the heel of his bottle to flatten out each word.

"Your poetic license is hereby revoked."

"I been drivin without it all my life anyway."

The Duke exhaled a thick stream of smoke.

"So," Zirque said to the Duke, "the Two-Flow Way is what you're talking …"

"Pure horse shit is what he's talking."

The Duke nodded. "See if I can align myself – rivers a gravity, you know, I read about those, move whole sections a galaxies more or less sideways and … I hear there are invisible rivers down here, too, carry you off it you let 'em."

"What're you readin these days anyway?" Earl asked. "*Goat-Fucking in Ancient Times?*"

"*The Decline and Fall of the Grand Emporium* more likely," Zirque said.

"Just finished *On the Origin of the Specious.*" The Duke's smile was only half visible through cigar smoke. He tapped ashes into a glass tray. "Fact a the matter is, I got holda some books on English voyages into the arctic, the Crown bent on cutting across the top a North America t'reach the rice, spices, and riches of the Far

East the quicker. Brits started after their waterway in the 1500s, Henry Hudson himself – the river between Jersey and New York's named for 'im – was abandoned in an open boat by his crew after a hard winter up there."

"Guess he had a time of it paddlin back t'England," Zirque said.

"Didn't even leave 'im any oars."

Earl shook his head. "Worse than any death row I was ever on."

Blue Jean rubbed the chill out of her arms. "That's about the awfullest thing I ever heard."

"Strange thing bein, after Foxe sailed that way 1631 or thereabouts, they knew there was no way t'cut through below the Arctic Circle, the fabled straight'd be frozen solid most a the year even if it existed. They kept up anyway. One ship named after Foxe was frozen in the ice 242 days, drifted 1,400 miles south and east – opposite a the captain's intentions unless back to England was the unconscious desire. The Franklin Expedition was the worst of all, 129 men and not one made it back home, abandoned their ice-wrecked ships but dropped one by one as they walked the Eskimos said. Starvation and exhaustion."

"Did anybody finally find it?"

The Duke nodded. "Took near 300 years, but only a modern icebreaker could make use of it. All those men died for nothin."

"I admire 'em though." Zirque finished his beer in silent toast to the frozen bones of lost explorers. "I never did get it down y'-know, just got tired is all."

The Duke nodded. "Maybe that's the best way, quit swimming upstream, let the current carry you some ..."

Zirque's whole life trying to wear himself out, a search for things that'd use him up but still leave something of him behind, something to hand down, pass on like an old farmhouse on a stone foundation. Stealing cars, chewing cactus buttons that made every thought a curveball, snuffing up nose powders so he could watch the night melt in the white glow, chasing after women and long-distance traveling on a drunken whim done with, he'd finally run himself down, an old dog settled in his musty pile a rags, sleeping peaceful.

The glass of wine disappeared while the Duke's cigar burned down to an ashy stump. He lit another and the freezing rain the radio had said might come began to fall. Another wine came and Zirque lit up a cigar, too, the four of them talking in a pocket of smoke and wine and beer and dusty amber light. When the Duke looked out the window he saw the cold coming on, icicles giving downtown ragged edges though it was still raining, a weird in-between temperature, he wasn't really looking forward to heading out.

Pushing back his chair, he swung a long gray coat over his shoulders, a gift from a West Point Cadet, a kind of slicker that probably hadn't looked any different during the Civil War. "One thing I'll say for you Granges, you didn't hug the shore."

Zirque thumbed over his shoulder at Blue Jean. "She's my homin instinct or I'd still be out there. Ain'tcha, honey?"

She threw him a glance but kept talking to Earl.

"She's the sweetness an light in my life."

"Zirque – "

"The kerosene in my heater – "

"You're such a jerk."

"The car in my garage."

"I'm not going to pay you any more mind. Go ahead, Earl …"

"The bulb in my lamp," Zirque said for good measure. Leaning the Duke's way, Zirque weaseled his fingers into the worn jacket hanging on the back of his chair (the same scrap of denim he'd taken with him when he was off doing fool things that were still catching up to him), pulled out a folded-up square of paper. "She gave me somethin just in case I lose my pigeon-like powers." A Blue Jean drawing of a woman not much more than a typical stick-man except for the hair, a dress, a bit more of a face. *You are here* she had written and put an X about where the stick-girl's heart would have been.

November 10, 1762

For some time now, I have known that there is no way out. Sixteen days have gone by that we have been inclosed in the ice. All is bleak around us. No description would serve for the netherlands of ice and snow encountered at these latitudes.

Moreover, what may prove fatal to my crew and myself is my failure to imagine more clearly the perils of these waters. Though locked in ice, we make slow progress farther north and east, as the ice itself drifts in a great pack according to its own inscrutable will. There is nothing we can do. God Almighty, what calamity!

It was folly to underestimate the vagaries of arctic weather. How well I know a strait blocked off by ice his year may have been free-flowing water only last season. The maze of navigable waterways and straits, of unfrozen bays and favorable harbors among the islands and peninsulas so often changes that a reliable map would be impossible. And how easily the chance arrangements of floes deceive one into believing new bits of land have emerged here or there. Most hazardous of all, perhaps, is the unknown course of the ice stream that circulates through this region in an entirely unpredictable manner, in which we are now trapped.

The first mate has informed me that the fire has gone out. God preserve us.

The night is hollow and what we don't fill with a few wisps of light from a neon sign or a streetlamp we fill with unmoored dreaming, imaginings strange as unheard-of sea beasts.

The Duke gets the same drifting-off feeling looking at the webwork of lines on a gilt 16th-century map as he does from the criss-crossing of telephone wires and cables, antennas and spun-iron fire escapes downtown. Telephone wires not exactly longitude-latitude, not so neat and predictable, more liked plotted courses intersecting with the spokes of wind roses. The wires (hung with icicles still dripping though the sky had dried) cutting across vast chunks of clouds – floating-overhead continents. A corner of clear sky measured off by the wires and cables, the telephone poles like transplanted masts of wrecked ships, wondrous in their stillness and the ice encrustings lavished on them by a frigid place breathing its cold metal-sharp breath, or maybe the poles are all that's visible of ships submerged in time disguised as asphalt.

A hot-water heater on its side, set out for trash, looked like one of those old-time lifesavers.

A tree, branches bent permanent, happened to be aligned with the clouds. Who'd've thought it could be so loud it its jacket, crinkling and creaking as a breeze went past?

That brick building over there, a single lit window against the dark sky near surreal, the whole crooked world aslant askew leanin toward something. The very top left corner a the building lined up with that star which is lined up with the Moon, which is lined up with that telephone pole, don't know why but they didn't put a pole in straight on this street and this one matched the slant a that building exactly. The same force movin through was out tonight, left a temporary trail in the clouds, left that telephone pole to point like a sundial needle.

Fourth Street, Hotel Besse with its thorny crown of antennas, a whole big uneven bunch of 'em atop its 13 stories haulin in signals. Cables hangin off them like saggin rigging, sails swept away, useless in this age of electromagnetic waves, wind left to babble to itself (like me). Zirque ought t'be standin stiffbacked among those steel spines, the crow's nest a the Besse, might pull in the music a the spheres from up there, the slappin and overlappin of the ocean a time, might even see all the way to the mythical Drifting Island of Memory.

This small-time city, kind of an accidental labyrinth, a maze a streets an alleys, a tangle a streetlamps, traffic lights, criss-crossin telephone wires an electric cables, downtown an architected reflection of some inner arrangement. From storefronts and storied buildings to the still-life of beer bottles glossed with yellow light, ashtrays with crushed butts (like tiny untended bones) on the tables in Farley's, memory becoming a city – we remember by arrangement, the names of a long-ago king's dinner guests crushed by the fallen ceiling recalled by their placement at the table. Memory has its alleys and streets and even parks with shimmering ponds at the center where words dissolve, some part of memory feelin without knowin how to say, just an electric tingle at the back a the neck, some part always under construction, imagination fills in the gaps, configurations tucked inside others like rooms inside buildings, furniture inside rooms. The city evolves, buildings topple, half-way fall, new ones go up, some're renovated, some joined, their uses switched up sometimes, new streets added, widened, changed into one-ways, renamed. All guided by ancient remembrances Jung dug up, those eroded forms somehow insinuate the layout a the new city.

Might be that with Zirque, somethin old in him leads the way, some kinda innate get-go, like those baby sea turtles flip-floppin frantic for the breakin vastness a the ocean soon as they hatch, knowin exactly where something they've never seen is t'be found. Maybe he's got rigged in him some kinda gyroscope generating a lopsided momentum always carryin him in a direction he's not thinkin about. Or is it he's adrift, carried off at night by the churning of his dreams, the rest of us not so unlucky as to have this always-spinnin mechanism that never leaves calm enough for a good night's sleep (though I ain't much at ease either come bedtime, might as well be lookin for the shadow a the Moon at nightfall). Might be Zirque's infused with something long-settled into the land, a magnetism of a kind drawin him along. Maybe all little a both – if we're all lead copper aluminum, he's iron always pulled at by a pole.

The Moon three-quarters tonight, the distance nothing the mind can close in on, its light reaches across the desert of empty black that's mainly what existence is, keyholed here and there by a star or an insomniac walkin the edge a the familiar, tryin t'peek over, yes empty mostly, same as the atoms that make up this over-weight body, solid enough to stop an arrow though, to be held to the ground by a fist of gravity.

The Duke wonders how to find his way, should he use that moon overhead to navigate? Or the tiny mercury-vapor moons on their hooded poles – sparks of dust in the three-quarter eye of a sleeping god?

Stars and headlights, a fluorescent sign announcing Crowell Drugstore, the lit end of a cigar pointing due east, the true source of light, all the rest pagan stolen fire, the flame jumpin up to grab holda the night before the darkness brings its inexhaustible weight to bear, crush the bright upstart. Pillar a cloud by day, star by night ain't so easy anymore. Now we even got to deal with the difference between True North and Magnetic North, the one unerring, constant, the other a variable, sometimes northwestin, sometimes northeastin. One found by measuring the elevation a the Pole star, the other by what your compass is doin, uncertainty a snaking wormhole into the everyday: just when we think we know where we are, we drop down through an uncovered manhole an come up on the other side a things, not a landmark not a familiar constellation in sight. Or worse, wind up like that happy-go-lucky young Frenchman, Bellot, disappearing in a sudden crack in the ice before anyone was sure he was gone. Like the Thomas boy, who had all the promise anyone could've hoped for in an 18-year-old, electrocuted one rainy night on farm machinery.

All right then, Magnetic North … center a the pull shifts dependin on where you're standin or floating (howsoeverbeit). True North on the other hand an arbitrary goddam thing, doesn't exist any more than a straight line on the Earth's curved surface.

The strange thing here, town's got its own pull same as a New York, a Chicago, a Far East, the poles. Maybe just for tonight Farley's is Magnetic North. On another night it'll be the Pan Club or might be so off-center so as t'get all the way to Frontenac. Might even be that ghost bar, Bartelli's, cast adrift backwards in time everybody might be headed over that way, tryin to look past the cardboard & painted-over windows without knowin why without knowin where they're headed, might go across the street to the Pool Hall instead, thinking there, *there* is where whatever's going to shake loose tonight will do its slow uncocoonin for anyone payin mind enough t'notice, the Northwest Passage just opened up, the straits are free of ice an mist, time's runnin in both directions, but you miss the boat if you're not icemaster enough t'see there's a moment of redemption over the horizon, a moment of clarity when we know what it was Pap was up to stripped naked in a drainage ditch where he drowned in six inches a rainwater, a moment when you can see where you should be standin (or flowin) in relation to everything else, the vanishing point is right there – what vanishes at this point being the horizon (you don't need to go any farther) you've found ground zero where all motion is at rest, where the two are one and from that place the world makes perfect sense, the city your memory has built up fits into the city you're standin in, all the *terra incognitae* – whatever the mapmakers missed – as familiar as the cracks in McKay Street.

Funny thing is, early on, those mapmakers couldn't agree on a flat, a round, an oval world. Debated which end is up – north or east – but had no doubt there were four rivers running through the underworld, no bickerin over the layout a where it is we'd all be headed one day. You might think Friskel's House a Dust one a the doorways, but the real way down is here (the Duke thumped his chest), we've all had a peek during a bad night's sleep or a gut feelin, a flash of introspection an we find ourselves spelunking the nadirland we're carryin around inside us though mainly nowadays we know maps better than the territory, we can draw America's outlines freehand, navigate town to town a hundred times better than we ever could the maze of our own hearts.

The Duke was standing outside Carol's Corner Café, glass brick on either side of the door, a big window to look out (or in) set in red brick, Lyman's regular place Sunday mornings, rain or shine. In rain, soaked except for his crew-cut head, that corduroy Depression cap of his sagging it'd been handled so much besides being wet. He'd pick up the *Pittsburg Sun* off the counter, mainly the pictures he gandered at, a serious look on his face, his tongue out, lips curled under when he tried to read the local goings-on (a football score put him on his surest footing) he wanted to be like everyone else while he waited for breakfast, taylor ham and eggs every time, sometimes a side of sausage or bacon, it was the grease he loved. Old Mary, shriveled as eggs sunny side up left out overnight, his favorite waitress, with those big glasses of hers, she always got him a side of cornbread no extra charge.

Rainy day shivery something cold had rolled in out of the north, had drifted in along with the mist, a ghostly chill off an ancestral burial ground of the Kansa (though there aren't any that anyone knows of anywhere near) the streets sunk in a quiet shade of shadowy gray cut by the occasional keening of a train whistle along the Santa Fe Line. Lyman with only that hat and an old corduroy jacket worn through at the elbows to keep the November dampness off him, his back eased up against the smell of brewing coffee and smoky bacon, he could see people out the rain-jeweled window on their way in long overcoats, umbrellas up, hats held and heads bent, shroudy figures in the fogginess, as if the shades of people were abroad, detached from owners, a supernatural shanghai left them downtown, wandering, wondering, the way obscured, a kind of natural sorcery at work to make a labyrinth of the familiar.

Safe inside the café, anchored to the padded stool at the counter, conversations around him like lazy bees buzzing past, settling their fat bodies on flowers on a warm day, a slap hello on the back from George Wilke, smiles nods waves from the other tables, he was just like them, lifted a hand and called *Good mornin,* Mary askin him about work at the bakery, about the Vaccas, telling him not to rush through his meal *Take your time* her smile making more wrinkles in her face, *just imagine you hear a far-off violin playin somethin slow and wonderful, the longer it takes you to finish the longer that violin plays. A slow old-time waltz, those people outside about the business can't hear it and aren't you sorry for them they can't?* Before he left, he counted up his change (tongue out), the nickels and pennies to add up to what he owed plus a nickel for Mary.

Drawn some nights to St. Elmo's neon, Lyman wandered down Fifth, stopped in front of Farley's to see who was there, never went in, just hovered. What did he know beyond the smell of the bakery or the bells of the fire engines? Was he ever anything more than a kid let loose in the carnival of the world, carried along by the rides, conned by barkers *Over here, over here my boy! You've got the magic key on your ring yes you do, that and a mere five cents Lyman for the ride of a lifetime!* Selling this to a man whose life was a ride he couldn't really get off.

Alone in the basement of the bakery did he sleep sound? When he woke to find no carnival music, no rides, nothing but the dark of the closed-up bakery, he'd pull on a long string, fire a bare bulb, try to read, but couldn't get much past the first pages of *The Happy Valley*, a library give-away, cover creased and bent from being in his back pocket all the time, a boy and a girl best friends growing up in a Neverwasville where nothing really bad ever happened.

Rae Anne's mom taught him – did he ever reach for his own mother when he was struggling with the words? All tongue when he concentrated, he wanted to read really did he just couldn't lift too many of those sentences off the pages though he talked about Robby and Sharon like they were his friends and he pretended to read the newspaper like everyone else in Carol's when he was really looking at the pictures the way he went though his life, just looking at the pictures. Even coins confused him sometimes, they had to be worth somethin because look how pretty they are an everyone carried them but adding them up he didn't always get it right – government backing, gold reserves, Marx's manifesto as far out of reach as Marco Polo's wondrous Cathay, which Arthur Stilwell thought to reach with a railroad through Mexico picking up where the Pacific waterway left off.

Weathervane might not be a Kansas invention though the state is named for the People of the South Wind, and dust is kicked up from the streets more or less sunup till moonfall but that kind of directional ought to be a Kansas original, Lyman a kind of human weathervane, no man more prone to the tilt of the Earth, the natural lilt that carries everything from a goose feather on up to a galaxy, he didn't have much control over anything, his head was as light as goose down, Lyman a weathervane for the unfelt gust that doesn't originate in one of the cardinal directions, wells up maybe from the nadir (a point you'll find on any Native American compass), keep an eye on him, never much got anywhere unless he got himself carried along, you'll know which way things are blowin.

August 12, 1775

This day has been witness to the strangest event I expect I shall see in my lifetime.

It began in ordinary fashion, the hours passing no differently than those of the day before – aye, of many days before. We now find ourselves off the west coast of Greenland, well above the Arctic Circle. With whales scarce of late, the lookouts have been cautioned to keep a keen eye on the sea.

The Herald, *an icy breeze snapping her sail, made her way through a sea choked with icebergs but otherwise empty. These many tons of ice are shaped as oddly and capriciously as clouds. Indeed, as they are also quite as white, they could have been great clods of heavenly stuff grown weighty and fallen into the frigid waters. It was among these same that the lookouts spied another ship. She was a three-masted schooner that seemed adrift and in a state of ill-repair. Ropes hung haphazardly from the masts and the sails had been reduced to tattered rags.*

I ordered the men to divert our course to intercept the strange visitor that I might hail her.

The attempt was made, but I received no reply. Nor could I see anyone on deck.

Ordering eight men into a longboat, we rowed to our silent companion in fairly calm waters. The elements had all but worn away the name, but after a moment's squinting in the midday sun, I was able to discern it: Octavius.

When we had pulled alongside, I again hailed the Octavius *but once again was greeted with a deep and abiding silence broken only by the slap of the sea against the hulls of the two vessels. One of the men crossed himself. The others began to complain, quite audibly in some cases, of being so close to such an eerie sight.*

Superstitious foolishness! What were the perils of a derelict schooner compared to those of the arctic region? I chose the four men who I deemed to be the stoutest of heart and ordered them aboard. Leading the way myself, I took hold of fallen rigging and hoisted myself onto the deck.

Third time maybe the Duke had doubled back up Broadway and come again to the Hotel Stilwell, Pap's haunt, a place to remember well. The year he died the last it was open. As famous for being the grandest built in Crawford County as for its founder, old Arthur Stilwell. Papish, dead near ten years now, use to perch like a gargoyle in a hall window a the Stilwell just to catch sight a Blue Jean goin in or comin out of Carol's Corner Café, climbed down the drainpipe now an again to sit in the booth behind her, knowin all the time Blue Jean herself was gazing up at a constellation reminded her of Zirque, due east where the light creeps into the emptiness of our hearts, points the way, they chase each other, Moon and Sun up there, eclipse bein the dark moment of embrace.

Pap never … unless at the end there maybe he came on the passage, which is what took him by the hand along the spirit trail.

It ain't sho easy. The streets, shometimes they move.

"Pap – ?" Or maybe just a ripple in the near-nothing of the air.

I mean don't you remember em bein jusht a shcant different from what you're seein now, ain't they moved?

"Well Pap who'da thought …? I'm glad you left Farley's, nothing for you there anyway, you know."

Shome kinda … Farley's is shome kinda – but that ain't the point, the point's the shtreets, they're still runnin east-west or north-south or bending around southeast and whatall, but just maybe they've shifted over a bit. This scrag a land we think's sittin shtill so we can shtand on it, the continents are all afloat adrift awash in the world's oceans, the earth itselfs ashkew on its axish, headin off with the entire sholar system in its own direction – what's heavy enough, anchored enough, dug in deep enough not t'be?

"Well I …" The Duke wasn't sure he'd understood. "Farley's, I guess."

Everything you know, or jusht think you know, it's all heaped up, sittin on the waters they used t'think shurrounded all the land there is, the earth disk-shaped back then, shurrounded by the Great Outer Sea of Boundless Extent. Nothin shtays put, memories ain't where you left em. 'Less you take the time to arrange em, line em up with your own personal astrolabe so every time you see scorpio up there – her sign – you remember Blue Jean and everything she is to you.

The Duke turned to say something else to Pap, but he was gone, dissolved in a bit of light under a streetlamp, a faint electric hum the only sound.

The Duke nodded to himself. Habit replaced natural laws out here, that's what ghosts are made of, routine, still going up a staircase torn down years ago – but what the hell do they know? They ain't there anymore either.

August 12, 1775

As I had feared, the deck of the Octavius *was deserted and the ship's wheel was unattended. We had to choose each step with great care for the planks of the deck were unsound and had been made slippery with both frost and some sort of moss.*

Below decks – there lay the frightful story! In the crew's quarters lay the bodies of 28 men, all thickly bundled, all uncannily preserved by the Artic cold. This time, we all removed our hats and crossed ourselves.

In hopes of discovering what had led the men of the Octavius *to their fate, we made our way aft to the captain's cabin. There we found him motionless in his chair, still at his desk, his head bent forward, his quill lying beside his hand as though he had gone to sleep in the midst of attending to his recording duties.*

A film of green mould had crept over the dead captain's face and hands, but otherwise, the body, like the others, was perfectly preserved. We tarried in his cabin only long enough to confiscate his log and then continued our exploration of the ship.

In another cabin, we discovered the remains of a woman, reclining, as it were, on a bed. She seemed held rapt by some event of great importance. Hardly did she seem lifeless at all but for the shrunken quality of her limbs. Not far from her, the ship's pilot sat cross-legged on the floor, a flint in one hand and steel in the other. Before him lay a little pile of wood shavings. Once more we offered a prayer for the dead and crossed ourselves.

The log book safely tucked inside my coat, I led the way topside whence we returned to the Herald.

Against my wishes, I left the Octavius *adrift; the men already feared disaster might follow this ominous encounter but were altogether convinced it would literally follow us were we to take the* Octavius *into tow. I watched her, a floating tomb among the icebergs of the North Atlantic, until she was little more than an indiscernible speck on the horizon and, at last, lost to sight.*

The final entry in the Octavius's *logbook is dated November 11, 1762. Here I feel it only proper to give voice to the dead captain whose last words fate has seen fit to place in my hands:*

> *We have now been inclosed in the ice seventeen days. The fire went out yesterday, and our master has been trying ever since to kindle it again, but without success. His wife died this morning; there is no relief.*

Their plight, relived in this passage with all the freshness of the dreadful moment it was written, was indeed poignant. Yet what is astonishing to discover is the ship's ice-bound trek: According to the captain's last entry, the Octavius *was at Longitude 160 West, Latitude 75 North. I returned to previous entries and studied these numbers as Pythagoras must have pored over many a theorem of geometry. I called in the first and second mates to be sure of what I had read. There could be no doubt. When the captain made his final entry into the logbook, the* Octavius *had been prisoner of the Arctic Ocean, north of Alaska, on the* <u>other side</u> *of the North American Continent.*

The Octavius *had weathered the onslaught of the northerly elements, all the while being pushed ever eastward by the capricious ice stream until she eventually emerged in the Atlantic where we came upon her. God Above but this ship with its captain and all hands dead for well nigh 13 years has navigated the fabled Northwest Passage!*

Still walking though the air had turned colder, the Duke had his mind on how Lyman got left by the twinkling electric-lit now-you-see-it-now-you-don't carnival, washed him up in a place that'd take care of him until, too old and without family, they stuck him in the Poor Farm (name like that gets somethin for honesty but you gotta take off for originality), since torn down. They gave Lyman a squeaky cot for sleeping, a chipped enameled cup for coffee, a night stand, a whistling radiator that peeled paint on the wall, stained and warped the floor where it leaked – nice folks over at the Poor Farm but they didn't have enough coal to shovel into furnace, the radiator didn't whistle enough. His breath turned to wintry mist in his room, he went out less and less, wasn't anyone to see anymore, he was lucky to have a place to stay hardly anyone came to visit though he could go into the lounge where it was warmer and play cards or checkers, a brotherhood of the unshaved the unwashed the unkept. Mr. Brunges with a bathrobe over his clothes, his chair set alongside the pot-belly stove, its chubby curved legs resting on the balding green carpet, old Brunges wore the same stained shirt every day, his robe worn through in places to match the carpet.

In Lyman's room two nails in the wall behind his cot, one for the big crucifix Father Pat had given him, the other for his cap gone flat and shapeless no one knew what was holding it together it was like a wet dish rag on his head, Lyman's rough hand putting it on and pulling it off had worn the corduroy smooth they used it to cover his face when they found him.

Not a one of those keys on that big ring he used to carry around opened the door he tried them all, a few must've fit but the lock didn't turn, he was at it most likely better than an hour before he gave up it must not have occurred to him how cold out it was how he wasn't dressed for it he should've broken a window but he never broke a thing in his life on purpose never stole a penny from the register used to bein locked out anyhow ain't much use complainin about it somebody'd show up by morning. Curled up against the cold, his back to the wind that'd be enough, they'd show by morning, think on a sunny day in *The Happy Valley* (weren't they all?) he wouldn't minding showing Robby and Sharon the bakery so long as Mr. Vacca didn't mind the big blackened stone ovens kept the place so nice and warm they thought he was asleep when they found him *Don't he look peaceful though?* still wearing bib overalls and his cap locked out for good this time.

The Duke had walked all the way back to Frontenac, was on his way past the silent houses lined up along McKay Street but it was the insectquiet of the fields he was after. Nothing showed in the eastern sky yet, but there was the vague sense darkness was giving way. He knew he had to keep walking, the only choice left was which road would take him to the place near the gathered dawn where something was waitin on him to do its slow uncocooning, the straits free of ice and mist, he would have to go no farther, no further. As he set off, he couldn't be sure considering how many porches were hung with windchimes of all kinds, but he thought he heard, somewhere up ahead in the near-dark, the jangle of keys on a ring.

FIRE FROM HEAVEN

...and their beauty shall be for Sheol to consume,
that there be no habitation for it.
— Psalm XLIX

(The speaker is Li'shilah, a temple harlot.)

From Gebal in Canaan, Gebal near the sea, he comes. So long has it been (that) the Chaldeans who study the skies have seen many shifts in the heavens of wandering light [for] it has been so long.

Zedebkiah was he anointed, as the Far-Ranging is he better known. No true dwelling place has he, but his legs are made to go astray. Like a strip of cloth driven by desert winds, he is beset by [the] fierce desires that come upon him. Since the time of his youth has he been thus. Yet his urgings do not master him, nor can they be altogether quelled.

From Gebal near the sea he comes, Gebal in whose harbor the curving boats of the Egyptians [are made] to lie low in the water with great trunks of cut cedar. From Palmyra, the oasis city in the sun-beaten desert came he to Gebal, his asses laden with trading goods [...the] glass trinkets and baubles of the Canaanites, earrings and drinking vessels, images of Ba'al, who is beautiful to look upon, [that are] no larger than a finger, and His consort, Astarte [...] Amulets inscribed with spells and incantations to divert the ill wind that seeks to enter through the open mouth.

By the stars he is guided [...] tak[ing] refuge in the shade of [his] tent during the noon heat.

May Zedebkiah never leave the shade of his tent to wander a night whose sky is empty!

For the vagabond augurs have foretold a night when there shall be no star, nor moon, nothing in the great vault of black overhead. As it was in the Beginning, so shall it be on that night (when) it is said the Chaldeans to the east [who] bear witness to the movements of the heavens, shall shake their bearded heads in wonder and astonishment.

For with the coming of the darkness that is like the First Darkness, Zedebkiah shall have no destination. Before the coming of light again to the sky, there shall be no city (here) for him to find.

Yea, long before the sun has risen, it is said there shall be a time of red lightning. Wide-eyed and snorting, our tamed beasts shall take to the plains. Man, woman, and child shall fall upon their knees [...] shall make themselves as low as the dust and plead [for] mercy.

Lightning shall strike the watch towers along the walls, lightning shall split sky and earth. Jeroaz, the toothless beggar-seer, has said the earth itself shall open and swallow this city and its dwellers [...]. The work of many hands shall [be] take[n] back into clay. Yea, the inhabitants of this city [shall be] mere clay again.

Hezacham, prophet of the Temple of Ba'al, has seen in his troubled sleep brimstone and ash, hot and black, all-consuming.

Who is to be believed? For 10 shekels, the seers will also say the Nameless One Himself will appear at the door of the most humble in the guise of a barefoot sojourner. These same soothsayers will offer the beggar closest at hand a shekel to fool the eyes into believing the prophecy has been fulfilled [and] keep for themselves (the other) nine.

Yet also I fear there is truth in the divinings. Just as the tame beast grows wild before the onset of a thundering storm, so something of great weight stirs in the heavens. Jeweled though the unfurled darkness is, there is something that menaces even [the] basalt bone of the earth at my feet.

Yet will I stay. [Not to] goad the Jealous God into making fools or prophets of the soothsayers, but to bear witness. Has not the end of this city been foretold a hundred times since the laying of its first stone? In dust I would see it lie. I would be visited upon by the wrath of the Vengeful God who has ...

(Several lines missing.)

[...] was not expected to live. A wailing infant left to the jackals roaming this city. My mother, she who broke the bond of all natural things, I have never known. A lowly street harlot. It was rumored no temple would have her, and [I] do not doubt it is so.

Mother who has never heard her child's voice, why did you abandon your daughter on the doorstep of strangers to be named Li'shilah according to their pleasure? Mother [at] whose breast I was never suckled, mother whose face I have never beheld, I would know why.

Yet it may be that I have indeed beheld your face. Perhaps in the market at the hour it is most crowded. Perhaps in the midday heat and the dust raised by sandaled feet, [you were] amongst the farmers and traders calling out their prices – the fat, bearded merchant who sells fine tunics; the yellow-toothed leatherworker whose skin is as creased and thick as the hides upon which he works; the white-haired hag, whose face shines like bronze, she [who] offers clay vessels baked in an oven fired with the dung of beasts.

It may be that I gazed upon you and you upon me, and that I did not recognize you as flesh of my flesh. It may be I was blind to the eye which looked back into mine and from which mine had come. I did not see in your shape the woman's shape into which I have ripened. Nor did you break the silence between us, if indeed we met. You left me joined by blood to no one I know in this city nor in any land, [even] were I to journey as far as distant Shinar. I am left the tomb of no ancestor to venerate. I am left no name that I may know of those who came before me. I will be no more than a hungry ghost when I die, my belly forever empty. Set loose among the solid things of the Earth, heralded by a howl travelers will mistake for the wind, I am never to know peace even in death.

Mother I have never known, have I not gazed at the bare foot of every woman in this city? Have I not seen those as gnarled as the roots of the olive tree with infirmity and age? Have I not seen those missing a great or little toe? And those with veins [that] lie curving beneath the skin like great worms? Have I not searched every harlot's place? Have I not been to the temples, the dens of iniquity, the dark streets and houses well-known among sojourning men? For it is said the needleworker has put a snake of green coils around your ankle. And upon the other foot, strange symbols whereof no one can read nor understand, but with which you are forever mark[ed]. The unwashed feet of the lowest farmer's wife reeking of dung, have I not seen them? The smooth pale feet of women of noble birth, have I not seen these also? Yet never have I gazed upon the Woman-Of-The-Coiled-Snake. Have I not promised gold to the beggar who brings me to her? Yet there is no word.

Shall I tell you (if you yet draw breath, if you so incline your head to hear) I am become a temple harlot? Yet it is not any coin to make me lie with a man but the coin of a man who suits me.

See, even now I wander the walled garden of a noble. I breathe air perfumed with the scent of dates [so] ripe with sweetness they begin to rot in the heat. Long-stemmed flowers brush against my knees and mingle their fragrance. Servants lie within the sound of the small bell (that) I need only strike to bring one forth. A balcony finds its way around the length and breadth of the garden. That the night may not overwhelm me as I take my leisure in this walled garden, braziers have been set aflame. Hanging braziers and those that stand have been set aflame. [F]or so I can afford to choose the men who seek my favor. Yea, pleasing to them am I. At a whim may I set them at one another's hearts [so] that they plot one against the other.

Before the eyes of the One God, those who worship Ba'al come to me. I bid Him watch. Him I offer insolence for the misfortune he has brought to me since I first crawled in swaddling cloths. Astarte, consort of pleasing-to-look-upon Ba'al, is my heavenly name, for like the goddess, I couple with the Ba'als of this city, I couple with the men who would be like Him. It is because of such as they and such as I [that] the One God seeks vengeance. Let it come. Though it may be as gathering into my arms hot coals, yet I shall embrace it. Let the flesh burn away and the scent of its burning fill my nostrils. Let the pain be as no other pain I have felt before. Let darkness cover my eyes.

Does He Who Has No Name not see also Canaan, where the worship of Ba'al is all? Has He not looked upon Canaan [in] the Season of Planting? During the spring festival, when couplings are numerous in the cities and in the fields, has the One God not seen? In the sacred groves, the devout aspire to be joined by Ba'al Himself. In the sacred groves, it is custom for the man to spew his seed upon ground to call Him forth. The Canaanite women, who are grown giddy with wine and (the) incense of ground herbs, the Canaanite women lie naked upon the fields in adulation of Astarte. Fathers are wont to give their daughters to sons for harlotry. Eventimes their own daughters fathers take. For such wickedness shall all of Canaan be destroyed also? Or is the Lord of Hosts lord only over our cities of sin in Palestine?

I have been to the Canaan of festival nights filled with flames as if souls of the departed came again to those hills. Sweet smoke from the scorched fields lay upon the hills like a mantle. Sweet smoke lay upon the hills for the fields were blackened with burning. [So was] the land made ready for new crops.

Amid the tended groves of tall trees, coupling did not cease. Amid the groves I saw women pressed against rough bark by their heaving mates. [Among] towering pillars of stone also and [the] great obelisks marking the presence of Ba'al, there was no end to the love-making. Beside the stone walls, beside (the) carved gods of the temple's outer courts, men and women lay. Worn with their efforts to arouse the gods of fertility, they lay. They lay with the cool surface of limestone against their thighs. To the murmur of the fountain, whence the waters flowed into a clear pool, I have listened. In those waters men and women bathe to be refreshed. In those waters, the heat and the dust are washed away. The sweat of labors and pleasures are washed away.

I say that I have been to Canaan and seen the evening fires burning upon that land's hills. In my wantonness I have coupled with those men and worshiped the great mystery of the bringing forth of life. The mystery of the sea of woman, which a man must enter like a silver fish, the sea of woman whence new life will be brought forth as by a god casting his net for that which swims. The mysterious sea of woman I have contemplated.

A child [it is] that comes of the sea of the womb. Why does woman not give birth to a serpent? A serpent it is that enters and begets the child. [A serpent] it was who first lay with a woman. The children's tale of a honeyed tongue and a forbidden apple is given credence only by the foolish. The phallus of God entered her in the enclosed garden. No more than a cast-off snakeskin she was left by His phallus. She [was] left the nearest to heaven living woman has been. Even now a man may make a woman call out His name [for] it is union with Him she truly desires. Her flesh-and-blood husband, who is ever jealous of his own god, she accepts in His stead. Imagine God entering His own creation. Imagine him entering she who was His daughter! The first act of love therefore incestuous and profane [...]. Think on a phallus the thickness and length of a snake. Think on that the screams [to] have come forth to lose virginity thus. Take heed: kings keep to themselves the privilege to lie with the virgin bride on her wedding night. Who in his heart would believe the ruler of heaven would not also do so?

(Several lines illegible.)

[...] the myriad embraces, men whose bellies are covered with black wool, as of the lamb. Against mine, bearded faces have pressed. A sweeter fragrance than many (belongs to) the sweat of donkeys. Yea, ten times a hundred embraces have I felt, yet it is the Canaanite trader whose name has been carved upon a secret place beside my heart. The word [that] enfolds his being lies beneath the rising and falling of my breast. It is [a] second heart lying in thick darkness beside the first. It lies without movement. Yet does it burn as if I had swallowed a cup of flaming oil.

Under Cannaan's broad-faced moon, he stood beside me. In an alleyway of the island city of Tyre, he stood beside me. The sea god's voice in the winds folded the waves as [if] the sea's surface [were] bed linens for (a) sky yearning for rest. In the joining of mouths we exchanged breath. When he sent himself forth (into me), it was to such a depth as no man who buys my favors might aspire to reach.

Yet if he is found within these walls, the Canaanite trader whose face is forever marked by the art of the needleworker, the Gebalite who will not dwell in one place, his heart would they cut out and throw to the dogs who scavenge the streets of these cities.

** ** **

(The speaker has been identified as Zedebkiah.)

Day rouses itself from the cradle (in which) it is kept by Night. Below the world still lies Shamash, the Sun, yet is His coming foretold by darkness that draws back like a tide of the sea. From the east we approach the city. Upon asses we approach the city. The towers of stone are gray-blue shapes in the distance. No more solid seem they than the pale shadow cast by moonlight. Yea, they seem but scattered shadow and dust [as if] a gusting wind would sweep these towers from the sky, as if (they were) a withered mirage.

To this city I come as one unknown. As a foreigner I come to this city. For my name alone is enough to bring the blade from beneath the robes of my enemies. With me I bring half the Chaldean dozen of asses [to] bear the wares of distant Tyre and mighty Egypt. Asses bear the unmatched work of artisans in Palmyra. They bear the goods of the Sea People, who sail from an island no one has ever seen in the Great Sea. The Sea People who know the fish that calls as does a bird. The fish [which] breathes the air they have painted on their wares and stitched into their robes.

Wide travelled am I, for am I not called The Far-Ranging? The watch towers of Jericho are common sight to me. The palace of Pharaoh in Egypt with its cities of the dead have I seen. Inside strong-walled Erech, whose great avenues are the breadth of a plaza, have I walked. A mighty king of Erech is said [to have undertaken] a great journey and held counsel with Utnapishtim the

Faraway. Utnapishtim [who was] favored of the gods, survivor of the Flood. If you would hear the story of Erech's great king, conqueror of the Bull of Heaven, the scribes will speak to you from tablets of baked clay. Yea, the words of this great king are preserved upon hardened clay. Upon hardened clay are his thoughts carried forth from the tomb. So have the scribes read:

With my forehead to the forehead of my enemy I have stood. I have stood with the sweat of his brow running into my eye, its salt bitter upon my tongue. And so it is with this mystery. My double-bladed ax have I brought to bear upon it as if it were the skull of my foe. It is vanity, for I am offered an airy target. Its silence mocks me like drunken laughter. It is not to be dealt with by a blade of steel no matter how finely tempered. The blood of kings moves it not. This mystery [which] straddles life and death like a giant astride a gorge, it is not of [the] Earth, yet it is in the Earth and in the heavens. From the top of Erech's great ziggurat, have I seen the light of the distant stars shining through it.

And what is this mystery, oh great and long-dead king? What riddle disturbs him who saw the House of Dust, where the other kings of the Earth had put away their crowns forever? You saw them sitting in darkness and silence. For their hunger there was no meat but clay, and for their thirst, only dust. From that unhappy place you, the greatest of Erech's kings, returned to the living with breath still within you, the One Who Saw The Abyss.

Yet now even that great king, founder of mighty Erech of the strong walls, like all the kings before him, that king stands beside Ereshkigal, queen of the House of Dust, her face forever sour. What was it he wished to wash from his troubled mind with strong drink? Has this legendary king not also commanded to be written:

Mired in the boredom of hours spent drunk, I do little more than watch the smoke of incense rise. I watch the fragrant smoke rise while the dancing maidens dance. Winged fears and cravings beset me. Al-

ways I am beset by winged fears that give me cause to question the performance before me. Is there no more than this? Aye, to this city with its crowded streets and broad marketplaces, is there no more? The exchange of one good for another, the sound of coin on coin – is there not more than this?

How I long to bite into the mystery that lies behind all things. How I long to bite into this mystery as if it were well-roasted meat. How I long to let its juice run into my beard. Aye, let my fingers grow sticky and wet with what my teeth have drawn forth! I would learn the art that turns that which is beyond my grasp into flesh. That magic I would learn which turns the ungraspable into the forehead of my enemy. I would wrestle this great unknown if only hands could be laid upon it.

So the great king of Erech has written. And have not the Hebrew prophets said: Everything a man does is for his mouth, and still his soul is not satisfied?

So it is with my restless legs: I am become a common face [among] distant peoples. Unchanged I return to this city and my temple harlot. Yet Ashnanna, my wife, is not a league distant. In that city Ashnanna waits. So close are these cities of the plain, were one to draw breath, the other would exhale. If one were one to fall asleep, the other would dream.

In the city of Li'shilah, in the city of my harlot, I killed a man by the blade of my knife. Though [he was] a thief with his own blade, yet (his) blood relatives are sworn to seek my death. So must I enter the gates (seated) upon the last ass in my train. So [must I dress] in the tattered robes of a slave. So am I forced to be still and know the shame of one who has no freedom.

Through the gates of thick cedar I move forward with my head low. My head I must bear low, yet am I able to see beyond [the gate]. I see words written upon the city wall. It [is] yet another fool augury. *The days of thy city are numbered.*

** ** **

(The speaker has been identified as Ashnanna, the wife of Zedebkiah.)
In the distances between the cities of the plain, a storm gathers. Dogs cower in the streets. Dogs scent on the wind (that) the long-dead have been disturbed. What was buried and forgotten once more is exposed. At night their howling does not cease. Sleep is no longer like the smooth-flowing river but is unquiet, like the cataract which falls upon broken rock.

In the narrow place between houses, the cat, who is beloved of the Egyptians, who walks upon the wall that separates night from the slow coming of day, the cat lies in wait. Its green eyes are as two moons in the thick darkness. Lovers have they have seen and adulterers. The incestuous, the men who lie with other men as though with women, the unhappily born and unjustly buried child they have seen. The fears of the man who has waited until the Moon has risen to bury a dagger in the heart of another for silver – all this have they seen. While blood is spilled for coin, while bodies lie locked in carnal embrace, a great wind rises.

Fire and brimstone are foretold. Fire and brimstone, it is said, shall sweep these sister cities from the face of the Earth. Fire and brimstone shall be brought down upon our heads [so that] no man nor any beast within the city walls shall find mercy.

Women heavy with child, who are mothers thrice (before) shall find no succor. Children, whose eyes see the wonder of all things, shall not be spared. The man and woman who have only just come to know love shall die in each other's arms. The man and woman newly married will die on opposite sides of the city, calling one another's name.

To the One God I pray. If thy mercy shall not be gained [then] before star and moon have vanished from the sky, bring to me Zedebkiah.

For my husband I wait.

The strength and grace of his forehead [are] worthy of the carvings of the Egyptians. The fear brought on by the storm riven by lightning, this fear in me his face blunts. [It is] a face burned with heat and wind. The color of [a] baked clay vessel is his skin. His face is the brown of a clay vessel touched by red. A glowing ember has been placed at the heart of him and warmed the skin. The black of the black glass of the Canaanites is his hair. Many has been the time I have feared my heart lost. Like the stone thrown into the dug well, my heart I have feared lost. Yet always to me he returns.

Dots of black travel across his forehead. Dots make a strange pattern as if left by insects engaged in a dance to attract one another. The markings on the right are mirror to those on the left [as of] the wings of a butterfly. More beautiful and terrible to look upon the needleworker's art has made him. [It is] the soul's path to Sheol, he has said. By a magus it was divined. [Although] it seems no more than a pattern woven into a rug, it is a map for the dead.

Forever is he marked thus. No hand may remove what has been engraved thereon. When his soul rises above his body at death, it will look down upon his face. His soul will look down upon his face and understand wither it should go. For mine his soul shall wait. [The] shade of him who was Zedebkiah shall await me. If he dies second, the underworld mazes he will search for me, for he has promised not to abandon me even in death.

Though he has left my side, to me he returns [in] tokens of the distant lands he has seen. From Canaan figures of fired glass he brings. From Akkad he has brought a gazelle of hammered gold. From Shinar, earrings of silver that carry the glow of the moon. To me he brings bright stones for the jewelers art and shells of the sea swaddled in cloth. The smallest of these sea leavings I heap in a jar even as the Egyptians are said to store the organs of the dead. Would that I could keep his organs while he were yet alive! Heart and liver, stomach and intestine I would keep (that) he would always know his home. Hair I am left to gather. The trimmings of his nails and sand and coins and threads that settle from his robes, these I keep in a jar. This jar fits in my hand. As sacred as the clay vessel that holds the organs of the dead is this jar to me.

Evening has come and I take pleasure in our garden.

In our garden, at my feet, a great beetle contends with ants. He is strong but they are many. It is a burrowing beetle. His great humped back rises high above his head. I wish this beetle free of the ants, for he is like Zedebkiah beset by the many ills that befall the traveler. An ant holding firm one of the beetle's legs – is it any different from a band of thieves setting upon Zedebkiah's caravan? Another ant pulls at a black wing – is it any different from a dust storm causing Zedebkiah to lose his way? The beetle does not yield easily. Yet if the beetle is pulled to their mound – see how it is dragged backwards! – he will not escape. Though I favor the beetle, yet I shall not interfere. So may the powers choose to speak to us even through lowly insects.

Lord of Hosts, hear my prayer! Across the desolate places of this earth, carry my voice to Zedebkiah. Lord of Hosts, whisper into his ear.

Be with me, my husband, when the end is upon this city. Be with me in the time of the red lightning and I shall not fear God's wrath. Your return shall I await [though] this city is but smoldering cinders. With the ash my dust shall mingle. Yea, [if it is] cast to the winds, even then would I find you, Zedebkiah. At your sandaled feet I would settle. You would not know (this) dust was your wife. You would not know that this dust had been carried over the desolate places of the earth to be at your feet. You would not know that only in your memory is there that which was our home and she who was your wife.

Ah see, they have gone now, ants and beetle. But wither? Has the beetle escaped? Or is he pulled beneath the mound of his enemies?

Zedebkiah, who is my love, be with me in the time of the red lightning. Zedebkiah, be with Ashnanna.

** ** **

(Zedebkiah and Li'shilah converse. A narrator also enters the text--though briefly--at this point. The inconsistency suggests the text as a whole is the work of more than one author.)

"Come with me, Zedebkiah. Come below the streets, where we have gone many times, come to the shadows where we have kissed, our mouths ashen with the taste of the smoldering leaf."

Zedebkiah, whose body was full of desire, Zedebkiah said: "I have not forgotten. For do I not bear the scar of the time we coupled in the embers of a dead fire? A deeper love of the clear sky and the distant sea took hold of me. By a hot coal my flesh was burned. [Even] as the goat's flesh was consumed by flame was I burned. [Yet] the pain was lost in our coupling."

So narrow is this street [that] no more than two may walk abreast. Like a serpent it winds through the rankest of brothels. Among the snake charmer's tent, among the fortune teller's room lit by the hanging brazier, it winds its way. It is home to the gaming stalls where a man may lose a year's wages, the gaming stalls where a man may [so] lose his freedom. For the law makes a slave of him whose debt is not paid. Many are the doors on this street. Men who are like scorpions nest behind these doors, (and) many are the doors this street seeks out in its meandering course.

"With me you have descended these steps many times, Zede-bkiah. Many times you have descended into this place of pleasure, but you shall see a stranger sight than any before. For the corpse of a slave was found washed upon the shores of the Dead Sea in whose waters nothing can live. The waters have prevented corruption of the flesh. There is no corruption of the flesh but what has been done to him."

** ** **

(The body of the dead slave has been identified as the narrator.)
"[Of what] would Habiru speak? Of my mouth, which is open wide. Thus my mouth is locked in the stiffness of death. With burning incense have they filled it. Smoke pours forth from my gaping mouth. Blackened is the pit of my mouth that is become a widening hole. Yea, the fire smolders in the vault of my long-gone breath. Upon a bed of stone I lie. Women pleasing to look upon approach me. I see women pleasing to look upon, but my nether region does not awaken. The soul of this withered body is in Sheol already, and it does not rise to the callings flesh. What it is to vomit, to defecate and urinate, what it is to hunger for the flesh of the roasted beast, to grow mad with the thirst induced by the waters of the Dead Sea, these are distant memories. For numerous things they use this body: the mouth to burn incense, the stiff fingers to hang their wineskins, the shrunken abdomen to pillow their heads.

"An empty wineskin am I, only the smell of wine remains. Here [where] nightly their mouths run with wine. Nightly their mouths take in the smoke of strong herb. Nightly the smoke of their mouths crawls across my withered skin. I see the smiles of men as they lean over me. I see women, well-formed and long-haired and naked. No day or night is there here, only comings and goings.

"Here is come a new one whose face is marked by the needle-worker's art. He accompanies a temple harlot. Her beauty is of black hair and a fine narrow nose. Her beauty is made of the rounded cheekbones and black-lined eyes of the Egyptian cat. Yea, the highest of prices her beauty commands. Into the well of my heart she gazes. Into the depths of my heart she looks when she caresses my temple with a finger. Yet no voice have I. I have no voice to speak of the fatigue my limbs have felt, the exhilaration that once lifted my heart, the cold grip of death that is like bands of bronze tight around the body.

"The Temple Harlot is not alone in her caresses. A woman of hair as wild as the weed which the farmer uproots from his field, her hair is as gray as [the] sky from which rain falls, she sniffs as (would) a dog at my nether region. With fingers given over to leather, she caresses the lower region where the hair grows thick. With oil pressed from olives she has anointed me. My toe she has anointed with the juices of her body. On the stiffness of my toe she grew frenzied and cried out with joy. Would that I were alive! For pain and pleasure do not reside in the flesh but only move through it.

"With the pungent blood that comes of women during their moon-phase have I also been anointed. With this blood have I been marked across the forehead and chest. My leg has been gnawed upon. I shall be gnawed away and crumble to dust. With fire I shall be consumed. Then shall I truly know the void where no memory dwells, where no thought stirs. The void whence nothing is brought forth. Smoke pours from my mouth as if the fire of a soul yet burned within me. Image of comfort!

"Because they fear the void, also they fear the emptiness of my body. Thus have they given me smoke for breath. Thus do they exhaust themselves with fornication and pleasures of the flesh, wallowing in the fluids of their bodies. So have they replaced religion with worship of the flesh, one for the other. So have they sinned. Like beasts they fornicate on all fours in sight of one another. Yea, in full sight of God, the All-Seeing, all they fornicate. Breath and sweat make the moist heat between a woman's thighs in this den of pleasure.

"Silence they fear. Darkness they fear. For are these not the void? In their fear of the void, they are wont to sting their senses.

"Yea, fear me, you who would cast aside the Commandments and the Sabbath. Neither fear nor joy, sadness nor foreboding, dread nor gladness comes to my still heart, [which] is as the discarded pit of the date, hard and dried. I lie as driftwood. As I have lain on the Salt Sea, so now do I float. Though on a bed of stone I have come to rest, yet do I float on the thick darkness of an eternal night. Here I lie and float beneath a city lost to the pleasures of the flesh."

** ** **

(Zedebkiah is the speaker.)
She sleeps the sleep brought on by strong drink. Amid the smoke of the dried-and-ground plant which dulls the senses and causes laughter to flow like wine. The hours are become a sweet sap, thick and clouded, the hours are the amber of fired glass.

My blood, [which] had been heated even as oil over flame, my blood turbulent with desire, is calmed. My blood is as calm as the pool of standing water.

In blind arousal we took one another beside the dead slave whom they call Habiru. My hand was not deterred by the finery of her robes. In blind arousal my hand pulled away her robes. As pleasing to the touch as the petal of a flower is her skin. To me her mouth opened. As sweet as the flesh of ripened fruit is her mouth.

Li'shilah lowered herself upon me, Li'shilah took me into the sweetness of her mouth. Gazing upon Habiru, I regretted [that] his withered phallus would never again rise.

I lay upon my back gazing upon the walls. Upon the walls, plastered smooth, upon the walls bordered in blue tile, the hanging braziers cast their light. Paintings of Ba'al the dying-and-rising god, and his consort, Astarte, took strange life from the wavering light. I looked upon those walls and my head became like smoke. Li'shilah's mouth moved upon me and my head grew light. I saw Ba'al, who was perfectly formed, struggle with Yamm the water demon. No weapons had he, nor armor, nor clothing. Naked he grappled with the sea beast where the waters wash upon the shore. Into the deep water Yamm tried to pull mighty Ba'al, there to coil around him and drag him to the bottom. From many wounds blood flowed from Ba'al. Stung by the salty water in many wounds he struggled in the waves. His own salty waters poured from him. His hair was matted and crusted.

Upon my back I lay as if fallen on the field of battle. I lay upon the cushions and pillows piled upon the floor. My limbs grew as light as smoke. Li'shilah's mouth sought to draw my soul out of me, and it was because she gripped my thigh that I did not drift upwards.

She climbed atop me. As if I were an ass [she] mounted me. Twisting as (does) the flame in a disturbance of air, she lost herself amid her own cries. [In that] burning light Li'shilah was more beautiful than Astarte Herself. [I] rose up. (As do) oxen in the mud we rolled. Her legs she clasped about my waist. Pillows kept us from the floor's hard embrace. Her black hair heavy with sweat, her cries grew louder. Harsh as the summer wind that rustles among the husks of corn after the harvest was her voice. More breath was there than sound in my ear. As if in depth of prayer, Li'shilah, whispered for me to leave within her the seed of a child, but her voice was lost within a cry as [a] trail disappears into the wilderness.

I swayed as if at the edge of a dizzying height, yet I held back my seed to prolong our coupling.

At Habiru's feet we joined as animals join. At the dead slave's feet we understood greater reverence for life.

At last I spilled my seed upon her back. Upon herself she smeared it as if it were a costly oil. Then I felt upon me the hands [that] had shaped her. I knew [such hands] belonged to no earthly thing. Thus do I cast my lot with those who worship the gods.

Li'shilah no more mistakes the union of our bodies for love than the Hebrew mistakes an idol for the One God. We are no more than jackals scratching at one another. Like jackals who groom one another [with teeth] that graze the skin, we howl in the pleasure of the deep itch relieved. We are as jackals rolling in the heat and dust, biting each other. We flood our pains with shivering ecstasy. Soon enough we leave each other, as if (we were) bones cracked open and gnawed upon. As if no more than bones sucked dry and cast aside.

She sleeps the sleep brought on by strong drink.

Though I lie awake yet do I feel (as though) my spirit [has] crawled off to a shaded place [...] a snake in search of shadow. The Sun lies in darkness. In mighty Egypt it is said that the Sun descends by night and journeys the Underworld. In the Underworld, it is said, He does battle with a great snake. Each night He is the victor. Each morning He rises triumphant. Woe to the world should the Sun lose!

I wander the darkened streets [for] my lust [has] abated. Dry in mouth I wander. My mouth dry as if full of hot sand, I roam.

Homes lie atop shops as though this city were a hive. This city is a hive less orderly than those made by bees. There are stones that are ill-fitting and loose. Yet the city piles itself ever higher as the population grows. So close is the mason-work, a man may leap from roof to roof. A man may [make] his way through the whole quarter without touching the street.

In a narrow passage I ponder the rubble of earlier cities. In an alley I contemplate the old bones and forgotten possessions that lie beneath the streets. Out of windows, chamber pots are emptied. Here the smell of urine is heavy in the stone. The Moon itself [is] confined by the walls rising above me.

The infinite heavens appear to my upward gaze as but a small plot. From the bottom of this [alleyway], the sky is but a plot marked off in the fields where wheat grows. The city is worn with living. The city is worn with our breathing and sweating, with our fornicating and eating, with our urinating and defecating. Far above the bile left by human habitation, the gods [are] untouched. Far above this city, the gods float in purity among the stars.

What do They know of the hungers and fierce desires [that] have shaped me as the ceaseless flow of water shapes unyielding stone? As the endless scouring of desert wind smooths the most unyielding stone, am I shaped by longings I do not understand. I am two-thirds man and one-third beast. Ashnanna is she whom I call wife. My love for her never tires. As the star in a field of sky never goes out, so my love (for her) never tires. So are we married. Yet also is she married to the hours I spend with Li'shilah. To that within me which will not be yoked, is she also married. To that which refuses the harness is she also married.

I would it were as simple a thing as the walling in of a city!

In this gated city, a man is measured. Five times his height the walls lord over him that he may reach no higher. His hand's breadth is the distance he must keep when passing another in the street. The criminal speared at the foot of the wall, the wall whose scaling was beyond him, [so] was the boundary of his life marked off.

Within our walls we do not fear the darkness that comes with night. Marduk of the Babylonians has slain Tiamat, she who is

Night itself. Tiamat, who knew no restraint, whose form was terrible to look upon. Tiamat from whose belly sprang screaming beasts of goats' heads and fish tails, bird talons and lions' bodies, She who opposed the rule of the gods. With comfort we look upon the rising walls built to hold off the terrors Tiamat would vomit forth. With comfort do we look upon these walls of stone. Yet does not night undo all that we have built up by day?

** ** **

(Zedebkiah has returned to Li'shilah. They sleep for most of the day. Darkness has fallen prematurely.)

"This darkness comes early, like the calf overanxious to free itself of its mother belly. This darkness will hide me [that] I may return to my house."

Li'shilah gazed upon the heavens. Li'shilah looked upon the sky and said: "Not a star is there. There is nothing which shines in this sky."

"Here is the night foretold. What else did the prophets mean when they said neither moon nor star shall give off their light?"

Li'shilah shook her head. "A storm is come, nothing more."

Zedebkiah answered: "It may be a storm like no other."

"Why do you not fly then to Ashnanna?"

"Will you not leave this city also?"

Li'shilah spoke to him thus: "Once was I saved. Once I was cupped by a hand no eye could see. Yea as cunning as the air, [this hand] lurks behind the storm with all of its force [...]. It leaves behind not so much as [a] path in the dust. It is not heralded by fierce winds [...] So airy [is it] stars shine through it [...]. Yet do I believe in it. A second time will I trust myself to it.

"Go now to your wife. Do not fear for me. My life is as the money of a man in debt – though it is in my own hands, yet it does not belong to me."

Angered, Zedebkiah drew his brows together. Angered, Zedebkiah said: "I will throw you across the back of an ass. Across the back of an ass I will throw you as though you were a sack to be taken to market. For if you have not fled this city (by) the time of the red lightning, you are doomed with it."

** ** **

(A significant section of the text is missing. Zedebkiah has not returned home but has called upon two friends, Israfel and Gazram.)

The house of Israfel was full of the burnt-grain smell of freshly baked bread. Round loaves of bread [lay] upon the table. Wine there was also and cheese newly broken. Shavings of wood lay in corners, shavings of wood lay upon the floor, for Israfel was a carver by trade.

Zedebkiah sat at the table of Israfel with Gazram the Dwarf. Gazram who ate of the cheese and bread, and drank of the wine. A goat tethered in the street called for something it lacked. Nor were dogs quiet in the street, but they howled as if agitated.

Israfel placed food and wine before Zedebkiah, but he neither ate nor drank.

To Israfel Zedebkiah said: "There is no hunger within me that bread can satisfy. Nor is there any thirst within me which can be quenched by water or wine."

"Zedebkiah, whom I have not seen in the passing of a season, why have you come to your friend Israfel?"

Zedebkiah answered: "Israfel whose beard is ever in need of trimming, whose hair is ever matted but whose eyes are bright and dart as quickly as does the hummingbird, Israfel whose memory is a plain of clay stamped by the reed of the scribe, is it not you who remember the raid of the Philistines and the tearing down of the southern wall? Is it not you who lived through the drought that withered the fields and left the breasts of women shriveled so that the children cried for milk? Have you not also heard the wandering poets who play music and sing for kings, and do you not swim in knowledge as fish swim beneath the waves? Have you not gathered the images of many gods, of Enlil who is the lord of the firmament over Shinar, of Thoth, the bird-headed god of the Egyptians, of Ba'al Who-Is-Beautiful-To-Look-Upon among the Canaanites, of Marduk whose monument towers six times a man's height in the plaza of mighty Babylon? The ways and worship of these gods are known to you.

"Israfel whose staff I used to pull myself up when my infant legs were too weak to stand upon, who took me to the gaming houses, who made me wise in the ways of men and took me also to the brothels to learn the ways of women, I ask you what is this night of early darkness and sky smooth with cloud?"

Israfel answered, "Zedebkiah, whose face in this city is enough to uplift my heart, I tell you I do not know."

Gazram the Dwarf, who drank wine from a clay jar, said: "Have you never before seen a storm approach?"

The words of Gazram the Dwarf, whose head came only to Zedebkiah's shoulder, were of little account to Zedebkiah. Gazram's words went unheeded, for Gazram was known to drink more of beer and wine than of water.

"Yet may this not be the night of which the prophets spoke? The long-dead are disturbed. Dogs are not quiet in the street. My own beasts of burden grow restless."

Israfel, who was of great girth, who bore a staff though he was (as) sturdy as the caravan mule, Israfel said: "It may be."

"Then will you give your word to go to Li'shilah and show her safe passage beyond the walls before the skies are stricken?"

Israfel nodded. "So shall it be done."

Gazram the Dwarf scratched at his black beard. It was known that Gazram, who consumed beer and wine nightly, desired Zedebkiah's wife for his own. Was he not betrayed by his gaze when Ashnanna was before him? Did his looks not revealed all that was in his heart? Gazram asked, "What of Ashnanna?"

Zedebkiah replied: "I go to Ashnanna now."

Zedebkiah the Far-Ranging said no more [but] embraced Israfel the Staff-Bearer. Saying no more, he entered the street.

The wind had begun to moan as does the soldier who grasps at the spear that has lodged in his chest. In the narrow street a beggar held out his hand. The beggar held out a hand with but three fingers.

To him Zedebkiah said: "You have I seen more than once upon my many returns to this city. A silver coin, then, for your three fingers to close upon."

The Beggar of Three Fingers bowed, but made no word. The three-fingered beggar made his way through the street while the wind heaped sand carried from the wilderness against doorways.

** ** **

(The speaker is Hezacham, a seer and friend of Li'shilah.)

"Thou shalt not lie with a man as with a woman, for it is an abomination." So say the self-righteous. Those who would teach the word of the One God. Yet what do they know of His will? Hezacham has seen when they have not. Hezacham foresaw the drought of three seasons ago. Hezacham prophecied the coming of the tribes during the Moon of Harvest. Now Hezacham has seen the end of this city in fire. The self-righteous, those swollen with importance like the river after the summer rains, they will say it is such as I [who] brought down such wrath from the heavens.

To hold off the wilderness, did we not raise a city? Yet is there not also within each man some of the beast of the field? Is [the wilderness] in each man not held back by walls made not of stone, but by the laws of the rulers? By the laws of the rulers and the pronouncements of the priests a man's heart constrained.

Evil these twin cities hold, yea, it is so. Yet it is not the men who lie with other men, nor the fornication of nobles with whores. Here is only the bestial appetite sated. In the infant left upon the refuse heaps, there lies wickedness. Yea, in the taking of life in exchange for coin, there lies wickedness. He who wears the robes of the self-righteous yet whose heart is black, this man who is full of sin. He who calls for punishment for what he himself has done, he is most wicked.

[...s]earch the shadows in this city. All that hides from the Sun lies in the shadow of a man.

(Several lines obscure).

Yea, we shall burn for our trespasses. By fire the dagger-wound [shall be] cleansed. Across the flat rooftops the assassin flees, yet he will not escape. By burning sulfur shall he be cleansed.

To Li'shilah I go now, for the woman [whom] she seeks I have found. Yea, of the numberless sinners who inhabit the cities of the plain, of numerous sinners who have wrought its end, I have at last seen the Woman-Of-The-Coiled-Snake.

** ** **

(The speaker is an angel.)

When an angel speaks, it is nothing for the ear but echoes in the cavern of the soul. From the Great Sea of Darkness on which wakefulness floats, an angel raises images in dream. Li'shilah, favored of the gods – for who has greater need of them than the child abandoned? Li'shilah, you spurn us. Yea, many is the blasphemy to have issued from your well-formed mouth. Yet were you not provided for? Who was it that brought your mother to a woman whose womb was barren, to a man and wife who would raise you in the warmth of their hearts?

The day of reckoning for your city is at hand. The evil done on the Earth is [what] man does to man, [what] woman does to woman. Have I not led Li'shilah away from Evil? Have I not lain before her all that is good? But it is for her to stretch forth her hand. Look closely, for an angel's hand may be missing fingers.

Yet so insolent have the citizens grown that they did not humble themselves before me, before a servant of the gods they did not humble themselves. Citizens of the plain beware! Look long upon that which you love, for these things you shall not see again.

** ** **

(Zedebkiah approaches his home.)

The smell of the storm that carries lightning within it filled Zedebkiah's nostrils, the taste of copper was in his mouth. What hovered in the air brought forth howling from the cat, [i]t caused the ass to bray and shake its head. So close to his home was Zedebkiah [that] he saw the light from the lamp burning within. So close was he that he saw Ashnanna's shadow pass before the lighted window.

Zedebkiah spoke: "I am returned to she who is rain to the thirsting fields and rest to the weary traveller, she who is light to the darkness everlasting. Yet the wind is cold and dry that moves across the plains of my heart. My soul writhes like a snake thrown upon coals. What am I that I have lain in Li'shilah's bed after many leagues of dust and weariness, burning sun and biting wind?

After many days of living upon food that is dry as dust, the withered fig and the wrinkled date, upon strips of meat as leathery as the sandal, what am I that I have not returned until now to she who waits for me with love in her heart?

"The floating glow of fireflies is not more beautiful than she. The fireflies, which are the wandering stars of evening, have not greater beauty than she. Her breath I feel within [me] when the city is before me, when the city is gray and blue in the pale light of the breaking day [...] when the city is not firm but wavers on the horizon as though it is soon to vanish.

"Just as the hot eye of heaven [must] set at the end of the day [and] travel the darkness of the Underworld, so the star of wakefulness in a man descends when the gates to the Land of Sleep open. [He] enters into the darkness which will one day become the Land of the Dead. The sleeping and the dead, how alike they are. [Each] night is preparation for travels in the netherworld. So a man must navigate the perils of his dreams [for] one day, when he travels the Land of the Dead, these (perils) will be demons. [During my] sojourns in foreign places, Ashnanna is the rising of a second moon. A second moon, Ashnanna lights the Land of Sleep, Ashnanna scatters shadows.

Zedebkiah observed the peace of his home. Unwilling to disturb the peace of his house, he stood unmoving.

"Ashnanna, my days of journeying between distant places are at an end. Have I not purchased land for a new dwelling in Canaan? Have I not secured land atop a steepness that looks out upon the Great Sea? [It is] like the brow of a god rising from the Earth. It is like a god gathering His form as He ascends. It is near the city of Gebal, the place of my birth. Near Gebal shall I trade with the merchants in the port. My legs shall no longer stray. My legs will be at rest in our house-that-looks-upon-the-sea.

From the columned terraces of our house, we shall watch

ships diminish upon the horizon. Here at last I shall lay to rest all that is fierce in my nature [...] We shall have the harvest of the sea, what is reaped by the fisherman's net. I shall be free of the noose of [the] men who seek my blood, the gamers and assassins, [those] who loan coin for profit.

"To Li'shilah I shall not return, nor leave word of our house-that-looks-upon-the-sea.

"This night shall purge me of all that is evil. In the fires of this night, all (that is) within me but refuses to obey me shall burn.

"Ashnanna, in sight of the sea we shall bring forth a child. We shall walk upon the very Beginnings [?], the edge of the Blue Deep, with our child. [He] shall be delighted by the strange and wondrous things which are cast up by the waters. Our child shall know only the comfort of his mother's arms and the salted breeze that moves unceasingly across the face of the Blue Deep."

Thus spoke Zebebkiah. Yet he was kept from his long-suffering wife, Ashnanna, and Ashnanna was kept from her far-ranging husband, for he was struck upon the head. Zedebkiah received a blow upon the head, and darkness covered his eyes.

** ** **

In a Land of Sleep darker than any he had ever visited, Zedebkiah dwelt. In a Land of Sleep with neither moon nor star, Zedebkiah lay.

At last the mists before his eyes began to lift. Yet nothing made itself clear [for] the ground was moving. Upon the paving stones he saw only hooves. Only hooves he saw for he was laid across the back of a donkey as though (he were) a sack of grain. Of the man leading the donkey he saw only sandaled feet. The odor that came of him was of the beggar's quarter. [It was] the odor of long fermentation. Coarse black hair grew upon the legs. The woolen tunic was of a color tainted with filth. The tunic was heavy with mud and the leavings of animals.

The hands of Zedebkiah were bound – tight are the bonds made of thongs of leather! His stomach was in turmoil. Yet the pain in his head surpassed the wretchedness of his stomach, the twisting of his bowels. His cheek was sticky as with honey. Old was the taste of blood in his mouth.

Bent upon the back of the donkey, Zedebkiah the Far-Ranging could raise up his head only with great pain. A single eye he saw, a single eye clouded over as is the Moon on certain nights. A scar as straight as the knife blade, above and below [the eye] was the scar he saw. Then Zedebkiah knew Ramaz, Ramaz who was forever scarred and the sight put out in his right eye. Many names had he: Ramaz-Of-The-Clouded-Eye, Ramaz-Whose-Dagger-Is-Purchased-For-Coins, Desecrater-of-Tombs, Ramaz Extractor-of-Teeth.

Zedebkiah was afraid [for] it was said Ramaz was a worshipper of demons, it was said he used teeth in his sorcery. For as teeth are rooted strongly to the jaw, so it was (when) Ramaz wished a spell to take strong hold, he offered (the) white dust of ground teeth to his demons. So would Ramaz seek to cause a man's heart to wither, so would he put a poison into his heart and lodge [it] there forever.

"You are not dead, Zedebkiah, for he who has sent me desires you to pay the blood money for Heroam's death. Yet shall I have your teeth for my own."

Ramaz spoke but required no answer. He spoke to Zedebkiah as if to the boundary stone between nations.

No answer did Zedebkiah make, nor did he lift his head.

Ramaz's sandals no longer moved. He-Of-The-Clouded-Eye stood as still as a boundary stone between lands. His frayed tunic hung from his body as a curtain hangs between rooms. His head was lifted and the skies he observed. Ramaz gazed up at the sky.

With great effort [for] his neck was stiff, with great effort for he was in great pain, Zedebkiah looked upon the heavens. The clouds had departed – and behold! No star was there nor the Moon. There was only blackness, only darkness there was, smooth and unending.

** ** **

(Hezacham has come for L'shilah, but she refuses to leave the city until she has confronted her mother.)
"Ah Hezacham, the brothels frequented by seafarers and those who wander the dusty land have I searched these many years. The crowded marketplaces and the smoke-filled dens of iniquity have I also sought out. How am I now to leave until I have seen her?"

Hezacham, who wore bracelets of gold upon either arm, whose ears were pierced by golden hoops, Hezacham who was fond of wrought necklaces and precious stones, said: "Even tonight I have seen her in her miserable hut, Li'Shilah. He who guards the gate to sleep has pointed his finger at her [...]. I have stood beside [your mother] as she swept straw and dung. Let her be forgotten! For by morning this city shall be no more. Woman who is as obstinate as the wild ass, look to the sky. Is it not as black as the First Darkness? Why do you not tremble before the wrath of the All-Mighty? Why do you tempt His anger?"

Li'shilah stretched forth her hand. She put her finger to a stone in the golden necklace Hezacham wore. To him she said: "On such a night is it fitting I find my mother. Let us go to her farmer's hut. Did you not say it lies beyond the walls? That it lies beyond the boundary of the city? Who can say but that is distance enough from the city?"

"Li'shilah, these many years have I known you, these many years have I loved you. My love for you is a fire that does not burn. [It] is as (the) love for a sister [...]. For you know that a woman's body stirs no desire within me. Have I not always loved you thus?"

Li'shilah answered: "You have."

"Have I not prevented evil from entering your chambers? Was it not Hezacham who kept the vilest of the temple (patrons) from you? Did Hezacham not show you (how) a noble would pay a hundredfold for such as you? Did you not suck from Hezacham as from a mother, until you needed milk no longer?"

Li'shilah nodded: "These many years have I understood [that] of all the loves I have known, yours is the purest."

"Will you not heed me now? Will you not abandon these cities to their doom?"

"Hezacham, I cannot." Li'shilah seized his wrist as if the hand (above it) were the head of a snake poised to strike. "Accompany me, Hezacham, or flee from this city. I do not fear the wrath of the Hebrew god. I go now to a farmer's hut beyond the city walls. Choose as you will. I will know why motherhood has fallen to such as you."

** ** **

(Some dozen lines are missing. Hezacham is not able to dissuade Li'shilah from going to her mother. Upon arriving, Li'shilah ties her mother to a post meant for tethering animals. Li'shilah is the first speaker.)

"years...

[...in] your looks, [though] your hair is as badly kept as the field that lies fallow, though your hair is gray with age and your face slack with the wear of years, even now do I see mine. Mother, you who call yourself Galia, you who left me to the city, so are you now tied to its fate. You shall bear witness."

Upon her knees, Galia was as low as the dirt, as low as dung. Galia, dressed in worn sackcloth, she pleaded with Li'shilah: "My child, free me from my bonds! I shall tell you all, from beginning to end, omitting nothing. I shall be your slave, a servant in your house shall I be if only you will loosen my bonds."

Li'shilah, whose hair was scented with oil, who was dressed in the white pleated cloth of the Egyptians, looked down upon Galia without pity. "You who left me without a mother nor any ancestor's tomb to venerate, you shall remain as you are until you have spoken."

The wind was full of the heat of the desert. Like the blast of air from inside the potter's oven, the potter's oven that fires the wet flesh of the earth like unto stone, this wind made Li'shilah's heart hard.

"Daughter who is flesh of my flesh, bone of my bone, forgive me. Hardly a child was I when you swelled within me. No father had I but him who used me as if I were his wife even from the time I came only to his waist. I cared nothing for what was to become of me – how could I care for another? Forgive me, for I commended you to the hands of a childless couple, I commended you to the mercy of the Lord of Hosts.

Li'shilah, who wore proud rings – of fine gold were her rings, fine gold (set) with precious stones – Li'shilah made no answer.

The nails of Galia's fingers were broken and full of earth. Upon her fingers only a copper band there was marking her bond to a farmer. To her daughter Galia spoke: "My child, you were not abandoned. Though I kept myself unknown, still I sent copper and silver so that you were robed. In secret I sent copper and silver to keep the gnawing emptiness from your belly."

Li'shilah stood over her mother who was bound to the earth, whose knees were in the dirt. To her Li'shilah said: "And still, these many years later, you have not sought me out, you have never shown yourself. Even the beast of the field shows affection to its offsrping."

"My shame burns ever brighter, my child."

"These many years have I known you were a whore of the street, for what temple would have you? My father was no more than a sack of coins. You would not know him were you to lie with him again. Any (one) of a dozen men is he."

Galia answered: "It is not so. A merchant of Gebal your father was. He alone was my consort. Even as I abandoned you, so he abandoned me before you were born."

"From Gebal?"

"To Gebal he returned. A wife he took in Gebal, who bore him a son. Hamurab was your father called. No more than this do I know of him."

Li'Shilah gazed upon Hezacham, but Hezacham answered with silence. To her mother Li'Shilah spoke: "I know Hamurab of Gebal."

"Has he come to you in the temple?"

"To what you abhor you left me, you who bestowed upon me no bloodline."

"My child, forgive me."

"I know of him. Yea, through the temples, through the intimacies of the flesh I know him."

"Ah, that you should have lain with your father!"

"Only through the son do I know the father, through the flesh of his flesh. It is his son who has known me, who has known all the passageways of my body."

No words went forth into the silence. Nor was there any wind heavy with the heat of the season, for it had stopped. Only the everlasting call of insects there was, the call of insects to one another in the darkness.

A tongue of flame flicked across the sky, and day dawned, false and brief.

Hezacham, whose voice wavered, said: "It is the time of the red lightning."

Again the sky flashed with bright anger, and they saw two riders. Two riders they saw, seated upon asses.

Li'shilah said: "Here are Israfel the Staff-Bearer and Gazram the Dwarf."

Gazram, who was drunk with wine, spoke: "Greetings, O Hezacham, whose anus is flung wide open like the gates of the city and admits men of all lands."

Hezacham answered him: "Greetings, O Gazram, whose breath could drop the bird from its perch and wilt even the sturdy tree. May the wind bear your blood to places undisclosed."

Li'shilah asked: "How is it that you have found your way here?"

Israfel answered: "Who but Hezacham could know this place? Who but Israfel could Hazacham trust with what he knows? Let that be. It is the time of the red lightning. We must go."

"I shall stay and my mother beside me. If the ruin stretches beyond the city walls, let it be so."

Li'shilah bent down to take her mother's face in her hands.

Close to her mother's face she placed her own. A snake of finely wrought gold that coiled around Li'shilah's arm gazed with ruby eyes. As cold as this ruby gaze was the kiss which Li'shilah gave her mother.

Israfel climbed down from upon his ass, saying: "Li'Shilah, well you know Israfel is a man of his word. My word I have given to Zedebkiah to find haven for you."

Li'shilah spoke to Israfel. "Ah Zedebkiah, husband of Ashnanna, he has not forgotten she who is slave to his desires [...] might have been were it not for [...]"

(The text breaks off here and what follows is badly damaged.)

** ** **

Ramaz turned away from the unbroken blackness of the sky, Ramaz started again for his destination.

Two beggars seeking coins beset him. Two beggars seeking coins cast their eyes down and held their hands out.

To them he said: "Do you not recognize Ramaz with his clouded eye? Why do you ask for coins when I show neither pity nor charity to the beggar?"

Still the beggars plucked at his robes, still they held out their hands and whined for copper and pity.

Ramaz lifted a foot against one of the beggars, in anger he kicked one of them.

Groaning, the beggar fell to his side and covered his head.

To him Ramaz said: "A curse upon you. May the disease which rots the flesh take your body. May you be exiled from this city and wander the plains with neither rest nor destination."

Yet even as Ramaz attacked the beggars, Zedebkiah felt his bonds cut. Before him the knife passed, before him passed a hand that had but three fingers.

Greatly agitated, Ramaz cried: "Begone!"

The beggars withdrew in the unwilling manner of shades unwilling to be on their way to Sheol. So the beggars returned to the folds of the city.

Free of his bonds, Zedebkiah gathered his strength [for] he feared his legs would be weak. Zedebkiah was afraid his legs would fail him. With the stealth of the creeping cat, Zedebkiah slipped from the saddle. Quietly he dropped to the ground.

Yet He-Whose-Dagger-Is-Purchased-For-Coin stopped after seven paces. In only seven strides Ramaz understood Zedebkiah had deceived him. Thwarted, he cried out in anger, yet did he waver, for he was loath to leave his donkey.

To the narrow places of the city Zedebkiah fled [though] his legs (were) uncertain beneath him, though the darkness was confusing [to] his weary eyes. He mounted a flight of stairs, and his head swayed as though he looked down from the height of a mountaintop. Dizzy, he entered an open gate, a courtyard full of scattered stones he entered. Zedebkiah reached for a stone, upon a stone his hand closed, and he hid himself behind a wall of the courtyard.

He tried to still his breath, for his breath came hard, and he feared the sound of it. He heard the footsteps of pursuit, he heard Ramaz coming up the stairway. With all of the strength remaining to him, Zedebkiah, who had hidden himself behind a wall, struck Ramaz. He-Of-The-Clouded-Eye fell to the earth unmoving. Ramaz lay still.

Zedebkiah returned to the street from which he had come. The donkey belonging to Ramaz had not wandered. Zedebkiah mounted the donkey and found his way through the city.

Revelers cavorted in the street. The voices of revelers he heard, for what was this black sky compared to the sack of coins held aloft by the gamer who had won? What is there to him but the game? What but wine to the drunkard? To the lecher, the prostitute?

Through the dark streets Zedebkiah rode until he had returned to his house.

To him Ashnanna ran, his wife ran to him. "At last you are come home. Have I not waited? How could it be otherwise?"

Zedebkiah slid from the donkey.

"Ah, but you bleed."

Ashnanna held Zedebkiah, Ashnanna kept him from falling. A soothing came to him as to one who sinks into the depths of sleep. Though he was in the arms of Ashnanna yet he felt himself immersed in the warm salty waters of the Blue Deep. He was in the depth of waters where the sunlight is broken into fragments like the shattered pot. With difficulty he found his voice, saying, "We must go."

Ashnanna answered: "Our horses I have made ready. What is most precious to us I have laid upon their backs."

Zedebkiah looked to the sky, studying it as one who tracks animals in the field. To Ashnanna, his wife, to her he said: "We will have a house near the sea."

Lightning flashed, and they saw that the anger of God was the color of fire.

** ** **

(Israfel has left with Li'Shilah and Hezacham. Gazram, for reasons that are unclear, stays. Li'Shilah's mother has been left behind also, probably as punishment for abandoning Li'shilah as an infant. She pleas with Gazram, who, in his drunken stupor, does not seem to realize the seriousness of the situation.)

[Galia s]aid to Gazram: "Will you not loose me from my bonds?"

Gazram gazed to the south. [The] towers upon the city walls came forward out of the shadow, beneath the sky that was riven by fiery lightning the towers came forward. Gazram drank from a wineskin. "So angry is the Lord that he will leave an entire city as ash. No mercy has He for the wicked. No mercy has He [for those] who walk the same streets as the wicked."

Galia pleaded with Gazram: "Watch if you will, yet will you not cut me free of this restraining leather? I beg of you, loose my bonds."

Gazram spoke of other things: "Shall this red lightning smite the cities of the plain? Shall the Earth itself open up and swallow them? Shall we not be among those who watch? It is a tale to be told among travelers for a thousand years."

"I beg of you! Take what you will, only untie what holds me like a goat!"

Gazram squeezed the wineskin until no drop flowed from it. Casting it at his feet he stood over her, for she was still upon her knees. "Farmer's wife, you were once a harlot. Be so again."

He drew aside his garment and his member was raised and swollen. As Gazram's hands were too large for his stature, so too was the staff that emerged from his loins. As badly formed as the root of a tree, so too was it thick. Taking her hair in his hand, he said: "Though you are old, yet you were once pleasing to look upon." So saying, Gazram entered her mouth.

No protest did she make but did as she was bade, as she had done when she took the silver of unknown men and fornicated. Ever deeper Gazram pushed into her mouth, yet he was not satisfied, for the wine had dulled his arousal. Though she was faithful to his wishes, though she allowed him to use her mouth as if it were the flower of her thighs, which holds the scent of the sea, yet he did not expel his seed.

She could not cry out for her mouth was closed upon Gazram's root, yet it was the time of the red lightning and she feared for her life.

To her Gazram said: "The wine has heated my desires, yet numbed my senses."

He withdrew from her mouth and lifted the sackcloth that covered her.

A false day passed in the time it takes for a bird to beat its wings.

She raised herself up that he might enter her.

He saw that her hips had grown broad. Rounded and weighty her hips had grown, yet there was firmness still. As if she were a beast of the field he entered her and she cried out. Her face [was] near to the dust and (the) dried leavings of animals. The sounds of one in pain she made.

Gazram grunted like the ox who pulls the plow, he labored at the task so that his sweat fell in the dust. His desires unabated, Gazram said to her: "By your third orifice shall I take you."

"Do not tarry, my lord," Galia pleaded. "I beg you."

With the very juices that flowed from between her legs did he annoint her anus. Spreading wide her haunches, he thrust his man-root into the smallest of the gates by which a man may enter a woman. A great cry she let out, Galia cried out as if she were again giving birth.

To her Gazram said: "Squawk if you will, for such is the lot of a woman who has lived by harlotry and broken the bond that ties mother to daughter." And with great zeal he thrust himself forward so that her cheek lay in the dirt. On her knees she moaned while Gazram plundered the treasure of her forbidden portal and grew frenzied with greed.

Gazram's head swam. He had reached dizzying heights. "Mother of Li'shilah," he said, "the heavens move within me."

Galia answered: "Come forth then. Spill your libation."

With a sigh Gazram came forth. Sighing, he flooded her with his warm seed.

"Are you not satisfied, my lord? Will you not cut me loose now?"

Still Gazram shivered, his head tilting up to the roiling sky.

"My lord?"

He collected his wits and covered himself.

"Let us away from here." Gazram found his dagger and cut the leather that held Galia fast.

He mounted his donkey and reached out his hand to Galia, to Galia he offered his hand.

The horizon grew [as] bright as if the hot eye of the firmament had risen once more. Gazram and Galia saw that the sky above the city was in an agony of burning.

** ** **

(Li'shilah, Israfel, and Hezacham witness the destruction of the cities from a distance.)

The burning finger of God touched each of the sister cities, arcs of fire reached out for the cities. As red as blood and as bright as the sun was the destruction. Li'shilah could look no more upon the sight. Hezacham stood beside her as one blinded.

Bearing the heat of the forge, a fierce wind swept from the place of destruction. In it lay the black ash of timber, the powder of bones ground as finely as incense, the shrieks and fear of the wicked, the prayers of the old and helpless, the cries of the mother and the innocent child – all was made foul with sulfur. Yea, the rankest stench that rises from the swamps to the east could not equal the reek of that evil wind.

Li'shilah and Hezacham turned from the hot ash and sand, they shut their eyes from the dust and ground bones. They fell upon their knees and covered themselves. Israfel's long robes snapped about him in the howling wind. His great weight anchored him. He stood as does the column of stone. His robes flying like battle standards, he stood.

At last the wind died, the wind diminished to a stirring of the air. As dust settles after a horse has passed, so the silence fell about them.

Israfel looked into the distance. "The cities are no more."

The sky had become black once more. Smooth and black was the sky. To the east there was a glow like the dawn, but it was the cities become as embers. To the east they lay in smoldering ruin. Coiling as if in torment, a great column of smoke rose to the sky.

Israfel held his staff aloft, for its copper bindings were aglow. "It is Gazram's soul. He has no other way to bid us farewell."

Li'shilah gasped in wonder at the light ringing the copperbound staff. Yet it did not last. The staff of wood and hammered copper soon became dull.

"Gone is the light," Israfel said. "It is on its way to Sheol."

And there was neither sound, nor wind. There was only a great void in which Israfel nor Hezacham nor Li'shilah moved. Nor would the beasts they had brought with them stir.

"Ah, but see." Lishilah pointed to the east. "Are there not two riders approaching?"

risen [...] shades tormented [...] the hot ashes [...].

(The rest of the section is too badly damaged to decipher.)

** ** **

(The narrator is impossible to identify. It has been suggested that the speaker is Zedebkiah, although this is conjecture based mostly upon stylistic considerations. Israfel is more likely the speaker.)

[...] scores of generations beyond the passing of this one shall wonder over these vanished cities. Stone laid upon stone with an eye to iniquity, so these cities were built. The din of their marketplaces are heard only in idle talk. It will not be certain whether or not they were built by human hands or (existed) only in tales. It will not be certain whether or not they were destroyed by God or an invading army. It will not be known whether their shapes were built by stonewrights or fashioned by wind among clouds. Who will set down the story of these two cities? Who will believe it? Their walls cast no more shadows, no one passes through their gates. What are these cities now but a strange dream a man forgets by the light of day? And yet all cities to come shall be built upon the memory of these that never were.

(The next three lines are illegible.)

And these themselves were built upon the memory of the far-off cities to the east and south, the cities whose foundations were laid by the Seven Sages, which shall also lie in dust.

[A] mirror held up to a mirror – [even as] man is held up to God – echoes again and again in the cavernous eye of the Infinite. [...] no more than the curving [de]sign [...] do we see [...] the snaking tattoo [...]

And so [it is].

AFTERWORD & POST SCRIPT TO ADRIFT IN A VANISHING CITY

Unlike most works of fiction, which begin with a familiar disclaimer, this one ends with more or less the opposite intent. The fact is, many of the characters closely resemble persons both living and dead. Notable among the living are Millo Farneti, Earl Kukovich, and Stevie (the Duke of) Pallucca. Lyman Kispaugh (that's the correct spelling) is one of those gone to the Kansas earth whom I've resurrected in fiction. It is, however, important to point out that while the characters may in places be reasonable replicas of their real-life counterparts, in others I've added or subtracted according to what the story called for. (Lyman was a stick-cross when I found 'im – a single black & white photograph & some hearsay. I decked him out in shirt & pants and stuffed him with straw, so maybe he's just a scarecrow of what he was in life, but close enough you'd probably recognize 'im.) And none of the stories actually happened as I've told it although there are *incidents* that did occur – the way the Pan Club got its name for example. Even here, however, I changed the sign from incandescent to neon.

As I implied, a good number of the places I've written about either have existed or still do, such as the Pan Club (unfortunately slated for the wrecking ball, last I heard, after a fire), Gutteridge Pharmacy, Pallucca's Market, Bartelli's Blue Goose Bar, and PiCCo (the building remains but it has been closed for years, mainly – I suspect – due to the presence of a more centrally located Dairy Queen). Other sites – such as Farley's Tavern and Carol's Corner Café – are amalgams of similar establishments I've seen in the Midwest (primarily Otto's Café & The 311 Club, both in Pittsburg).

The incidents, rumored history, and people who found their way into this collection were to me much like found objects, and what I've tried to do is put them in a kind of scrapbook … and painted in the background.

On July 2, 2008, Stephen R. Pallucca died of a heart attack at the age of 57. He was the last of the Frontenac/Pittsburg locals to lend his name to a character in these stories.

Earl Kukovich, a member of the same club, died of cancer around 2000 (after the book came out, Stevie told me, Earl took a yellow marker and highlighted every line in which he was mentioned). Earl, whose whole life had been sketchy, loaded with misinformation, and self-serving legend, was probably in his sixties.

Millo Farneti died of heart failure in the winter of 2004. He was found on the lawn of the Sacred Heart Catholic Church on Mckay Street on the morning of January 31. Millo survived the longest – 83 years.

Eduardo Lerma, whom I had met in Mexico City, died well before the collection was even published. I learned of his death via a long-distance phone call I had made to El Congreso (the real name of the hotel where he had lived). I took the loss all the harder, knowing Eduardo would never read about himself or ever realize how much he'd been in my thoughts in the years since I'd met him.

In August of 2014, my wife, Neslihan, and I stopped in the Pittsburg-Frontenac area because of a pair of sneakers Stevie had given me in spring of 2006, which was the last time I'd seen him. They were well past their expiration date, but I couldn't bring myself to throw them out, so we drove half way across the country and put the sneakers on Stevie's grave with a note – laminated with packing tape and tied to a lace – explaining their significance.

A couple of days later, Tom Moody, who had been a close friend of Stevie's, took me (and our wives) to the lot where the Pan Club had once been. Dusk deepened nearly to night by then, I didn't see the slightest evidence that the bar had ever been there.

Of the people I had hung out with in Frontenac, only Tom and Kenny Krumsick were still around – and Kenny really only visited Frontenac as his job, which often kept him on the road, permitted. Mostly Books in Pittsburg, a grand little bookstore I always rummaged through when in town, was boarded up. The owner, whom I had known only as Roger, had died, and the windows of the store had been nailed over with plywood sheets – all painted chocolate brown. Pallucca's Market in Frontenac, once a supermarket with an impressive Italian import section, had rented out three quarters of its space to a used-furniture shop and operated out of the back, mostly as a deli. Of Bartelli's Blue Goose Bar, which had been a standing ruin the first time I had visited Frontenac in 1985, not one red brick remained. Millo had had a key to the place and stored his manuscripts in a filing cabinet that stood a little surreally amid the rubble inside. Most of the building's roof was already gone – some of it was on the floor – though rafters still notched sky. The Blue Goose was eventually leveled for parking-lot space back when Pallucca's had been a good deal busier.

The last time I visited Stevie, I think he was at peace with himself and how his life had settled out; he'd found equilibrium. He'd made a daily routine of riding for miles on an old-time, heavy-framed bike with chubby, white-walled tires – permanently borrowed from Millo. Fire-engine red, of course. The plaque on Stevie's gravestone, which lies flat as a granite trapdoor in the grass, has a raised image of a guy on a bicycle in remembrance of Stevie's habitual pedaling. The bike, Tom told me, now hangs in Bear Cub's garage – Bear Cub being the nickname of one of Stevie's oldest friends. (Sidebar: Lara Preston, a friend of mine from nearby Joplin, MO, took Neslihan and me to dinner the same day we left my sneakers with Stevie. I asked for a beer instead of an appetizer. The waitress offered the usual suspects, none of which

I was in the mood for, along with one called Fat Tire. I had to ask twice because it didn't sound like a name for a beer. "Okay," I said, "I'll try that one." It turned out to be a Belgian brew, and on the label was a red bicycle almost identical to Stevie's.)

A favorite topic of conversation for Stevie back in 2006 was a t-shirt he had designed: BUllSHit (he was not a fan of George W.). If he had ever marketed it, he probably would have had his retirement fund. But that was Stevie. He rarely if ever followed through on his ideas – some of which could have been cooked up with Ralph Kramden. He never finished the short stories he started. He never more than roughed out any of the articles he got stoked up about. He did, however, put together quite a few poems he called alternatively *The Broke-Heart Ballads* and *The Cellar Cantos.*

Somewhere I still have the original copy of one of these, which Stevie typed out on a Congressional memo pad using a manual typewriter.

> A cool wind moved the leaves around.
> Swirling brown in front of me.
> Autumn music without a sound,
> And then a certain face I see.
>
> Just a moment from a season.
> Has it happened long before?
> Only the wind and I remember,
> The leaves and a friend at December's door.
>
> Sleep well, you big palooka.

ABOUT THE AUTHOR

Born in Orange, NJ, **Vincent Czyz** is a graduate of Rutgers-New Brunswick, Columbia University (MA). He spent three years at the *North Jersey Herald News* in Passaic, NJ, as copy editor, book reviewer, and feature writer. In 1991 and again in 1994, he won fellowships from the NJ Council on the Arts for excellence in prose writing. In 1994 he was awarded the W. Faulkner-W. Wisdom Prize for Short Fiction. He spent a total of nearly a decade in Istanbul, Turkey before settling in Jersey City. The 2011 Capote Fellow in Fiction at Rutgers-Newark, his short stories have appeared in *Shenandoah, AGNI, The Massachusetts Review, Tampa Review, Quiddity, Georgetown Review, Tin House online, Camera Obscura, Southern Indiana Review, Louisiana Literature, Skidrow Penthouse, Hot Street, Wasafiri Journal of International Contemporary Writing* (London), and *Archaeopteryx*. His fiction has also been anthologized in Turkish. His essays have been published by *New England Review, Boston Review, AGNI, Poets & Writers, West Branch, Logos Journal, Rain Taxi, Translation Review, The Arts Fuse,* and *New Millennium Writings.*